A Retelling of the Story of Esther

CHOSEN

Well Versed Publications

Copyright © 2026 by Allison Wells

Well Versed Publications

whatallisonwrote.com
wellversedpub.com

All rights reserved.

Print ISBN 979-8-9856800-9-6
Ebook ISBN 979-8-9940631-0-1

No part of this book may be reproduced in any form or by any electronic or mechanical means, including information storage and retrieval systems, without written permission from the author, except for the use of brief quotations in a book review.

AI was in no way used for the book, nor do I allow any part of this book for AI training purposes.

Cover & interior images from depositphoto.com, used with permission
Cover design by Allison Wells

For every little girl who wanted to be a princess when she grew up only to realize she was already a queen.

Contents

Epigraph	1
Part I	3
CHAPTER 1	5
CHAPTER 2	15
CHAPTER 3	23
CHAPTER 4	29
CHAPTER 5	39
CHAPTER 6	45
CHAPTER 7	55
CHAPTER 8	67
CHAPTER 9	77
CHAPTER 10	81
CHAPTER 11	89
CHAPTER 12	95
CHAPTER 13	101
CHAPTER 14	111

CHAPTER 15	119
CHAPTER 16	133
CHAPTER 17	147
CHAPTER 18	159
CHAPTER 19	167
CHAPTER 20	177
CHAPTER 21	185
CHAPTER 22	193
CHAPTER 23	197
CHAPTER 24	207
CHAPTER 25	211
Part II	217
CHAPTER 26	219
CHAPTER 27	227
CHAPTER 28	237
CHAPTER 29	245
CHAPTER 30	253
CHAPTER 31	261
CHAPTER 32	269
CHAPTER 33	277
Epigraph	285
Acknowledgements	289
About the Author	291
Also by Allison Wells	293

Mordecai had a cousin named Hadassah, whom he had brought up because she had neither father nor mother. This young woman, who was also known as Esther, had a lovely figure and was beautiful. Mordecai had taken her as his own daughter when her father and mother died.

Esther 2:7 NIV

PART I

CHAPTER 1
1536

Esme watched in horror as her mother's face hollowed out and her skin practically melted. Her father and sister were already gone. She could not lose her mother as well. The feverish body of her tiny little brother laid in her arms as her mother slipped from this life into the next. What would become of her and Aaren? Sobs wracked her body as she clutched the too-thin boy to her own small chest.

She woke with a start, bolting into an upright position in her bed. Drenched in sweat, Esme tried to catch her breath. Hair was matted onto her cheeks and neck, serving as a reminder of the hardships she endured as she fought the fever. Now, however, she was fine. There was no fever, only nightmares.

Esme willed her breathing to return to normal when a knock sounded on her door. "Es?" The familiar voice of her cousin Maurice helped her relax.

"Come in," she said, her voice hoarse. She pulled the blanket further up over her arms for modesty.

Maurice entered her room and sat at the end of her bed. His touch on her face was tender and paternal, just like a father's. "The nightmare again?"

She swallowed the lump in her throat and nodded. The frequency of her nightmares about her family had decreased. In the fourteen years since her family's death, they slowed and only visited Esme about once a year now. In the beginning, she would have to relive watching her parents slip away nightly. Then, it slowed to weekly and monthly. Now, they only came when Esme felt stressed or worried. It was an annual reminder of the heartbreak she endured as a child.

"Will you be able to get back to sleep? It's still too early to rise." Maurice glanced out the window. "There are probably still two hours until the sun is up." He turned back to her, worry lining his face.

Only twelve years her senior, he raised Esme from the time she was eight, after her family died from a horrible sickness that had taken many of the residents of her small town. She survived against all odds, and the local doctor, desperate to find someone to care for the girl, tracked down her only living family member. Since then, Maurice had been a fatherly figure and a loyal brother to her, always there to offer his love and protection.

She looked into his deep blue eyes and noticed the slight etching on the edges. Maurice was certainly not old, but he was no longer as young as he once had been. His dark blond hair gained a few silver glints in the past year or two as well. *He is nearly thirty-five; he needs a family of his own to look after,* Esme thought. He deserved happiness after all he had given up on her account. Esme smiled at her cousin, and he kissed her forehead.

"Yes, I will be fine, Maury. Thank you for coming to my aid. I need to clear my head a little," she replied.

Maurice nodded and left her room, leaving the door slightly cracked open in case she were to have another nightmare.

With her breathing back to normal and the sweat gone, Esme tried to get back to sleep but could not. There was no light outside her window, and the world around her still slumbered. She did not think sleep would return to her, so she lit her candle and thrust her hand under her mattress. When her fingers wrapped around the piece of parchment, she carefully pulled it free from its hiding place. Her heart sped up as the paper came into view. *It was still real.*

While receiving missives wasn't entirely unheard of, receiving one that could lead to courtship was new to Esme. It was from Carden Wallace, one of Geoline's Peace Keepers. He was part of the country's elite protection force, tasked with keeping the city of Atelina and the country of Geoline as safe as possible. Carefully, she unfolded the hand-written missive.

Esme, I have thought of nothing but you for weeks. On Friday evening, the king will be giving a proclamation from Atelina Palace, and I hope you will consider accompanying me. I assure you my utmost protection and attention.
-Carden

Being asked to accompany Carden was no trivial matter. Being seen in public with a man was a sign of a true courtship, yet they had never spent time together before. Over the years, they crossed paths multiple times, but Esme had never suspected Carden had noticed her. The fact that he had been thinking of her for weeks sent a shiver up her spine and raised goosebumps on her arms.

Her two best friends, Sandrine and Yasmin, had said Carden recently took notice of her, but Esme dismissed their words as silly, infatuated thinking. They were in love with the idea of love and wanted her to find happiness as well.

Esme furrowed her brow, deep in thought. Was she ready to be seen on the arm of a man? Especially a man as noble as Carden Wallace? He was an upright man from a good family. She would be well cared for and live in a nice house if she were to marry him. In an attempt to regain clarity, Esme vigorously shook her head. The request had been for a single event, not her hand in marriage. She knew better than to put the cart before the horse.

Esme swung her feet over the side of the bed, feeling the cool wooden floor beneath her toes as she made up her mind to start the day and focus on her daily reading. She moved soundlessly to her desk as she pulled a night robe around her shoulders. Moving her candle, Esme opened her Testaments for the day's chosen verses.

Most of the people of Geoline worshipped several gods, deities that each had a specific purpose. There were gods for food and fertility, peace and protection. Esme had been raised to follow a single Eminence. In contrast to several self-absorbed gods, the true Eminence genuinely cared about the well-being of the people. Many Geolinians misplaced their faith and lived with complete disregard for others. Maurice had asked Esme to keep her faith to herself and she obediently complied.

At this time of day, Esme sensed the deepest bond with her roots. Her family had been from Cartrelle, a day's ride from Atelina. A separate world as far as Esme was concerned. The people looked much the same, but they were so vastly different. Most Cartrellans were believers in the Creed and peaceable. While people cared for their neighbors in Atelina, it wasn't as friendly as she remembered Cartrelle. But then, she had only been a young girl.

When her devotion was complete, Esme stretched and thought it best to ready for the day. There was no servant to cook for her or dress her as some of her friends had. She and Maurice were on their own, and she quite liked it that way. Though they had few fineries, they were comfortable.

Opting for a muted lavender day dress, she delicately draped it over her head of jet-black hair. If she chose to go with Carden, she would need to pull out her best dress. The light blue and silver dress perfectly complemented the blackness and sheen of her hair. Esme smiled to herself and twirled around on her tiptoes. This was all *if* she even decided to go with him. She would need to ask Maurice what he thought.

She brushed her hair while looking into the mirror. Her pale, heart-shaped face was fringed with inky bangs. A piece of twine wound around her hair, gathering it into a tail down her back. Esme had blue eyes that looked like pools with glints of green flashing on occasion. She was small for being a full-grown woman, most of her girlfriends were several inches taller than her, but it was not something Esme ever really minded. It made her feel dainty and precious, and she thought every girl deserved to feel precious.

Once Esme was dressed and ready for the day, she sat on the edge of her bed and looked around her room. It was stark white as all rooms were. It was furnished sparsely since Maurice was not a wealthy man. Her bed was familiar and adequate, her desk streamlined and angular. They were the same starched white of the walls, making the shadows extreme and almost grotesque.

To her left was a small closet filled with the few dresses she owned. She had a few for every-day wear and two fuller, fancier ones for special occasions. Esme had a limited collection of shoes, carefully chosen for specific activities—sturdy boots for outdoor work, comfortable slippers for indoor chores, and stylish footwear for social outings beyond their garden.

She heard wealthier families had closets as large as her bedroom full of dresses and shoes and jewelry. She had never aspired to such wealth but at times wished for things to have been easier or different. Still, Esme knew there were those who did not have what she did, so she chose to be grateful for what she had.

Esme's thoughts again returned to Carden Wallace and his offer. She would need to ask Maurice's permission. *But*, Esme thought, *I'm twenty-two*. It was time to be thinking of marriage and getting out of Maurice's way so he could also work on beginning his own family. As far as Esme could remember, Carden mentioned an older sister who had become a widow a year ago. Perhaps she and Maurice could accompany them. Together.

Satisfied with the idea, she went to the kitchen to begin preparing breakfast. She cracked several eggs and mixed in cheese, mushrooms, and some leftover ham. She fried them up and sliced some bread as the eggs cooked.

Maurice emerged from his room and kissed her temple. "This smelled wonderful. What prompted this?" Usually they prepared a simple meal together.

Turning to her cousin, Esme heaved a large breath. "Maurice, I have been asked to attend the reading of the king's proclamation by Carden Wallace. I think—I think it would be best for me to accept." She plated their food with shaky hands and passed one to Maurice.

Maurice raised an eyebrow as he passed Esme butter for her bread. "You think it would be best? Or you are incredibly excited and can't wait to go? You don't look or sound like the latter."

Esme sighed as her throat tightened. Truth be told, she wasn't sure. "I'm twenty-two, Maury. Sandrine is engaged to be married; other friends are moving that direction. It's time I did as well," she said, more to herself than to her cousin. The lump in her throat did not dissipate.

"He does come from a good family. Do you care for Carden?" He waited for an answer.

Unable to meet his gaze, she pushed her eggs around on her plate. "I—I'm not sure. I know he's a Peace Keeper. I know he's an honorable man and would always hold me in high esteem. But I don't know if I've developed affection for him yet. But he does have a sister who was widowed this past year."

Taking a bite of food, Maurice tried to hide a smile as he shook his head. "Are you trying to match yourself or me? I will marry when the right woman comes along and not until then. I would advise you of the same."

Admonished, Esme ate the rest of her meal in silence while she thought. When she finished, she took Maurice's plate without asking if he was done and carried them to the basin to wash them. This was how they had done things for fourteen years. The routine between the two of them was never different.

"Carden Wallace asked me to go tonight, and I think I will tell him yes unless you tell me not to, Maury. I am unsure if he's the right one, but I won't know for sure if I don't try." She leaned back on the counter, her hip jutting out as she tilted her head toward her cousin.

"Just remember the Eminence will lead you to the man you are meant to marry somehow. We are to trust in His ways, Cricket." Esme blushed at the use of her childhood nickname. Maurice had not called her Cricket in a very long time. Even though she was still diminutive compared to him, she was well past the age for childhood nicknames from family.

But she knew he was right. The Creed would lead her down the path of His desire for her. The dishes were left in the basin to soak, and she quickly found paper and a charcoal pencil to send off her own missive.

Carden, It would bring me great joy to accompany you tonight. I shall expect you before nightfall. -Esme

She opened the door and flagged down one of the many runners in the city. One of the benefits of living in Atelina was the numerous children always willing to run missives back and forth for a half-penny.

"Where to, lady?" The grubby young boy, Gerald, couldn't have been more than ten, but she had seen him many times before. He reached for the parchment, but she held it away from him until she gave the address.

"Carden Wallace on Pennton Street, please. Straight away, no dilly-dallying." She gave him a pointed look before handing him the note and the half-penny.

"I'm a professional, Miss Gustoff. I'll run straight there." With his promise, he darted off. Gerald was able to weave around buildings and between people as if it were a race. Soon, he was out of sight.

When evening approached, Esme was pleased to see that Carden was right on time. Maurice ushered him into their living quarters, and Esme spied on them through a crack in her door.

Carden Wallace was one of the most handsome men she had ever met. His hair was light blonde, almost white, and cut short the way all Peace Keepers wore their hair. His gray eyes were piercing, like the color of a summer storm. His square jaw flexed as he spoke to Maurice, making Esme wish she could overhear them. Carden wore dark sage green slacks with a pale butter colored shirt, topped with an overcoat to match the slacks. He looked marvelous.

One last glance in the mirror told Esme she looked good as well. Her black hair shone in a low ponytail. The blue and silver dress was large and heavy as they tended to be when made with so much material. Pacing her room, Esme adjusted to the sensation of the dress trailing behind her, making sure she wouldn't trip over her flowing skirts.

"I hope I haven't kept you waiting too long," she said as she emerged from her room. It was customary for the lady not to appear until after her date had been greeted by her family, so she knew she was not actually delaying him, but she apologized regardless.

"Not at all," came the reply from Carden. "And might I say, it was worth the wait to see you enter the room looking so lovely." He dipped his head in her direction. Esme caught Maurice wink at her from the corner of her eye.

"You both look dashing," Maurice interjected. "Have her home at a decent time, Mr. Wallace. I'm off to work, but I'll be home before too long."

"Of course, sir," Carden said, shaking Maurice's hand.

"Have fun, Esme," Maurice said, patting her on the back.

She nodded and they departed for the walk to the palace.

"I have to admit, I was surprised at your invitation, Mr. Wallace," Esme said as they walked side by side. She kept her gaze down but watched his feet move in sync with hers.

Carden chuckled but didn't look at her. "Really? I thought I had been pretty obvious in my admiration of you. I've seen you around town and always thought you were very smart and lovely. And everybody knows Maurice, so you're from a good family."

Esme tried not to blush at his words of flattery. They walked side by side for a few moments, but the silence was too awkward for her. "Tell me about being a Peace Keeper," she requested, more to fill the silence than actual curiosity.

Puffing his chest slightly, Carden radiated pride at his career. "It's not an easy job—catching thieves, protecting the city. I love being stationed here in the city where there's always action to be had. But it's nice that it is not always as dangerous as some other areas. I could be stationed anywhere in Geoline if needed. I understand those on border patrol have it harder than in the bigger cities, what with illegal immigrants coming in to Geoline, but that's nothing for you to worry over." He stepped closer to her as if to protect her, and Esme was flattered at the gesture.

"I would love to be promoted one day to Palace Keeper. Those are the elite few who are chosen to guard the king and his family. Geoline only has a dozen Palace Keepers, as they are so good at what they do, there is no need for more. Of course, we Peace Keepers are there to back them up if ever necessary. It's not easy, what I do, but it is truly a satisfying lifestyle."

Carden's smile was wide and inviting. He placed his hand on the small of Esme's back and a small tremor of pleasure registered in that spot. She tried to determine if this was a match from the Eminence or not. She would have to figure out how to ask Carden about his faith.

"I know your cousin works in the palace, but you stay away from it and take your wares to the market." Carden's bright eyes turned to slits as he spoke. "Why do you not work in the palace when it would be so easy for you to become one of the queen's ladies?"

The warmth she had been feeling was replaced with hot pricks of alarm. Was he interrogating her? He mentioned illegal immigrants, and she was an immigrant—a legal one, thankfully. But did he know that? She chuckled nervously.

"You are right. There is no need for me to be in the palace, though. I love being in the open air and talking to the people in the market there in the shadow of the palace. And there's something special about growing your own food. I love watching my vegetables grow and flourish. I enjoy talking to my chickens and having their little chicks race around. There's something satisfying about providing for yourself." Esme sighed as she thought of her garden and her chickens.

"But being inside the palace would be an honor. Serving Veva or other noble ladies would raise your social status. You could have people to do all that dirty work for you," Carden argued.

"That might be true, but I like doing the dirty work," Esme rebuffed. She did not appreciate Carden Wallace's appraisal of what she should and should not enjoy doing.

Thankfully, they arrived at the gates of Atelina Palace at that moment. As they approached the opulent archway, Esme glanced up at Carden. "Oh, look, we have arrived so quickly." She shot him a quick smile.

Esme could not have imagined the walk taking much longer had she crawled.

CHAPTER 2

LEVAN SCRATCHED HIS HEAD as the servant tossed the bright yellow curtains open. With the sun steadily rising, he knew his ability to lie in bed was coming to an end. But Levan had been up late the night before planning his big feast and proclamation. He was still tired. But the life of the king was never ending, and he rose with much growling and protest.

While another servant dressed him, members of his council came in to brief him on the day's activities. "The announcement for the week of feasting will be made tonight," said Marcutin, one of his councilmen. "Making it a city-wide proclamation is a stellar idea. It promises to be a grand event. Most of Atelina—of Geoline—is expected to want tickets, Your Grace."

"S-splendid, Marcutin." Levan nodded, he always stuttered more in the mornings. Closing his eyes, he took a moment to try to tame his words. "Dinald, how does the announcement look? Am I as s-s-strapping as ever? How does Veva look?"

He looked to his Minister of Propaganda for a response. Portraits of him and his queen had been made for the occasion, and miniatures had been sent to all the cities in Geoline so they would have a commemorative portrait of this grand occasion.

In addition to the lavish week-long feast, he would be proclaiming a celebration in honor of his wedding anniversary and making the announcement of his eldest son's betrothal to Princess Josefina of Beedaley. Not that the boy had anything to do with it. He was only six years old.

With a nod, the small man was quick to reassure him. "Oh, yes, Your Grace. Everything looks perfect. Veva is as fetching as ever, and you will come across as the most generous king on record."

"More than Orwell of Viriland?" Levan teased. Orwell was a staunch, stout old man. Levan would love to acquire his lands.

"Naturally, Your Grace," came the reply.

"Hesten," Levan snapped to his right-hand man. "Is Veva done with the children? I need to speak to her."

Hesten Egold, a man almost as tall as Levan, hastened to do his bidding. The darker man snapped his fingers, and a servant went to the quarters of Levan's wife.

While he waited, Levan looked into the mirror. His dark chestnut colored hair was cut short to keep the unruly curls at bay. His eyes were the color of blue ice, making him look like a cool and calculating dictator, which worked well when it came to doling out commands or looking imposing—both of which he did frequently. He stepped back to see his full reflection. He stood six-and-a-half feet tall, larger than most mirrors in his castle, and his shoulders were as wide as most doors. He had to turn slightly to fit through. Levan knew he was a commanding presence, and he relished the notion.

Within moments, his wife Veva arrived from sharing breakfast with their two sons and gave a brief curtsy. She was not yet dressed and still wore her night robes, the sash accenting the curves of her figure. Despite being married for eight years, she was still in the prime of her youth at twenty-five.

Levan was thankful she was still so fetching and had proven to be a good breeding wife. Otherwise, he held no affection for his raven-haired bride outside the physical.

Levan shot a look at his advisors, and they all filed out of the room in quick order. Only Hesten remained. "Anything else, Your Highness?" Hesten positioned himself at the door and waited for instructions.

"When I'm done here, Hesten, I w-want to be briefed on the presentation I will give at the feast. Have everything ready for me," Levan said.

The dark-haired man nodded and exited, his heels clicking on the parquet floor as he went.

Levan approached the queen. She was beautiful—that was what had drawn him to her when she was a girl of seventeen. Veva boasted black hair that fell in soft curls past her shoulders when unbound. Her eyes were as dark as her hair. Levan could never read anything into them, not that he ever tried. Among all the women presented to him, only Veva's beauty led him to choose her as his bride. It had been a well-made, if loveless, choice. Still, he kept up the appearance of doting husband for the sake of his kingdom.

"Today is the anniversary of our wedding, Veva," he said as he trailed his hand down her arm. "D-do you recall?"

"Of course," she said coolly, her Mayonian accent coming through her words. She did not move a muscle. "I could not forget such an event." She did not seem pleased he remembered their anniversary and that angered Levan. Did he not deserve some sort of accolade for remembering?

"L-look at me, Veva. I will be treated with respect," he commanded. "Especially on such a momentous day as our eighth wedding celebration." Veva turned her gaze towards him, her eyes filled with curiosity. Levan nodded. "Yes, a celebration. Just for you, my darling. We shall dine tonight with dignitaries and revered guests at a banquet given in your honor. And the honor of our two sons."

A flush rose in Veva's cheeks. "You flatter me, Levan. I cannot express my gratitude at this display of affection." Now she turned toward him and lifted her hand to his cheek. He moved away before she could touch him.

Levan had not thought the feast was a display of affection. He only thought it lined up perfectly with their son's betrothal and a chance to show off their vast wealth. And it never looked bad to play the caring husband and father.

He was quiet a moment before speaking, willing himself not to stutter. "Think nothing of it, my darling," he replied. Then he approached his wife and kissed her cheek. "We will dine at six. Be sure you are ready."

Levan cleared his throat and straightened the folds of his coat one last time. The bright crimson color helped him stand out and be easily seen on the balcony. If Atelinians were standing far away, there would be too many people to guess which one was the most important. The red colors helped them to know where to look.

Beside him was Veva in a voluminous dress of dark green. She would blend in with everyone else, as she should. Only the crown on her head gave any indication she held some importance to the masses. Behind them stood Hesten, Marcutin, Dinald, and other men who thought they had a right to be there.

Off to the side but still close enough to hear his words sat the only man who knew he wasn't worthy of being in such a place of honor. The scribe and newsman—Levan's favorite one with the light-colored hair—sat off to the side ready to record the announcements for posterity.

With a dazzling smile on his face, Levan extended his hands in front of him, patiently waiting for the noise around him to fade away. "Good evening, Geolinians. I hope your day is bursting with happiness, each moment cherished and leaving you with a feeling of contentment that mirrors mine. Tonight I am thrilled to celebrate the eighth anniversary of my marriage to the lovely Veva, my bride and your queen." He stopped and looked at Veva as they practiced in rehearsal. She looked at him adoringly as she had been instructed.

He knew there were men placed throughout the crowd repeating his words so they carried far and wide. He waited a moment so his words could trickle through the mass of people before him.

"And my love of life is spilling over to you, my esteemed friends. In one week hence, we will have a celebration of unforeseen proportions here in Atelina." He paused both for applause and for the repeaters. "There will be music, food, dancing, and anything else you can think of as we celebrate everything Geoline in a weeklong festival right here."

He boomed, "We will also celebrate the betrothal of Prince Lester to Princess Josefina of Beedaley." Another pause. This time the people's excitement was palpable. An engagement was always something to celebrate. "What an exciting time we are living in. We want the world to know of our happiness and wealth in all things that matter: friendship and family."

As rehearsed, he took Veva's hand. "You won't want to miss this amazing opportunity to be a part of something that will go down in history. Let's show everyone out there just how wonderful Geoline is. Thank you so much for your continued support and your outpouring of love." Levan lifted his and his wife's joined hands as he leaned forward toward the people below. "Have a sensational night, Geoline. Until we meet again, you are always in our heart."

Veva's hand wrenched free from his own as she hissed at him. "You are marrying our son off already? He's a child!"

Levan had forgotten the engagement was news to her. He had been negotiating with Prince Iosef for months. The group behind them parted so they could walk back inside first. He turned to her and shrugged. "It's all politics. If they both survive to be sixteen, they will be married. Who knows, maybe the girl will die before then."

Veva wrinkled her nose and furrowed her brow. "You are a callous man, Levan." She didn't wait for an answer before she strode off, yanking the crown from her head and thrusting it into the hands of her maid.

Levan pinched the bridge of his nose as the men around him congratulated him on a wonderful speech. He didn't need their brown-nosing. He sought out the scribe who was always honest with him.

"How was it?" He raised an eyebrow at the blond-haired man. He wished he could remember the man's name.

With a smile, the scribe nodded. "That was wonderful, sir. Short and sweet. I think everybody will be thrilled for the betrothal. The celebration sounds like the party of the year, naturally."

"Thanks so much, er..."

"Maurice. Maurice Gustoff, Your Grace."

"Maurice, of course. I'm sorry," Levan said, wishing he was better with names. He repeated it in his head. He liked this guy; he always seemed genuinely happy.

"It is quite alright. You have more important things to remember than the name of the man who takes down your words," Maurice said with a chuckle.

"It is a big job, Mr. Gustoff, and one worth remembering. I shall remember it next time we meet," Levan promised.

As the man walked away, Levan wondered if he should invest in name signs for all people around him so he wouldn't be caught fumbling for a name again.

But before he could ponder on that thought any longer, Hesten approached him along with several of his other men. They were still singing his praises, and while Levan usually enjoyed it, it grated on him at times. This was one of them.

"That was exceptional. The people will clamor to attend," Hesten chortled. "Well done, sir." Hesten was flattering him as he always did, and Levan rolled his eyes as he turned his head away.

He believed he had performed exceptionally well. The voice coach he requested had done an excellent job teaching him to project his voice with confidence and enunciate each word clearly. His stutter was hardly an issue anymore as it had been in his youth. It would never have done for the leader of a country to speak in public with such an impediment, even if it did come out on occasion in private.

Levan's parents had insisted on the voice coach in his youth. Their only child and heir to the throne could not have a speech impediment. Levan employed one ever since, and only those who saw him daily knew. His parents had done their best to make sure Levan never felt weak because of his stutter. Thankfully, he had outgrown it for the most part before his parents had been killed on a voyage to see snow-capped mountains in Sweden. He had only been seventeen at the time.

CHAPTER 3

ONCE THE KING'S SPEECH concluded, a murmur rippled through the crowd as people dispersed, their voices blending together in excited chatter as they formed smaller groups. Some spoke about the King Levan's marriage or the young prince's betrothal. Esme figured most were catching up on the latest village gossip, the hushed tones and excited whispers carried on the breeze. While palace life enthralled them all, it paled in comparison to the goings-on of people they knew.

It had been exciting to be close enough to hear the king's low, booming voice. Usually, Esme was on the outskirts, listening to one of the many speakers who repeated the words as it came to them. She realized the people on the outside of the crowd typically received a watered-down version of whatever had been announced and wondered if the king realized they were not getting a verbatim echo of his words.

Carden paraded Esme around and through the throngs of people. Esme felt a little foolish and she blushed as people noted their pairing and whispered. "Isn't that the Peace Keeper with that market girl?" she imagined them saying.

Never mind. She shook her head to clear it. She would enjoy this night. Social customs were not her strong suit, though she followed them all the same.

Several people stopped them and chatted briefly before moving along to someone else. Being this far up in the crowd, Esme didn't see Sandrine or Yasmin, though she knew they would be milling about somewhere. After twenty more minutes, she yawned, signaling she was ready to head back home.

Esme usually took great pains to avoid anything political and generally disliked what came from those in command. The news was always unpleasant, whether it involved an invasion, a threat, or people giving more money to the already affluent. But because they all lived in the shadow of the palace, Atelinians were a captive audience.

As she and Carden walked, Esme thought of the king. She had never seen him so close, though she had still been a good hundred paces—and fifteen feet in height—away from him. The paintings of him passed around the city did not do him justice. He was a handsome man. While she didn't get a good look at Veva, Esme imagined she was even more beautiful than her portraits as well.

"Isn't the celebration a wonderful idea? What do you think, Carden?" she asked as they walked home. He had been mostly quiet as they canvassed the city mingling. Esme thought such good news would have had Carden talking her ear off.

The scarcity of good news made King Levan's eagerness to share it understandable. A weeklong celebration sounded like something enjoyable and profitable for everyone in Atelina. Esme risked a glance sideways at Carden. The thought of him inviting her to any event, big or small, made her heart race; she wondered if he would. She wondered if she would accept if he did.

Carden nodded, but his face remained solemn. "It is. It is an excellent opportunity." He was so deep in thought, a frown etched onto his face, oblivious to the bustling world around him.

"An opportunity?" Remembering her desire to get her life started, Esme batted her eyes at him and brushed her shoulder against his. Then she felt foolish. She needn't try so hard.

"Yes, for me to advance as a Peace Keeper," he explained. He licked his lips and his forehead wrinkled. "They will need tighter security, more guards inside the castle with such a party going on. This could be my chance to show my captain what I'm made of. This might be my big break, a chance to achieve my dreams and leave my mark at last."

Did he always think about his job and career? The smile on Esme's face fell as fast as her heart did. Any girl would come in second place to Carden's career. "Do you not want to attend the festivities as a guest? Not just as a Peace Keeper? It sounds like such a jubilant occasion."

"There's a time for fun and a time for work. This will be a time for work while everybody else is looking unawares and caught off guard," Carden said, his mouth still turned down. But Esme saw the excitement in his eyes.

"Oh," was all she could muster in reply. Was she willing to be with a man who allowed other things to come before her? Not that being a Peace Keeper was a job to be taken lightly—she knew the call of duty would always take priority. But was she truly at peace with that? She wasn't sure. All Esme knew was that she was ready to get back into some comfortable clothing and curl up on the couch with a good book.

"You know," Carden said suddenly, "a promotion equals more money, and more money equals greater security. And that would go a long way in providing for a family one day."

Esme's eyes opened wide. Was he implying something? Did Carden think she was the right person with whom to raise a family? Trying to appear composed, she nodded, a small smile playing on her lips, unsure of the proper response.

They approached the blue door of her home, and Carden took her hands into his. He smiled at her for the first time since leaving the gardens outside the palace. "Esme, this was a magical evening. I should like to call on you again if you would be inclined."

She looked into his big, gray eyes. Would she be so inclined? He looked at her, a silent question in his eyes, expectantly awaiting her answer. She glanced down at her hands in his and felt heat creep into her cheeks. His hands were large but soft and well-manicured while hers were small and rough. Without knowing what else to say, she answered, "That would be lovely."

She felt him bend down toward her. With bated breath, Esme remained motionless as Carden planted a delicate, cautious kiss on her cheek. She felt like a little girl again, recalling the night when she was twelve and a young Marsalis Winston had given her a sloppy and unsteady peck on the cheek. Despite its difference, this kiss resulted in the same feelings for her. Nothing.

Carden's gaze met hers and he stepped back. He gave a curt nod and she returned it, the pink still flushing her cheeks. She hoped he thought the blush was from him and not from the memory of a boy's touch so long ago. She quietly opened the door and slipped inside, closing it behind her. She stood just inside the door, with her head resting on the wall, for a few moments before she realized Maurice was standing behind her.

"That good, huh?" Maurice chuckled. "Ah, young love."

She jumped at his words. "Maury. You scared the life out of me, cousin. How long have you been watching me?"

"Long enough to see that young man kiss your cheek through the window, and now you're resting your head in thoughts of love," he said with a teasing tone.

Esme scowled at Maurice. "I don't think so. All he did was talk about himself. He scolded me for my decision to not work in the palace, and then he talked about himself some more. I didn't think feeling love, let alone feeling affection for someone, was so... I don't know what to call it." She looked up as if the ceiling had the word she needed. "Dull. It was so drab and dull."

Maurice sat in a chair and patted the one next to him for her to sit. He grabbed an apple and took a bite, chewing as he thought. "Dull," he said, raising a blond eyebrow. "What an archaic word. I didn't know anybody used it anymore. So your date, who kissed you on the cheek, left you feeling dull and not giddy? That does not bode well."

"No, it does not," she agreed. What had been a light, airy feeling before now weighed her down. "Though he asked if he could call on me again and I said yes. I'm not sure why."

"Give the boy another chance. Perhaps he was nervous, Esme." Her cousin took another bite from his apple.

She nodded. Maybe that had been it. Nerves on both their parts. She should give Carden another chance. Changing the subject she smiled slyly while turning to her cousin. "Tell me about this big celebration next week."

Maurice raised an eyebrow. "The one you won't be going to?"

"What? Why not?" Esme's eyes widened in shock. She was an adult now. She should be allowed to attend.

"It will be nothing but debauchery and gluttony. No place for a good Follower of the Creed like you. The palace is a den of destruction. Everything there is a farce, a show put on for the benefit of others," Maurice explained. He gave her his best fatherly look and she knew he was serious.

"There must be some good there," Esme argued. "I know Levan's little speech tonight was put on and rehearsed, but surely, he was trained to be a good man and a good leader."

"Perhaps he was brought up that way, as Heins' only son, but those around Levan are despicable and immoral. Hesten in particular I see no reason to trust," Maurice said in a low voice. Even though nobody could hear him, he still feared what might happen if anyone went against the king or his right-hand man.

"Well, I want to go to the celebration."

"Only if that boy takes you," Maurice said. He stood and exited the room.

Esme shook her head and went to her room to change.

CHAPTER 4
Two Weeks Later...

"Just how much money do you have, Levan? Surely, not as much as you claim," sneered one of his guests, a man named Viggot from Barcelona. It was clear he had been overly liberal with the drink as the man's nose was flushed, and his words were becoming increasingly difficult to understand. It wasn't even dusk yet.

This was the last night, the conclusion of the week-long celebration. Not only was Levan celebrating the engagement between Lester and Josefina, he was celebrating a magnanimous success in terms of impressing his guests and allies. Not to mention lining his own pockets. The people of Geoline had been in rare form with this celebration and had been all too happy to share their riches with him. Levan was filled with happiness. And wine.

"Enough, I tell you. I have more than enough money to invade Hanstrup and Cartrelle this coming year," Levan replied, feeling a little tipsy himself. "Within two years, I think we could expand the borders of Geoline down to the Bay of Missico."

"Bah," said Hawkingsworth from Louishire. He had been naysaying Levan the entire week. "It's all talk. These rulers never have as much as they claim."

Levan never liked being challenged. How could he prove his wealth? A stupendous idea came to him. "Why, my wife's jewels alone could fund a war. I'll call her to show them to us. Then you shall see, Hawkingsworth, just how much we have here."

The men at the tables clapped and cheered. The allure of Geoline's vast wealth was surpassed only by their longing to see the queen, whose stunning beauty was legendary and had captured their imaginations. Levan wouldn't mind setting his eyes on the shimmering gold of his bounty either.

Levan smiled and turned to his second in command. Levan's words held sway, even over a significantly inebriated Hesten, who would promptly topple backward to sniff his own behind if so commanded. "Bring Veva to me. Tell her to wear her royal jewels." Levan's smile was crass, his eyebrow lifted up suggestively.

WITH A RESPECTFUL NOD, Hesten hurried through the palace corridors to deliver the urgent message to the queen's chambers.

Hesten thought he was indispensable to the king, and he intended to keep it that way. He would do just about anything for Levan. With his voice in the king's ear, he was one step away from being the ruler of Geoline himself. Running errands could have been done by a servant, but he liked to give things a *personal* touch.

When the maid opened the door for him, Hesten brushed past her to the ladies who mattered and bowed deeply. He couldn't help but smile at the sight of the noblewomen lounging lazily, their voices filling the air with lively gossip. "Surely, this is the most beautiful gathering of women I have ever seen." Hesten knew he was handsome and that the women of Geoline adored him almost as much as they did Levan.

His eyes found his wife amidst the throng; he moved purposefully toward her, a showy kiss to her hand emphasizing his affection for all to see. "Lady Egold, your beauty outshines every other woman here."

The truth was she did not outshine any of the other women. With her mousy hair, full figure, and beady eyes, Nicie was far from striking. The dowry that came with her, however, had been plentiful. As she was the only child of the Duke of Brumoldy, the title would pass to their eldest son, Marhest.

Nicie puffed at the attention. "If it isn't my doting husband. What brings you to the queen's quarters?"

He leaned in close to her and kissed her cheek. She had proven to be a good wife, having borne him four sons, her belly swollen with another. "I have a message for Veva."

"She speaks with the Countess of Asbury in the back," Nicie said as she ran a long fingernail around Hesten's jawline. He patted her cheek before rising to his full height and scanning the back of the room.

Hesten's eyes fell upon Veva; immediately, he approached, the scent of woodsmoke and spices filling his nostrils as he bowed deeply. "Queen Veva, the king requests your presence at once." She sat higher than the other women on a dais, a small tiara nestled in her nest of black hair.

She peered down at him. Veva was a tiny slip of a girl several years younger than him, but she knew how to command a room. Her personality and ego took up most of the space. She caused feelings in Hesten with one glance his wife had not produced in nearly ten years of marriage. Veva ran a slender hand down her neck and batted her heavily made-up eyes at him.

"It must be truly urgent for you to come yourself, Hesten," she said slowly. Veva lifted the heavy, crystal wine goblet and took a long sip, the cool liquid gliding down her throat. "What is so crucial that my husband's second in command comes to the queen's chambers?"

He cleared his throat and rolled his shoulders back. "Your king and husband requires you to come to his banquet at once. Wearing the royal jewels," Hesten said, moistening his lips. In a quiet voice, he added, "Only the royal jewels."

"You must be in jest, Hesten." A nervous smile touched her lips, barely concealing the wide, startled eyes behind them.

Veva's charm, a captivating force that consumed the entire room, was only overshadowed by Hesten's colossal ego. With his position just below the king, Hesten outranked everyone else in Geoline, and he had every intention of making sure the queen understood this.

"He said for you to come dripping in nothing but jewels, my queen." The men would enjoy the show, and he always wondered what was under Veva's skirts.

Veva sat straight up, lifted her chin, and scoffed. "Only the royal jewels? As in, no other clothing? I realize the jewels are vast and numerous, but they would not drape over my body in order to protect my virtue. I shall not do it."

Hesten shifted his weight impatiently. He smiled grimly through his thin lips. "Your husband and ruler commands it."

With a wave, Veva brushed him off. "I care not. I am no harlot. I will not come to him in such a fashion."

All eyes were now on the two of them. Women in the front of the room silently crept toward the back to witness the exchange. A vein throbbed in Hesten's temple as his anger flared, his breath coming in ragged gasps. People did not argue with him or with the king. How could he make Veva see he meant business?

As calmly as he could, Hesten tried once more. "My queen, your beauty is widely known. All Levan—all *your king*—wants is to display your beauty and the beauty of the jewels of Geoline. Surely, you cannot deny him that." His smile widened into a painful, joyous rictus, muscles screaming in protest. When he spotted his wife from the crowd, he immediately noticed her furrowed brows.

If Veva refused this, wives everywhere would then believe it acceptable to refuse their own husbands. This did not bode well for any man in Geoline. A furious energy thrummed in Hesten as he clenched his fists, his smile strained and unnatural.

"Please, my lady."

Veva stood to her full height and descended the few steps to stand in front of Hesten. Even then she only came to his chest, but that did not intimidate her. "I said no. You are dismissed."

He firmly believed she did not possess the authority to dismiss him from her presence. He was second in command, not her. But still, he went, a knot of apprehension tightening in his stomach as he stepped into the throng of wives. Of witnesses to the queen's refusal. With each stride, the sound of his boots reverberated through the room, the black and white flooring contrasting beneath his feet. The door before him suddenly opened, and he exited without hesitating. What would he tell Levan? He thought quickly.

LEVAN HAD FORGOTTEN ABOUT the errand he sent Hesten on until the man returned, his face red and veins throbbing in his neck. It would seem Veva got under Hesten's skin, which didn't surprise him as they both thought they were the most important person around.

"Did Veva ruffle your feathers, Egold? Where is the queen?" He chuckled and looked behind the man but saw nobody enter after him.

Hesten leaned in to Levan's ear. "She refuses to come, Levan, dressed as you requested."

From his vantage point, Levan could see the masses of men anxiously anticipating his words or the arrival of Veva. A forced smile spread across his face, a feeble attempt to hide his true emotions. "Wh-what do you mean she's refusing?" His voice was barely audible.

"She flat out said no, Levan. And then she dismissed me." Hesten looked to him and added, "In front of all the other women."

By now murmurs were rising through the room. Where was Veva? What was the problem? Old Marcutin and the other advisors approached Levan and Hesten. Levan knew, with a sudden tightening in his chest, that he would have to do something.

"Your Highness? Is there a problem?" asked Marcutin. With deep concern etched onto his face, the aging advisor stood nearby.

"Veva refuses to come. She refused the king." This came from Hesten. Loudly.

Levan might not have chosen to disclose that. He might have said she did not feel well or was walking the palace grounds. Now he would have to address her blatant disrespect; his jaw clenched with barely controlled fury.

"You must be jesting. What queen would refuse her king such a simple request?" Hawkingsworth called out. The room was filled with a deafening uproar.

Marcutin put his hands up to quiet the din of the crowded room. There was no other sound when he announced, "Men. Men. The queen has refused to come before her sovereign king."

Levan could hardly believe his ears. What was going on? The anger swelled inside him, a bitter taste in his mouth, as he seethed over Veva's rejection and the blatant way his men had shared the information with the dignitaries and commoners. He looked from Marcutin to Hesten, then to the rest of the room. Men chattered back and forth, their faces angry and their fists balled at their sides.

Hesten stepped forward, his arms raised high, commanding the room's attention. "My concern is that all the women—your wives and daughters—were in the room when Queen Veva denied her husband's incredibly simple request." With the men murmuring once more, Levan saw Hesten smoothly assert dominance over the room.

"It wasn't just a denial, it was outright refusal. What's to stop the other women from having such a blatant disregard for their husbands and fathers? As sure as the sun rose this morning, something must be done to prevent this from happening in our own homes." Hesten's voice was loud and crisp. Levan cringed.

Now the men in the room became nearly riotous. They were all well into the drink and easily agitated. They shouted and threw any objects they could get their hands on. Levan had to do something quickly. Without thinking, he stood and raised his right fist high into the air.

"Men of Geoline, I see the outrage this has caused you," he said in a booming voice. He struggled to think as he waited for them to be quiet. He hoped his voice would hold steady. "What can be done after such a refusal by the queen?"

Marcutin wasted no time in quipping up, "Remove her crown! Veva can no longer be our queen." With a resounding roar, the men expressed their approval, their voices a powerful wave of sound.

Levan's eyes widened as he turned his head toward his oldest advisor. What was Marcutin thinking? Had this been part of the plan all along? Levan wondered if Hesten had even spoken with Veva. Certainly, there was another way. But the mob before him had made up his mind.

With his voice low, Levan reluctantly announced, "Guards. Arrest Veva at once and bring her before me." He downed what was left in his glass of wine, then added, "Drag her if you must." The crowd cheered approval at his words.

Levan sat, suddenly exhausted. What would he do with her? Divorce was only something a few religious factions did. The only way to be rid of her as a wife was to be truly rid of her. But what about their children? The thought of Lester and Lennox losing their mother over such a trivial matter was unbearable. Did they really deserve this pain?

The pressure was immense; he felt the cold sweat on his palms as he racked his brain, desperately searching for a way to avoid executing his wife. But the crowd of men around him chanted and cheered, making it hard for him to think. Nobody spoke to him, but all around him were shouts and banter.

Though his brain was foggy, Levan tried to understand how this had come to pass. He wanted her to show off the crown jewels. Veva was a vain girl; she should have loved the idea of showing off herself and her sparkly things to a horde of appreciative men. Hesten and Marcutin's call for her removal as queen had been too quick, too calculated. His head throbbed, a dull, insistent ache that clouded his mind and stole his ability to think straight.

Before long, Veva was brought into the great hall. Her head was held high, her face stoic. Her hands were bound behind her, but that did not diminish her imposing stare or the magnitude of her beauty. She wore a pale pink dress lined with sequins and a sequined train trailing behind her. Atop her inky, silken hair was her coronation crown. Levan figured one of the guards must have gotten and replaced her social crown with this one. How befitting for her to literally lose her crown.

He stood before her, hands shaking, unsure of anything in that moment. He aimed for a look of regretful authority; wanting to soothe Veva while commanding respect from the onlookers, a difficult balancing act of expression. In the doorways, women gathered, their curious eyes eager to witness what would unfold. This day would live on forever in Geoline—or at least until Levan took another woman as queen. Would he take another woman? Plenty of time to figure that out.

He closed his eyes a moment to steady himself and hopefully his words. "Let it be known throughout Geoline that Queen Veva is no longer my wife and no longer the queen my people deserve. She is hereby stripped of every title and sentenced to..." he swallowed, "sentenced to her end. Please hear this lesson. When your king calls you, you are to obey." It pleased him that he had not stuttered. He avoided the pleading stare of Veva's dark eyes, instead seeing the approving nods of the men listening.

A hush fell, then a ripple of nervous whispers and excited chatter spread through the crowd. Out of the corner of his eye, Levan saw his advisors nodding vigorously.

He looked over the form of the woman who had shared his life these past eight years. Despite his harsh decree, her regal bearing, evident in her posture and the way she carried herself, commanded respect. But he knew his next words would crush her.

Levan lowered his voice, but it was still loud enough for many to hear. "Veva. This saddens me greatly, but I must do this." He gulped, his own eyes filled with moisture. "You have one hour to make your final goodbyes to the c-children for you will never see them again. In the morning, you will be gone."

Veva's face was immediately panic-stricken. Her eyes filled with tears and her stoic face crumpled. "No, Levan. Please! I love my children. Our children." Her posture changed from composed to broken. She fell to her knees, her glittering train twisting as she went down. "I will do as you ask. I did not know it would come to such extremes." Tears slid down her face as she looked up at him.

He had to resist her. He could not reach out to her, but he crouched beside her. As quietly as he could, he responded, "I did not know either. It is out of my hands. I am sorry."

He abruptly turned his back, a grim set to his jaw, and walked away, leaving her standing alone. He could hear her wails over the roar of the people who had just witnessed the first-ever execution sentencing of a royal. This was something only done in England. Was he as cruel as Henry?

He gave himself permission to be upset. His children were losing their mother. He was losing his wife. But Veva had gone against him. Something had to be done, right? Regardless, it was done now. Veva would spend a long, restless night in the cold, unforgiving prison cell. Her life would be taken at sunrise. Preferably before he rose for the day.

He snapped his fingers, and a Palace Keeper came to him immediately. "Give Veva one hour with the children. Then lock her up and send MacJames to me once that is completed. I'll be in my chambers." The Palace Keeper nodded and took off.

Levan collapsed in his own bedchamber and told the guard not to grant entry to anyone, regardless of who it was. He didn't want to see Hesten or Marcutin. He shuddered at the thought of hearing about Veva's final moments with the children. He wanted to sleep off the alcohol that plagued him. Maybe tomorrow things would look different.

A few hours later, Levan woke, still dressed in his finery. Reaching the door, he urgently requested the Palace Keeper on duty to send for his secretary, MacJames, discreetly, making sure nobody else was informed. He needed to make sure Veva would never look upon him or Geoline again.

CHAPTER 5

THE NEXT MORNING, LEVAN awoke to the sound of his council's hushed voices and footsteps pouring into his room. It would seem they did not nurse the same hangover he did. Their chatter caused a ringing in his ears.

"This is madness." Levan was still in his bed, and the sun was barely over the horizon. Each one thought they knew what he needed to do next with his life. A wave of nausea washed over him; he was so sick of it all. "Am I n-not still the sovereign ruler of Geoline? And now a grieving widower as well? All of you, leave me be."

A throat cleared and Levan looked up to see Marcutin raise an eyebrow in his direction. "If you would, sir—"

"Out." Thinking better of it, Marcutin shut his mouth and turned. As the room cleared, he called to the last man to leave. "Hesten, s-stay."

Hesten smiled and turned back to Levan. "Yes, Your Grace?"

A grudging dependence on his commander was hard for Levan to swallow, especially in moments when a lack of direction left him feeling lost and unsure. "I need a voice of reason. What do I do now, Hesten?"

"You must carry on as the ruler of this great nation. Show the people you are still here, with them," Hesten urged.

"How d-do I do that?" Levan certainly did not know. He threw off his covers and sat up straight. Someone had recently placed a steaming cup of tea next to him and he took a fortifying sip.

"Perhaps you could take a new queen?"

Levan silenced the man. "No, I need to be respectful of mourning. The people would keep comparing me to Henry in England if I married again straight away. You know, none of this would have happened if she had come to me as I asked." He stood from his bed, his chest bare, his legs covered with light linen pants. "W-why did she refuse you, Hesten? What happened?"

"I cannot say, sir. I went to her with your request to come before the people with her jewels on, and she said she would not be paraded around like a harlot," Hesten recounted. "I begged her to please comply, but she said I was dismissed and then ignored me. I left then, sir."

Chuckling, Levan shook his head. "How like Veva. How could she think showing off her jewels would make her look like a harlot? All she needed do was put them on with that shimmery pink number she already wore and wave to the people. She would have looked splendid."

"Of course, sir. Will you be ready for the day's briefing in thirty minutes?"

As far as Levan knew, the man lived only for his work, but Hesten was right. The only way to move forward was to put one foot in front of the other.

"I'm not sure. Perhaps we need to dismiss everyone for the day." Levan's head throbbed as he disappeared into his water closet. He was used to his council talking to him no matter where he was or what privacy others would have been afforded.

"How about making a morning announcement to reassure the people?" Hesten suggested, redirecting their conversation. "Let them know you are still one of them, just a man. Now a man in mourning."

"I do n-not think I can, Hesten. You do it for me, p-please. Let the people know that the palace is in mourning for at least...a month. They are to go about their usual business but in a somber fashion. Have it posted throughout the city." Levan came back into the room and looked out the window into the misty morning. It was dreary, just as he felt.

"Yes, Your Grace. I'll go at once," Hesten said. With a brief bow, he departed and left Levan to dress for the day.

A FLICKER OF SURPRISE crossed Hesten's face before he composed himself, his features carefully arranged in a neutral mask. It had not been Levan's intention for Veva to come without any clothes on, with only the jewels as her attire. He had wanted the queen to wear her dress as well. How had Hesten misinterpreted that? The key now, Hesten thought, was to make sure Levan never found out about that part of his request to Veva.

He found Dinald Waters, the Minister of Propaganda, in his office with the scribe Maurice Gustoff. Hesten sneered. "We need to make an announcement throughout the city. Levan wants a month of somber mourning." He snapped his fingers after the men stared at him, their expressions blank and unresponsive. "Let's get this moving. Now."

He watched as Maurice jumped to action. With a practiced ease, he set up his paper and quill, thanks to his nimble frame and quick fingers. The man's carefree nature and incessant cheerfulness filled Hesten with a burning hatred.

"We are ready, sir," Maurice said as he held his quill at the ready. "You may begin."

His train of thought was lost as he looked at the scribe. "Why are you always so cheery, Gustoff? It's distracting."

"My apologies, sir. I don't feel very cheery today. It's a sad day for all of Geoline, Atelina in particular. But I know the Eminence will see us through. I hope Queen Veva has had the chance to encounter him already," Maurice said with a weak smile.

Maurice and talk of his religion made Hesten scoff. While the faith was not forbidden, it was certainly a minority—and a small one at that. Nobody believed in antiquated old gods anymore. Hesten had been raised on the words and works of many gods, but he didn't believe in them either. He believed in himself. Nobody was more important than him except Levan. Maybe Maurice needed to be taught that lesson.

"Gustoff, you and all your Creed Followers are fools. There is no higher power. Except for Levan. And just below Levan... Is me. I am your god, Mr. Gustoff," Hesten hissed.

"I think not, Commander Egold. I have no god aside from the one and true Eminence," Maurice smiled calmly. "Now, if you would please relay the announcement as you want it, I will make sure the copy is good, and Mr. Waters will get it sent all over Atelina." He again poised his quill over the paper.

Hesten was caught off guard, but he regained his composure and squared his shoulders. "We are all saddened by the loss of Veva, mother of Lester and Lennox Haras, heirs to the throne of Geoline," he started, keeping his face solemn. He was careful not to call her the queen as her crown had been stripped of her before her execution. "I have spoken with King Levan this morning, and he expressed his gratitude at your outpouring of love and support in this time. He asks that you do your best to carry on with your lives but to observe a month-long period of solemnness and grieving alongside the palace.

"The royal family wants all the people of Geoline to remember Veva for the vibrant life she led and the two handsome boys she leaves behind." Hesten wanted the message to be short, so he wrapped it up. "Today is a day of mourning, but we can overcome this sadness and carry on. Long live King Levan."

It wasn't until Maurice said he had gotten it all and read it back to him that Hesten moved. He relaxed for a moment, then cracked his neck and confidently left the building without saying another word.

CHAPTER 6

"The queen was scheduled to be executed this morning before sunrise," Maurice said to the room of people around them. "We must be in prayer for Veva's eternal life, Levan, and the royal princes."

The men and women of their small church group murmured and nodded. Yes, they must pray for her soul and for everyone affected by her death, especially the two small princes. Esme had been shocked at the announcement that had gone out just as the sun went down the night before. She lay awake most of the night trying to make sense of it.

A tearful woman named Marjory Nirwerth dabbed at her eyes. "What about her children? Everybody in Geoline knows there's no love between her and the king, but she loves the princes. How could the king do this to her?"

Esme listened to the various accounts of the incident; some were filled with anger, others with grief. It seemed as though the king's advisors forced his hand. "From the accounts Maurice recorded, the king didn't seem to have had much choice. Even as supreme ruler, he still has a council to which he answers, and then there's the pressure put on him by that room full of drunken men."

Everybody looked at Esme, shocked. Even she was taken aback by her response. They all knew her aversion to anything political or having to do with the goings-on at the palace. "Don't get me wrong. I think this is a terrible tragedy. But the people in that room were out for blood. It looks as if King Levan didn't have much choice but to dethrone her. And since Geoline has never seen a broken marriage contract, this was the only option he had."

"Wouldn't divorce have been better than murdering that poor girl? We aren't uncivilized like the English." This came from Helene Carter, Marjory's next-door neighbor, who was vehemently anti-English.

"No matter," said their pastor Nermal Hobbes. "There is nothing we can do now for the queen, or former queen, but pray for her soul." Please bow your heads."

They all followed his direction, and he led them in a lengthy prayer for the Eminence to deliver not only the soul of the deposed queen, but also that of every person in the palace.

Sundays were a day of rest for those who followed the Creed. Even though they were a minority in Atelina, the quiet hum of the city on this day was a welcome change from the usual weekday clamor. After the execution of Veva, it was even quieter than normal.

The next day, Maurice was reluctant to go to work. "The execution will be the top of the news today, and I'm loathe to report it. I'll probably have long meetings with Dinald and have to once again interview those who were there. And I'll have to talk with Hesten. It's a sad day all around."

The morning had been somber, with a thick, grey haze hanging heavy in the air, muffling the sounds of the city as Esme stared out the window. "I don't think anybody looks forward to today. It's bleak. Even the angels are crying; there's mist in the air, and it's cold outside. I keep thinking about those poor boys. They're so young, and their father had their mother killed. How could a just ruler do such a thing?"

"You had a different stance before. You seemed somewhat sympathetic to Levan's situation. What changed?" The steam from Maurice's tea curled around his face as he took a slow sip, then leaned back, the chair creaking softly beneath him.

Esme thought a moment. She had been more sympathetic yesterday. Levan's announcement revealed a man torn between appeasing the crowd before him and saving his wife. She was uncertain of whether he had loved Queen Veva, though it hardly mattered now. The deed was done. It must have been a wrenching experience, a brutal conflict in his soul, to order the death of someone who had been a part of his life for eight long years.

"Hearing the announcement, I could only imagine it was not the decision Levan wanted to make. I think he got so swept up in the outcry and passion from those around him, and he believed there was no other choice," Esme sighed.

Maurice leaned back and cocked his head to the side. "You could tell that from the reports that came from the palace? I *spoke* to the people and did not gather that."

"Yes." Esme returned her gaze to the window and the sad world outside. "He allowed her to say goodbye to the children. From the way you described his face, I don't think it was a decision he wanted to make."

With a sigh, Maurice left for work, the weight of the day heavy on his shoulders, while Esme soberly prepared her cart for the market. Today, she would take some extra of her most popular comfort foods. She had been making cakes and pastries to go along with her fresh produce. The city of Atelina would need them. The sounds of the city overwhelmed her as she shook her head and weaved through the crowded streets. While still busy, the air held a different quality; the usual clamor was muted, replaced by a less intense, but still present, level of activity. Even though the queen always kept her distance from the common people, they were still reeling from the unexpected turn of events.

A week later, the whispers about the execution were fading away, and the atmosphere in Atelina started to brighten once more. People were so fickle, but Esme was no different. After a few days of feeling shell-shocked, she returned to her usual buoyant self.

"I'm going out with Carden again this evening, Maurice. Is that alright with you?" Esme was pleased with the way things were going. She and Carden had been out several times over the last few weeks, and she was starting to look forward to their outings.

Esme wasn't sure if they were serious or not, but she did have feelings for him. What she was not sure of, however, was if it was love. She enjoyed his company. Escaping the confines of her home, she reveled in the bustling energy and vibrant happenings of the city, finding immense enjoyment in simply being a part of it all. Atelina Square had become their go-to spot, where they joined other couples in leisurely walks, savoring the opportunity to see and be seen. They had taken in a theatrical performance and strolled along the city's historic waterfront district. Esme loved every outing. As their courtship neared the four-month mark, a question began to form in her mind about what the future held for them, or if there would even be a future at all.

"Of course," Maurice said. "Go and enjoy. Things are progressing with him it seems. Shall we begin the wedding planning?" Maurice's constant teasing filled her head with thoughts she knew she shouldn't entertain.

"I don't know, Maury. I do enjoy being with Carden. I wasn't sure at first, but he's grown on me. And he seems to appreciate me in return," she said with a shrug. "But should I not feel a spark? Something that makes me want to be with him all the time?"

"That's only lust. Love is different." A serious expression settled over Maurice's face as his gaze locked onto hers, studying her intently.

"How do you know?"

Pausing, her cousin came to a stop and firmly planted his hands on the table as he struggled to find the right words. "That is the age-old question, my dear. If I knew, perhaps I would be wed myself." He sighed in resignation and shook his head. "Might Mr. Wallace be the man for you?"

A blush, hot and prickly, rose on Esme's cheeks, making her turn away, embarrassed and flustered. "I can't presume to know. I certainly have not been courted by any other man. But I don't know if he's the one for me. How does one know, Maurice?" She looked back at her cousin, hoping he would have the answer.

"I've never been in love myself, Esme. I would be a fool to offer you advice on marriage," he admitted, scratching the stubble on his face. "But I hear you just know. You have a feeling in the core of your soul. Like you would cross oceans of time to be with that person. I think the Eminence would reveal that to you if you ask Him."

"Maybe I should spend some time in prayer before I meet up with Carden tonight," Esme said with a grimace. She remained emotionless. She didn't believe his absence would kill her, not even a flicker of emotion rippled the surface. But she just did not know.

Perhaps her friends would have sage advice. Luckily for Esme, she had plans with them. "I'm going to have lunch with Sandrine and Yasmin today. Sandrine gets married tomorrow, you know."

"Yes. I look forward to it," he said. "Thank you for inviting me."

"You can thank me when you meet her Aunt Lindal. She's twenty-eight and still unmarried," Esme said with a laugh as she quickly exited the room. She could hear Maurice calling after her as she walked down the road to meet her friends.

On the eve of Sandrine's wedding, lunch was a lively event with the three friends, filled with the sounds of joyous conversation and the delicious smells of their meal. Their excitement was palpable. Esme had grown up with Sandrine and Yasmin. From the moment she arrived in Atelina, they had been best friends.

Yasmin was a lovely girl with an overprotective father. While a few men had called on her, none made it past his rigorous standards. Esme was jealous of her friend's pale blonde hair and eyes the color of a cloudless sky. Yasmin hoped to one day run her father's butchery with or without a man at her side.

The bride-to-be, Sandrine, had tanned skin with eyes and hair the color of caramel. She was an exotic beauty. She'd had many suitors, but Kasen Kartrite captured her heart earlier in the year. He was a skilled cooper and woodworker, his shop filled with the scent of freshly cut wood, just a few blocks away. Sandrine was happy to get away from her six brothers and sisters.

The three friends giggled and laughed over childhood memories while eating sandwiches and listening to the actvities around them. Esme tried her best to deflect questions about Carden but had been bombarded. She eventually asked Sandrine how she had come to realize that Kasen was the man for her.

It didn't take Sandrine long to come up with an answer. Her lilting voice brightened as she talked about her intended. "Because he makes good money, he treats me like a princess, and he shares the same faith as we do. And because every time I leave him, I can't wait until I see him again. Do you not feel that way with Carden?"

Esme smiled nervously, which her friends took as admission. Esme easily admitted she anticipated seeing him, but she was uncertain if it was as urgent as Sandrine described. As she thought on it, Esme realized she looked more forward to the outing itself rather than the man beside her. The thought, sharp and unsettling, pricked at her conscience. She had never been a social butterfly before being associated with Carden, and she enjoyed it. Would it make a difference if she were with someone else?

She continued to deflect while out with her friends, instead turning all the attention to Sandrine. As they checked on final preparations for the wedding, Esme mulled over her relationship with Carden Wallace.

Back in her bedroom, Esme thought of the scripture that spoke of husbands and wives. She recalled the poetic words of Solomon in the love story he had penned. It was clear the two people were deeply in love, as their descriptions of each other were filled with affection and tenderness. In the story, the man said his love was a lily among thistles, something beautiful.

Esme didn't have time to dwell on the question because the doorbell rang and Maurice let Carden into the house. She could hear them greeting one another. Esme gave a final glance at her rose and gold dress, its rich color catching the waning light, and nodded with satisfaction. Her skirt swayed as she opened the bedroom door and greeted the men before her.

Many young couples gathered for a picnic and promenade around Atelina Square. The lush trees and luminous flowers nearly glistened in the last rays of daylight. She and Carden walked arm in arm, admiring the lilies and greeting those who passed by.

After nearly an hour of meandering, they found an empty bench and sat. Esme made sure there was space between them, lest people talked. Carden leaned in to her, though, and spoke in a low voice. "I have been wanting to ask you something but haven't known how to say it."

Esme's heart quickened. Might this be a marriage proposal? How would she reply after her revelation earlier? "Yes? What is it?" Waving a hand to cool herself, she was flushed from exertion and excitement.

"You live with your cousin, I know. But you've never mentioned your parents or any other family," he said. His statement, though not a formal question, carried the weight and intonation of one. The unspoken query hung heavy in the air.

The warmth she had been feeling turned to ice. Although his words weren't accusatory, she perceived them that way and instantly became defensive. Esme's fingers curled around the armrest beside her. She was not ashamed of her family or of Maurice, but Carden's blunt wording made her suddenly feel inadequate.

Her brain fumbled for words, and she struggled to open her mouth. Finally, she said, "My parents, sister, and brother all died when I was eight from a terrible illness. Maurice was the only family I had left. He took me in and raised me as his own." She gasped for air as if the words could have cut her throat. "Why do you ask?" Her grip on the armrest tightened, and she had to remind herself to take a deep breath. Why was she reacting this way?

Carden shrugged. "I've been wondering. But since you haven't brought it up, I thought I would inquire. I'm sorry for your loss." His face was straight. That was it. No emotion, no follow-up. It was almost as if he read from a parchment.

If he was asking burning questions, she had one as well. She licked her lips and inclined her head. "Can I ask you something?"

"Naturally, ask me anything," he said. His face still bore no smile, no emotion.

Esme made herself release the armrest and face Carden. "You are aware that my faith is important to me, but you have never expressed your own faith. Why is that?" Esme held her breath. She was almost afraid of his reply.

"Yes, I know you are a one of those who believes in a higher power. My parents are as well, actually. But I am not. It's just not logical to me, and the palace agrees, given their stance. How can there be only one deity? Or any at all? We can only look to ourselves for guidance, Esme." His voice showed no emotion; it was simply stating facts. "But I'm fine with you being a believer in your Eminence. I was also led down a path of fantasy." At this, he finally chuckled a little.

Feeling completely deflated, Esme slumped her shoulders and let out a sigh, the weight of her disappointment settling heavily upon her. A path of fantasy? Who was this man? She brought up her faith on occasion to see if he would express the same inclinations, but he never had.

When Carden asked if she wanted to make the rounds once more, she declined. Though she said it was because of the next day's wedding, her heart no longer felt as light and open as the night air alluded. It was then she decided Carden Wallace was not the man the Creed intended her to marry.

When she returned home, she marched up to Maurice with her hands on her hips. "Maury, I need you to forbid me from seeing Carden again."

Maurice put down the book he had been reading and took Esme's hands in his. His eyes were full of questions, but his voice was soft as he said, "I forbid you from seeing him again."

"Thank you."

He gave her a half-smile. "You're welcome. Want to talk about it?"

She shook her head and picked at her sleeve. "No. He's just not the man for me."

CHAPTER 7
Six Months Later...

Levan woke in a sour mood. To the north, Tentakay was invading Viriland. Levan, and his father before him, had always wanted Viriland and Tentakay for himself. The fertile soil of both countries would be an asset for their own. And yet, the Geoline army was doing nothing about this.

More than anything, Levan missed the comfort of confiding in someone he trusted, the cathartic release of sharing his frustrations and feeling understood. Someone like his wife. He realized he had respected her and trusted her in a way like no other on his council. He appreciated her honesty; Veva never hesitated to voice her opinions, even if they differed from his, and he found this refreshing.

Levan muttered under his breath, "Council. Bah. They have grieved me far worse than Veva ever did. And yet she paid the price for that." He paced his office then called out for Marcutin to come to him.

The small man, who had been on his own father's council, came immediately. Levan snarled at him as he entered.

"Your Eminence, what troubles you today? I see you are not pleased this morning." Marcutin positioned himself behind a large chair.

"Viriland is being invaded by Tentakay. They're both weak on their southern borders, and yet we are doing nothing about this? Why is my council not counseling me? Why is it you are always doing things that benefit me in no way?"

"Sire, please, I don't understand," Marcutin said as Levan hurled a crystal glass across the room. "What is the matter?"

"Do you even work for me? You have given me nothing but bad advice for the past six months. First with Veva, and now, you are ignoring this is opportune time to try to take on Tentakay and Viriland," Levan snapped at Marcutin.

Marcutin's wide, desperate eyes darted around, searching frantically for an escape from the king's rage. "I'll get the army generals to you right away, Your Grace."

Levan waved his hand but stopped Marcutin before he exited. "Send MacJames in." Marcutin nodded as he scurried off.

Slowly, MacJames entered the office. "You needed something, sir?" Despite the sounds of Levan's furious yelling and shattering glass echoing, the man remained unnervingly calm, his face betraying no emotion.

"I cannot think straight, MacJames," Levan said, looking at his secretary as if he should have all the answers. "And there is glass on the floor."

MacJames snapped his fingers, and a maid scurried in with a broom. She swept up the shards of glass in complete silence and disappeared.

"Do you require a doctor, sir? Why can you not think straight?" MacJames did not move from his position in the center of the room. He commanded it as easily as Levan did.

"Honestly, I am lonely. I did not think I would miss having a wife as much as I do," Levan admitted, falling into an overstuffed red couch.

"There are countless harlots in the city, sir, if you are lonely. I can bring the finest to you within an hour," MacJames suggested with a half-smile.

"I don't want a bedmate. I want a life-mate," Levan said, slamming his fist on the arm of the couch. "And my council all but did away with her for me. I didn't realize how I appreciated her, even if the affection was not there."

Stepping forward, MacJames spoke plainly. "Why not find someone who can fill that role, sir? It has been several months. You can take another bride, another mother for your children, another queen for this great country. Someone whom you can truly love. Why not set a search in motion? You can choose from all the finest ladies in Geoline."

Find someone from amongst the ladies of Geoline? The idea made sense to Levan. It could be a contest of sorts. It would boost his popularity and visibility after everything with Veva and give him a new bride. She wouldn't be a conditioned princess with her own country's agenda in mind. If the Geolinians were her own people, she'd ensure their well-being, fighting for their rights and prosperity. Maybe he could actually love his wife this time.

"Brilliant. Set up something where women can come in and apply to be considered," he ordered as he sat back on the couch. "I want their name, vital information, family, background, and more. I want families to nominate their daughters, ladies to come in and put down their own names. Then, we can narrow the pool by factors I deem necessary and get down to a few women I can meet and choose from."

The resounding clap of Levan's hands signaled MacJames's dismissal; the man bowed low, his departure marked by the quiet rustle of his clothes and the closing of the heavy oak door. Levan already felt better, knowing the search for a new wife had been launched.

Six months she has been gone, Levan thought. True, he did not miss her the way a husband should miss his wife, but he missed her as mother to his children and as someone not afraid to speak before him. Levan longed for a partner whose intelligence shone through her gentle nature, whose beauty was matched only by her humility. Did such a woman exist? And if so, would she already be taken? Or would she want him? Levan sat at his desk and thought about what he desired in a new queen and bride for some time that afternoon.

Just as Levan was contemplating, Guy, the personal assistant to the queen, entered his office. Guy was tall and broad with skin almost as dark as obsidian. When Levan first met him, the man's imposing stature and stern expression had intimidated him, until a warm smile softened his features. Guy Hart's smile could put any person at ease. He had been a perfect choice for Veva's assistant, and he had seen to her every need. He must have heard about the call for a new queen.

"Your Grace, I am sorry to intrude," Guy said with a smile as he bowed before Levan.

"It is no imposition, Guy. I assume you have heard we will begin the search for a new queen." Levan shuffled some items on his desk. "Please, have a seat."

Perching lightly on the edge of a chair, Guy was quick to ask, "I understand you plan to use a process of elimination, which is an excellent choice, sire. Might I suggest when you narrow your selection down to a few ladies you employ the Belin House on the grounds as a location to house those you wish to…get to know better?" He gestured with his hands and nearly made Levan laugh.

Nodding, Levan agreed. "That is a wonderful idea, Guy. See that it's prepared and ready within a month's time. How many rooms does it have available?" Levan took notes on the parchment in front of him.

"Fifteen, sir. If you would want me to stay in the house with the young women, then fourteen."

"I think you better stay in one. Best to stave off the catfights, yes?" Levan laughed. Would there be fights amongst those he would meet? Perhaps.

It would liven things up. And Guy would let him know about the girls' characters.

A great, big laugh erupted from Guy, shaking his shoulders. "I see what you're thinking, Your Grace. I'll keep those ladies in line."

"Keep the largest room for yourself. So we shall narrow down the list to fourteen women. One of whom will become my bride."

Guy smiled and pressed his hands to his midsection as he stood and bowed. "As you wish, sire. I look forward to helping out the future Queen of Geoline. Is there anything else I may do as you begin to search?"

"You spent all day with Veva, didn't you?" When Guy nodded, Levan continued. He chose his words carefully, knowing the man before him probably adored his former mistress. "I have often wondered if she truly loved me. I cannot hide that while I did respect her as the queen, I did not feel any romantic love that would link us for all eternity the way most love stories tell it. I want a wife who will love me and whom I can love in return. Not just physically, but all around. Does that make sense?"

"Yes, sir, it does," Guy said, leaning closer to Levan. The man's face softened. "With her gone these past months, I think I can tell you Veva felt much the way you did. She admired you but did not feel that love of which you speak. But please don't doubt her loyalty to you and you alone."

Shaking his head, Levan reassured the man. "No, I do not doubt that, Guy. If you can, help me find a new bride who will honor me, who will love me for me. That is my greatest wish in a new queen."

"It is noted, King Levan. I shall do my best." With that, Guy gave a curt bow and exited.

Levan turned his attention back to the countries to the north and waited for his generals to aide him.

One of Esme's favorite things about market days was seeing all the people as they shopped. It never failed that she saw Sandrine and Kasen and usually Yasmin as well. With a whoop of delight, Yasmin came around the corner, her pale hair streaming behind her, a wide grin stretching across her face.

"Did you hear? Have you seen the announcements?"

Esme returned the smile and tucked a strand of hair behind her ear. "No. What's going on? Something big?"

"King Levan will be looking for a new queen. It was announced this morning. He's practically auditioning women from all over Geoline," Yasmin exclaimed, her breath short.

Sorting her wares, Esme smiled at her friend. "Really? Auditioning women?" Who had ever heard of such a thing? Yasmin was easily excited.

Yasmin jumped and clapped her hands together. "Pretty much. Families can send their daughters or ladies can sign up on their own. Sandrine is nearly crying that she's no longer single, the silly girl. You and I should put our names in."

With a chuckle, Esme replied, "I'm not surprised he's finally looking to remarry. It's been half a year. But I am not interested in doing it."

"Why not? It's such an incredible opportunity."

"He had his wife, the mother of his children, killed," she reminded her friend.

Yasmin crossed her arms and pouted. "He didn't kill her himself. And besides, she publicly humiliated him and caused him so much grief. He deserves to find a wife and queen he can truly love. Maybe it will be me," Yasmin said, batting long eyelashes over blue eyes.

A peal of laughter escaped Esme's lips as her friend twirled, the bright salmon of her skirt a vibrant splash against the green background, pale yellow hair dancing around her head like sunbeams.

"Why don't you put your name in, then?" Esme encouraged her friend.

"Come on, Esme, you should too. Especially since things didn't seem to work out with Carden Wallace," Yasmin pointed out. "It can't hurt to get on the list."

Laughing, Esme rolled her eyes. "I'll think about it."

"All right. I better go before Father notices I've gone from the shop. Goodbye!" Yasmin bound through the crowd, which now buzzed with the news of the king's decision to find a new queen.

An hour later, three people asked Esme if she was going to be nominated for queen. Each time, she shook her head and said no. She wasn't interested.

As she bagged a handful of squash and tomatoes, a shadow came over her. Looking up, Esme saw Carden Wallace's imposing form before her.

"Esme, it's been a while," he said as he picked up a yellow squash. "How are you?"

She told him months before that she needed space, and he had mostly been respectful of her wishes. She'd sometimes see him at the market, a fleeting figure amongst the crowds, or near her friends and Maurice, his presence subtle yet unsettling.

A wide, genuine smile, showing her perfect teeth, graced her face. "I'm well, Carden. I hope you are, too." She licked her lips. "Are you looking for something specific?"

He stepped closer. "You, Esme. I'm looking for you. I've missed you." A tight smile touched his lips, but his eyes remained cold and distant. That worried Esme.

Taking a few steps back behind her display, she wrapped her hand around a length of lumber. She didn't intend to use it, but she liked to have an option. "I appreciate that, but I've been so busy. I'm sure you have as well."

He leaned on her table, a scowl on his face. "I don't understand. We were seen together for a number of months. We were courting and you disappeared."

This was a delicate situation, she knew. She needed to let him down gently, despite believing she'd already softened the blow with careful words. But apparently, she needed to do it again. With her eyes closed, she rolled her shoulders back. "You are very nice, but I don't see a future with you. I'm sorry."

As she opened her eyes, she was met with Carden's nostrils flared and his eyes wide with surprise. He stood to his full height, his chest heaving. No words came from his mouth, but he turned on his heel and strode away.

"That went well," Esme whispered to herself.

After packing up, she went back home a little more solemn than she had set out. As Maurice greeted her, his brow furrowed after a quick glance at her. "Is everything well with you, Esme?"

"Carden," she said matter-of-factly. "He approached and asked to court me again, and I declined. I told him we were not suited. He did not reply. I hope he understands."

"Are you sad?" Maurice tilted his head to the right, the way he always did when he was really concerned. His yellow-red hair flopped over his forehead.

"Sad? No. He was not the one for me. But I am disappointed. I feel... I don't know. Ready?" She struggled with the words she needed. "Yes, ready. I'm ready to find the one I am to marry. I'm ready for that next stage in my life. I enjoy working in the market. But something is missing, Maury. There's a greater purpose for me out there."

Maurice led her to a seat and sat next to her. "You are so smart and could be a tutor in a noble household. Why not pursue that? Or try to become the new queen. Outrank us all."

It was so hard to know what the Eminence was calling her to do. Becoming a tutor wasn't a bad idea, but Esme knew it wasn't for her. For some reason she could not pinpoint, however, putting her name in the search for a new queen sounded like the right thing to do. She prayed for direction.

She tilted her head and laced her fingers together. "Would you really want me to try to be queen?"

Maurice chuckled and bumped his shoulder against hers. "Well, only if you wanted a life of glamour and rumors. It's a very public life, though Veva managed to keep fairly private. I can't imagine why anyone would want to marry someone who had his first wife executed the way he did, though."

"I don't know what to do, Maurice," she said. "I think for now, I'm going to go back to my garden." And with that, she went outside, picked up her hand rake, and pulled at weeds.

One of the best things about working in her garden was the way her mind wandered. Esme often thought the clearest while tending to her vegetables and flowers or taking care of her chickens. She would pray, figure out what to get Maurice for his birthday, write songs in her head, and ponder life's conundrums.

The idea of submitting her name as a queen hopeful stayed in her mind. It was a ridiculous idea. There would be hundreds if not thousands of girls for Levan to choose from. From what she had heard, the list would be whittled down to just over a dozen girls. There was no way she would make it past the first round.

The announcement said Levan was looking for a regular citizen and not necessarily someone of noble birth. Still, Esme was certain those with more money and power would make sure their daughters and sisters were at the forefront. It would be silly, but she and Yasmin could put their names for the fun of it.

That night, she went to Yasmin's house and knocked loudly. When her friend opened the door, Esme blurted out, "Let's do it. Let's submit our names to the search for a queen."

Yasmin clapped her hands together as she rushed outside. "Really? You'll do it with me?" She hugged Esme tightly. "Maybe we'll get to live at the palace together."

Esme giggled. "He can't choose us both."

"No, but the top contenders will live at the palace until he chooses someone, and we could both live in the lap of luxury." Yasmin threw her hands up over her head and twirled around. Her carefree nature was contagious and soon both were dancing in front of Yasmin's home.

They made plans to meet up first thing the next morning and get it done before they could change their minds. The office collecting the nominations was right next to the market.

It made Esme nervous to be there filling out the form. Holding hands, she and Yasmin walked into the room as if they were meeting Levan himself. Esme was lucky she could read and write. Not everybody could. One of the workers was helping a family fill the form out for their eldest daughter. Esme turned her attention to the man handing out the parchment and quills.

"Thank you," she whispered and hurried over to where Yasmin sat looking over the form.

It was simple enough. Provide the name, age, address, and family of the girl being nominated. According to the rules, if you successfully passed that stage, the king's officials would thoroughly examine the girl's background. From there, a handful of chosen ladies would be introduced to King Levan. If he so desired, he would choose one to be his wife, and she would rule beside him as the queen.

Knowing she would never make it past the background check, Esme filled out the form. An orphaned woman with no social status would never be chosen as a wife by the Geolinian ruler. Nor a woman of faith, not that she was putting that on the form.

When Yasmin finished, they handed their papers over to one of the men manning the desk and took off, arm in arm.

"That wasn't quite as exciting as I thought it would be," Yasmin admitted as they walked down the street, their arms still linked.

Esme laughed. "Not exciting at all. That started and probably ended our running in the search for a new queen. Though wouldn't it be amazing if he chose someone from right here in Atelina?" They could be walking past the next queen and not realize it. She studied the faces of the ladies walking by.

"I better get back," Yasmin said "My father had a large buck to butcher today." She stopped and hugged Esme. "Thank you for coming with me."

"It was an adventure. One day, we will tell our children we were in the running to be the queen of Geoline." They laughed and parted ways. Esme thought it would be a fun story to tell her children and grandchildren one day, how she filled out the application to become queen. It was like taking part in history.

"What has you in such a good mood, Cricket?" Maurice asked when she came home. "You look absolutely elated."

It didn't feel right to share her silly adventure of filling out a piece of paper with Maurice. Instead, she hugged him close and kissed his cheek. "I took a stroll with Yasmin, and we were talking about how the next queen might be in our midst. She might have walked down the street beside us today, even."

With a roll of his eyes, Maurice smoothed her hair and pressed his forehead to hers. "You two are amusing girls. I feel bad for the families lining up to offer their daughter as a sacrifice to the king. But one day, you will be the queen of your own household."

She laughed off his comment about the girls being a sacrifice. If that was his opinion, he wouldn't think her application would be an amusing story. "I won't be the queen of anything if I don't find a suitable man."

Maurice stood and patted his tunic. It was about time for him to head to the palace for work. "You'll find that person one day. I think perhaps soon. I have a feeling. And until then…"

She stepped up to her cousin and smoothed his hair as he had done to her. "Until then, I will focus on my garden, my friends, and deepening my faith."

Maurice kissed her forehead. "That's a good girl. You truly are remarkable, Esme. Don't settle for second-best when it comes to a life mate, and don't spend your time waiting around. It makes the wait even longer and lonelier."

Esme suddenly felt like she had been given an insight to Maurice's own prolonged singleness. Had he been waiting and pining all these years? "I won't, Maurice. I love you truly."

"I know you do," he said. "And I love you. We'll just have to keep each other company until we find the ones meant for us."

Esme watched as Maurice left for the palace where he would record all the day's goings-on. She prayed he would find his own life partner soon, a wife to be his helpmate and to raise children with. He deserved all the love the Eminence could give him.

CHAPTER 8

HESTEN WALKED BEHIND ROWS of men ready to flip through each and every application. There were hundreds of submissions pouring in from all over the country. After a month, the volume hadn't slowed. At some point, he would tell the messengers to simply burn any remaining submissions, but he wanted a good pool to show Levan.

Of course, Hesten would make sure his own younger sister, Wilma, was among those who made it to the final round of fourteen. But that need not be common knowledge.

"His Majesty the King wants a specific type of woman," he said. He glanced at the men before him. They were educated men searching for a single girl. It was like looking for a needle in a haystack. "Every applicant must be Geolinian and live within our borders. Eliminate anybody who does not. The king also asks the applicant to be older than twenty and younger than forty. Once you have removed those who do not qualify, we will begin again with new parameters."

There was a little groaning from the readers, all scribes. They needed men who could read quickly to move through the stacks of papers efficiently. Hesten chuckled when he saw Maurice Gustoff in the second row of readers. He hoped the man got several paper cuts.

It took the better part of two days for the readers to go through nearly a thousand applications. After the first round, roughly eight hundred named remained. Hesten had to whittle it down to only fourteen ladies.

That was when he called in Guy Hart, the queen's official assistant. He was to help groom the fourteen finalists for life as queen and help with the selection process.

Hesten looked towards Guy and shrugged his shoulder. Guy Hart devoted his life to serving a woman, something Hesten believed to be unmanly and beneath him. He loathed Guy. But then, he loathed many people. Like that perpetually happy scribe—Maurice. Hesten frowned at all the negativity he was surrounding himself with and tried to shake it off.

"How did you do?" Guy asked cheerily as he clapped his hands together. His smile made Hesten want to slap the man. Maybe he just disliked cheerful people.

Sneering, Hesten snapped, "Down from over a thousand to about eight hundred. The house set aside for them has fourteen rooms. You figure it out." He picked up a stack of papers and flung them in the air. He was through trying to find a new wife for Levan.

Guy bent down and gathered a few papers and happily announced, "Let's find our new queen." He licked his lips before settling in with more specific parameters to narrow down the applicants.

Hesten shook his head. If only so much attention had been paid when he was taking a wife, maybe he'd like her a little better. While Nicie wasn't a terrible wife, her looks—particularly when she was expecting—were plain. She was a good breeder; he had to give her that. But she didn't hold a candle to Veva's beauty. Pity Veva had to get herself executed.

Making his way down the corridor, he passed Maurice Gustoff. What an arrogant fool of a man. Hesten knew Gustoff not only had foreign blood, but that he also believed in some religion known as the Creed. *What nonsense,* Hesten thought, *to believe in some being other than yourself.* The sight of the man made his blood boil.

"Get a move on, Gustoff. Why are you loitering around the palace halls?" Hesten snapped his fingers, and he heard a Palace Keeper jump to attention.

Maurice turned slowly. His face was the definition of calm, making Hesten all the more agitated. "I am simply sending a messenger on an errand, Hesten. I am sorry if I'm delaying you."

Feeling his face turn red, Hesten stomped his foot. "Quit being sorry and actually do something for once, Gustoff."

The man did not miss a beat. "How's the search going?"

Hesten grabbed a decanter from a nearby table and drank straight from it. "From the eight hundred left, we whittle it down to only fourteen ladies. Then, I must endure the distasteful notion of those fourteen women coming here to the palace for three months so they can be taught how to be a queen. It's all a farce."

Maurice took the drained decanter Hesten thrust at him. "I don't envy the job of narrowing it down to fourteen girls." He carefully placed the decanter back on the table, off to the side so a servant could refill it.

"It means we'll have fourteen dribbling women taking up space on the grounds. The sooner this is over, the better," Hesten said with a roll of his eyes.

"I don't doubt you there," Maurice replied with a lazy smile. He took a final sip of the cup in his hand and scratched his head. Hesten hoped the man did not have fleas. He took a step back.

"Get back to work, Gustoff." Hesten stormed away from Maurice, cursing the man's casual ways as he went. With so much on Hesten's plate, he had little time to concern himself with Levan's choice of a future wife.

Guy Hart spread applications across a table. Thirty faces stared at him, his top selection. He had carefully sorted through the lists, ordered portraits of each one, and left several hundred names to be swept away and placed in a firepit. Of course, Levan would have final say over the fourteen invited to stay on palace grounds, but Guy was the one who narrowed down the list and presented it to the king. Time was of the essence. The fourteen had to be selected by the week's end.

He carefully glanced over the miniature portraits of each one, checking to see that each could be held to the standard of a queen. Some had yellow hair while others had hair the color of night. Some were right at the age cap of forty, while others barely made the cutoff on the younger side. Of course, Guy had his few favorites, but he was not the one looking for a bride. Since the day his young bride passed away, Guy devoted his life to serving others. It had been ten years since he had become the personal assistant of the queen, and while he missed Veva, he looked forward to training a new one.

After serving Levan's mother, Carlotta, for two years, he went on to provide eight years of devoted service to Veva. They had been the closest of friends. Guy held both Lester and Lennox even before their father did. Veva had been a demanding but kind queen, despite what the king thought. She had not loved Levan, but she had done her duty to him, putting her own desires aside to align with those of her husband. Veva had been the daughter of a duke, raised for a life of both luxury and high demands. Guy wondered if the new queen would be able to handle the demands that came with the position.

Unable to cross any more names off his list, he prepared to present the thirty profiles to the king. He hoped Levan would be able to narrow them down by more than half. Guy gathered the ladies' profiles and went to Levan's office to wait for admittance.

"His Highness will see you now," bellowed MacJames. He raised his hand, and the door to the office swung open. Guy quickly went through and bowed, waiting for recognition.

"Come forward." The king's voice boomed in the small room, and Guy nearly startled.

"Your Grace, I have narrowed down eight hundred applicants to thirty. I thought you might want a hand in selecting the final fourteen." Guy stood between the chairs facing Levan's desk, papers clutched in his hands.

"I appreciate your hard word, Guy. Let's get on with it," Levan said without looking up. "I cannot imagine whittling that list down to only thirty. Tell me about these women who have made it past your scrupulous eye." Levan pushed a stack of papers aside to clear room for Guy's offerings.

"I have the basic information for each of them, along with their miniature ready to show you," Guy said as he turned the stack toward the king. He was sweating profusely, hoping he had done well.

"No portraits to start," Levan said, shaking his head and holding his hand out for Guy to stop.

The smile on Guy's face fell. "I beg your pardon, sir?" He had not anticipated the king not wanting to see who his choices were. Beauty had been his top reason for choosing Veva.

A scowl crossed Levan's face. It was the reason so many people thought he was a ruthless monster, that scowl. While Guy knew he was hard to please, he was a loving father and a fair ruler.

"I want to start with their credentials first. Name, family, age, where they're from. If I'm still interested, then I shall request to see their portrait." He propped his elbows on his desk and folded his hands together in anticipation.

"Of course, Your Grace. That will take me but one moment," Guy said as he pulled portraits out of the stack hastily. Thankfully, he had penciled each one's name on the back. Once he had all thirty removed, he pulled five from the top and laid them out before the king.

"These are the first five, sir. All are from right here in Atelina." Guy watched as Levan read each short list, looking for some sign of approval. Levan nodded, shrugged, and smiled. Guy was pleased.

After a few nods and grunts, Levan handed over three of the sheets. "Save numbers one, two, and four. Three and five can be crossed off," Levan said with a flourish if his hands. "Show me the next set."

They continued until Levan had been through all thirty names. He eliminated eight. Twenty-two still remained. Guy paused after showing Levan the last set and picked the pictures back up. He rearranged them so they were not in the same order as before.

"Here we are again, sire, with their miniatures. I'm sure you can agree every single one is lovely," Guy said, laying the pictures on top of the information on each girl. "Here are the first four of those remaining."

Four beautiful women with demure smiles vied for attention. Each one different from the other. Levan smiled in appreciation. "This is why I wanted to hear about them before seeing them. This makes it much harder. Tell me about the first one."

"Her name is Wilma Egold," Guy said. She was Hesten's sister, but he was not about to offer that information willingly. Wilma had straight blond hair with heavy bangs and eyes as black as pitch. She was stunning with golden skin and rosy cheeks. "Wilma is from right here in Atelina, from a well-known family. She's twenty-three years old."

Levan eyed the girl in the picture. "Egold, huh? Suppose I should humor Hesten and allow his sister into the running?" Levan chuckled.

So he knew the girl was Hesten's sister. Guy thought it was tempting fate to allow her into the finalists, but he kept his mouth shut.

Levan had read basic information on thirty women perfect for the role of queen. Guy's careful selection and refinement make each candidate highly qualified. Levan trusted Guy's judgment completely. Now he sorted through twenty-two pictures to see if any of these women might have the chance of being his wife.

Levan longed to feel that jolt of lightning that would make his heart skip a beat. He noted Hesten's sister among the group immediately, having met Wilma a few times. She was an attractive girl who had been properly groomed for a life of high status and in the public eye. Levan always found her striking. But he was still waiting for one—or a few—to make him long for her.

"Can we look at them one by one, please? I think seeing all the photos side by side is impairing my ability to decide," Levan said to Guy. The queen's personal assistant quickly laid out Wilma's picture again. "Yes, keep her. Just to be nice."

Guy presented another miniature. A cute little redhead, but Levan felt nothing. "No, not her." They proceeded through three additional Levan was not interested in.

Then came a portrait of a girl who could have Veva's twin sister. Levan gasped as the resemblance. She had the same wavy black hair, but this girl's face was framed with fringe. And instead of Veva's inky dark eyes, this girl had eyes the color of the summer sky.

"Your Highness? Is everything well with you?" Guy looked concerned.

"Who-who is this?" Levan implored. He looked at the picture again. There it was. The jolt he wanted to feel. But was it because she reminded him of Veva?

At second look, she was not so similar to Veva, aside from the hair. And she looked small like Veva. But she wore a smile that could light the sun, her black hair shone brilliantly, and her eyes danced before him. Veva had never possessed such animated qualities. Those were what caused his heart to leap.

Looking to Guy, Levan asked again, "Who is she? I must know."

Guy's signature smile broke out onto his face. "She is also one of my favorites, sir. Her name is Esme Gustoff. She's from right here in Atelina. She's twenty-two years old and comes from a small and gentle family. She's very well liked by her community."

"Tell me more," Levan said as he picked up the small portrait and gently touched the face of the girl.

"More, sir?"

"Yes, more. Please."

"It says here she enjoys being outdoors and loves music. She also tends a garden at her home. She lives with her cousin here in the city," Guy read to him.

"And her n-name again?"

"Esme Gustoff. I knew you would like her, Your Grace."

Levan returned to his chair and tried to clear his head. "I do, very much. Something about her drew me right in." He shook his head. "Please, let's continue."

It took another hour, but they finally had it down to fourteen. Each woman had been lovely and intelligent. And Esme Gustoff had not been the only one Levan asked to hear more about, but hers was the name he remembered the most. Her name and her beautiful big eyes.

"Today is October twentieth. Prepare fourteen letters to be hand-delivered to those chosen. If any decide not to come, we will not replace them. Their formal invitations to come to the Belin House should go out on the twenty-fifth. The ladies are to arrive November first at noon," Levan instructed. He stood and paced the room as he spoke. "Let them explore the grounds and throw a gala in their honor—just for them, though. Lavish them. The next day they will begin their preparations."

"Yes, my king. I will do it gladly," Guy assured him.

"If we begin in November, they will be ready in February. I shall meet each one then and not sooner. If any decide to leave before then, so be it," Levan said. "I plan to wed my bride and crown the next Queen of Geoline on March first. Is that understood?"

"Of course, sir. I look forward to the wedding with much fanfare."

Levan assessed Guy. He was the perfect man to prepare the next queen and wife of the king. He always appeared well groomed and tidy. He always wore a smile and was willing to go above and beyond the call of duty. Guy had the mind of a ruler and the heart of a servant. He had been chosen well for his job. If memory served, Guy Hart had even been present when each of Levan's sons had been born.

The memory brought back images of Veva to his mind. Her small stature, so reserved and refined, her beauty, which until today Levan would have argued was unrivaled, and her willingness to do as Levan asked. At least until the end it seemed. Levan cursed under his breath at the hand dealt to him.

"I beg your pardon, sir?" Guy was still in the room, Levan realized.

"Nothing, nothing, Guy. I am looking forward to meeting these ladies. I wish you the best of luck as you work with them. I w-will ask you for updates as things progress. Until then, have a splendid day." Levan dismissed the man with a cordial smile and sat back down.

His mind wandered back to the women who had been presented to him. There was another factor he had not yet considered. Something Guy had unknowingly reminded him of. The new queen would not only be his wife, but a new mother for Lester and Lennox. Suddenly, the task of choosing seemed much more daunting than it had an hour ago.

CHAPTER 9

"October twenty-fifth is tomorrow, Esme." Yasmin, in her usual giddy nature, twirled around as she and Esme walked to the square together. They were going to meet up with several of the girls they had known in their school years.

Esme laughed. "I pray you are among those chosen, Yasmin. You certainly have the spirit of a queen."

Yasmin paused in front of a glass window and peered at her reflection. "Do you truly think so, Esme? I would love to be chosen as one of the fourteen, even if I didn't get to marry King Levan. I would relish the experience." She posed as she looked at the glass.

That was something Esme had not considered—the experience. She was interested in the inner workings of the palace but hadn't placed much merit in the experience of training to be a queen. If—and she counted it as a hefty if—she were among the selected few, the chance to experience life as the queen would be something few people could claim. She stopped alongside her friend and also peered into the glass.

Her hair fell down her back in long, soft waves, the color even more brilliant against her light blue dress. Even in the dull reflection, Esme could see how bright blue her eyes were. She always tried to carry herself properly, keeping her shoulders back and her head up straight. But that did not mean she was trained or prepared to be a member of the royal household. Or anything else for that matter. But she liked the idea of learning. Esme smiled at herself. Remembering Yasmin, she hugged her friend and peered at her in the glass.

"King Levan would be lucky to have a wife such as you. He could use your vibrancy, I think," Esme laughed. "Come on, the others are waiting for us." The pair ran off as quickly as their skirts would allow, giggling along the way.

The evening was full of laughter and fun. Esme enjoyed the outing because of the company she was in. It had been far too long since she gathered with her friends. As they walked home, Yasmin stopped, blocking her path.

"What is the matter Yasmin? Did something disturb you?" Esme looked around her friend to see why she stopped. Staring back at her was Carden, heading into the square with his own friends.

He spotted her immediately, and his jaw clenched. "Esme," Carden started. "It is a pleasure to see you again."

Yasmin turned to her, standing between Esme and Carden. "Ignore him, Esme."

"That would be rude," she replied softly. She did not smile, but she did move out from behind her protective friend. "Carden. Hello." She would not say it was nice to see him because it was not.

"Esme, may I have a moment with you? Alone?" His expression was sincere, his cool blue eyes pleading. "Please."

Even with Yasmin's disapproving glare, Esme agreed. "Only one minute, Carden. I'm with friends, and I will not be rude to them." After receiving a nod from Yasmin, it was clear she would monitor them closely.

They walked to a quiet corner, and Carden tried to take Esme's hand, but she pulled it away and folded her arms in front of her. Maurice taught her it was a position of defense and aggression, and Esme decided she needed to defend herself against Carden Wallace. The hairs on her arms stood on end.

"Esme, I am so sorry for everything. I have had time to think, and I believe you are the girl for me," he said. "I ask for your forgiveness and to see if you would allow us to continue courting."

Esme studied him. His voice and look were both sincere. But Esme shook her head. "You did not seek me out to tell me this, Carden. You happened upon me accidentally. I'm sorry, but I do not accept. I do not wish to go anywhere with you anymore."

"But, Esme I came here..." He raked a hand through his blond hair and tried to reach out to her again.

"You did what? Came here looking for me?" She glared at him. When he nodded in confirmation, a wave of heat come over her body. Esme thought she might be sick. "How did you know I would be here? Have you been following me?"

His face contorted as he searched for words. "Understand, Esme, please. You are all I think about. I felt a longing for you, even before I first asked to court you. That has not changed. Come with me."

He pleaded with her, but Esme only harbored disgust for the man. A chill ran down her spine as he stepped toward her.

"No. I'm sorry, Carden. You need to leave me alone," Esme said firmly, skirting around his outstretched arm.

The pleading look on his face changed to one of fury. Through clenched teeth, he seethed, "Esme, I said come with me." He once again reached for her, but she jumped out of reach and ran to Yasmin's side.

"And I said no. No is a complete sentence." She folded into Yasmin's protective grasp and whispered, "Let's go."

They left without speaking, but once out of earshot Esme exploded. "I can't believe the nerve of that man. He admitted to following me here, seeking me out. I wonder how often he follows me, Yasmin. I feel dirty and sick," she said loudly, waving her hands as she stomped in a circle.

She looked around for Yasmin, who was standing stock still, shocked at Esme's outburst. "I'm sorry, Yasmin. I'm irritated and disgusted. I do not mean to yell at you."

"I know that," Yasmin said with a smile. "I have never seen such an extreme reaction out of you before. I'm quite surprised."

Esme laughed. "I am so sorry. I'm not usually prone to such displays, but I could not believe the gall that man has." She took a deep breath and tossed her hair over her shoulder.

"For what it's worth, Esme, I think you're far superior to Carden Wallace. And I also think you would make a fine queen if given the chance." Yasmin smiled and added in a teasing tone, "Not as good as me, perhaps, but not terrible."

As Esme lay in her bed that night, she shuddered to think what might have become of her had she been heading home alone. Carden had been a polite gentleman at first, fooling both her and Maurice. But this side of him, the side that followed her—stalked her—was unhinged and scary. It was a relief she had not continued their relationship.

Sleep was hard to come by as dreams of Carden coming through her window or snatching her from her garden plagued her all night.

CHAPTER 10

Esme woke the next morning with a strange feeling in the pit of her stomach. With the sun's gentle warmth on her face, she knew she needed to complete her morning tasks before the day's activities took over. She got dressed in a hurry, wearing a dusty purple dress with black piping. Even her clothes reflected the odd mood she found herself in.

Looking into her small mirror, she noticed circles under her eyes. *Drat that Carden Wallace.* He had not only made her evening unpleasant, but he had also disturbed her sleep, leaving her feeling restless and irritable. She would tell Maurice about their encounter; he would know what to do. If nothing else, he would tell Carden to leave them alone. Though not physically imposing, her cousin possessed a quiet firmness that commanded respect.

She brushed her hair quickly and sat down to read the Creed. Perhaps a lesson in the Eminence's Word would help her spirits lift some. "Choose joy, and when worry creeps in, take time to pause, reflect, and give thanks for the good the Eminence provides. Let peace take the place of anxiety.

Focus your thoughts on what is true, good, and beautiful—and peace will follow."

A silent prayer filled Esme's lips, a heartfelt thank you to the Eminence for all His blessings, a warmth spreading through her chest. She had a home and family when hers vanished. Friends who would bring her up when she was down. The opportunity to pursue her dreams. They were all hers, and she was grateful. She asked the Eminence to show her the path she should be on and to help her maintain a better attitude.

As she finished her prayer, she heard a knock on their outside door. Most people were not outside for another hour. Dread filled her. Would it be Carden Wallace again? Tears filled her eyes at the thought. Maurice met her at the door.

"Esme? What's the matter?" Maurice ignored the door and put his arms around her.

"Carden approached me last night. I'm afraid that is him at the door," she said in a hushed tone. She didn't want Carden to hear if he was on the other side.

A scowl came across Maurice's face. "Let me peek and then we'll deal with this." He carefully let her go and looked at the peep hole. He looked back at Esme and shook his head. Not Carden.

He swung the door wide open, apparently recognizing their guest. "Guy, what brings you to my door so early in morning? May I help you?" he asked. A man, his jacket bearing the weighty, embossed Geoline seal, entered their home.

The man was tall and wide in the shoulder, which might have been intimidating if it was not for his broad smile. Esme could see his nearly black eyes dance. "Maurice, I am sorry for calling unannounced, but I am looking for someone." He looked from Maurice to Esme. "Esme Gustoff?"

"Y-yes. I am she." With a nervous glance at Maurice, Esme saw his bewildered expression, his brow furrowed in complete confusion. "Is everything well?"

The official produced a sealed envelope from his coat, and suddenly Esme knew what this was. She had made it. She was one of the fourteen. Could it be so? A mix of fear and elation came over her. She had hoped for this chance but had not really considered what would happen if she made it into the final.

"My name is Guy Hart, and I come from the palace. I have news for you." The man handed the envelope to her with a grand bow. "Congratulations, Miss Gustoff. You are among the fourteen women chosen to train as the next Queen of Geoline."

"Is this true? I am one of those chosen?" Esme smiled with nervous energy. She had not mentioned it to Maurice at all. Who would have thought that out of hundreds of ladies, she would be one of fourteen selected to try to win King Levan's heart?

"What on earth is going on?" Maurice's face was red as he looked from Esme to the palace official. "Esme, would you like to explain all this to me? Or am I to stand here ignorant to what is happening?"

"Forgive me, Maurice. Did you not know she had applied? You were one of the men who read through the parchments," came the reply. Guy put his hand out for Maurice to shake, but he slowly retracted it when Maurice did not offer his hand in response.

Maurice raised an eyebrow to Esme.

She grabbed her cousin's arm. "I'm sorry, Maurice. I should have told you. But I filled out the paper on a whim and thought there was no way I would be chosen out of hundreds of girls."

With a nervous laugh, Guy continued to speak. "I am just beginning my journey to hand deliver each of these letters. Esme happened to be the closest to the palace, so first on my list. I know it's early.

"Esme, no need to pack much. Just your essentials and favorite things. You will be completely outfitted with new clothing and shoes upon arrival at Belin House. Be there on November first by noon." He looked between the cousins. "If you do not show up, we will not come for you, and your spot will be forfeit."

Leaning in closer, he lowered his voice to a hushed tone. "But I will tell you this in confidence: you are my personal favorite for be chosen as Queen. If you can be there earlier, all the better. It will give you additional time to prepare. You may arrive as early as sunrise. I will already be in residence. If you need anything, don't hesitate to ask me."

A blush crept over Esme's cheeks. "Will you tell the other thirteen ladies they are your favorite as well?" She could not help but ask.

The man put a hand to his chest and gasped. "Good gracious, no. I swear on the very lives of heirs Lester and Lennox, your beautiful face and your credentials stood out to me from the moment I saw them. I think you are the girl to beat."

"Esme?" Maurice looked at her, his gaze heavy with unspoken pain, the silence amplifying the hurt in his eyes. His hair was sticking up in every direction, and his cheeks were still coated in the night's stubble.

She looked to her cousin and thought it best to explain things without the palace official in front of them. "Thank you so much, Mr. Hart. I look forward to seeing you in a few days' time." She showed him to the door and ushered him outside before turning to Maurice.

Her cousin's face was drawn tight and his color was pale. She steeled herself for his response to what had transpired. "Esme? Did you? I mean, what? How?" He rubbed his chin and stared at her in disbelief.

"Let's sit down, Maury." She led him to the couch, and he landed on the seat without ceremony. His face was still ashen. "I did fill out the application. It was entirely on a whim on the day I broke things off with Carden. I was upset and filled it out for no particular reason."

"And yet you did not tell me."

"I truly saw no reason to. Yasmin was so full of fanciful ideas. I thought nothing of it outside of girlish giggles and imaginings," she said, resting her hands on his. "Never in my wildest dreams did I think I would be invited to live on the palace grounds for three months and learn from those inside the walls."

"Wildest dreams? Wildest dreams?" He stood and paced before her. "You mean worst nightmares, don't you? Would you really compete with other women to make the ruler of a nation choose you as his wife? After he ordered the execution of his previous wife?" Maurice flung his hands in the air. As he walked, his rust-colored shirt billowed, the mismatched buttons catching the light, a testament to his hurried nature. He still did not have his outfit completed for the day.

"I still don't imagine Levan would ever decide I was the one the Creed had chosen for him," Esme began. "But what a unique opportunity..."

"Levan does not believe in the Creed or the Eminence, and neither does anyone else there. They are not Followers of the Creed. Do you forget that I have met these people, Esme? I work with them. I have seen them behind their grand curtains. They are absolute evil." His eyes searched hers, silently begging, pleading with her to say no.

"The man who was just here did not seem evil," she countered, though her voice was quiet. She looked down at her lap.

Sitting next to her again, Maurice took her in his arms. "He is one of the only ones I would trust in that place. Now tell me, dear Cricket, do you mean to go?"

With a silent prayer on her lips, she looked down around her as she breathed deeply. Looking back at her cousin, she nodded. "Yes. I intend to go. This is the experience of a lifetime, Maurice. You have to understand. I do not expect to be chosen. I am different—as you just pointed out—as I have faith in more than just what's tangible. Levan would not choose me because of that simple fact."

With a nod, Maurice's anger gave way to grief. "Esme, promise me one thing. If you go... When you go, do not tell any of them who you are or from where you came. Do not mention our faith in the Creed to anybody you meet in the palace walls. They will not understand, and what they do not understand, they destroy."

Shaking her head, Esme tried to reason with him. "But Maurice, why? How can I?"

"Promise me." His voice bellowed as he interrupted her, causing her to jump where she was seated.

Esme nodded. "Yes, Maurice. I promise. I will tell no one I am a believer in the Creed. But—"

"Not right now. We will talk again about this before you leave. But for now, let's act as if everything is normal. I need to get ready for work. They are announcing the delivery of these very envelopes this morning," he said, waving the stark white envelope in front of her.

With that, Maurice tossed the missive down on the table and left the room. Esme picked it up and studied the official royal seal on it. She had not even opened it. Gently, she broke the seal's fixture to the parchment and unfolded it. It smelled of lilacs and fire.

Congratulations to you, Esme Gustoff. You have been chosen to join thirteen others in the Belin House at the Geoline Palace in Atelina. You are expected on November 1st by noon. You must bring this invitation with you for admittance at the gate. Congratulations again, and best of luck, future Queen.

Esme carefully folded the crisp cream-colored invitation, its embossed lettering catching the light, before carrying it to her bedroom. She was one of the fourteen finalists! The sheer magnitude of how this would change her life made her head spin in confusion. Had she not just been reading in her Testaments about not worrying but instead asking everything of the Eminence, and He would bring her peace? She lay back on her freshly made bed and prayed in earnest.

CHAPTER 11

LEVAN PACED BACK AND forth, knowing Guy was out delivering those envelopes to the selected few who lived in and around Atelina. In other parts of the country, messengers bearing the familiar, embossed Geoline seal, diligently delivered their packages, the scent of freshly printed ink faint on their documents. Some were from as close as Savanne, others further from Myante and Augustine. Guy told him one of the final fourteen was from beyond Gwynberg. There was nothing beyond Gwynberg except rural farmland, which intrigued Levan. He was filled with curiosity and a strong desire to learn all about her experiences and daily life in the rural countryside.

He attempted to compile a list of the most crucial qualities in a new queen. He'd stared at the list, a growing sense of frustration welling up, as he failed to prioritize its items. Lists were important to Levan. They helped him see clearly and make the wisest choice. He had scratched things out, added things in, and reordered them all. He had only succeeded in confusing himself thus far.

"I beg your pardon, Levan. Might I have a moment?" Hesten stood halfway in the door and bowed. "MacJames said you were not occupied at present."

"Hesten, just the man I need to help me," Levan said, waving in his right-hand man in without looking up. "You're happily married, are you not?"

Hesten's eyes grew large. "Of course, sir. Nicie is a wonderful wife. We had another son born to us two months ago if you recall."

"Excellent. I will admit, Hesten, that I am allowing this matter of finding a new queen to occupy too much of my mind lately. I thought perhaps a list of top attributes for her to have might come in handy. Help me out, would you, friend?" Levan motioned to the list before him. Hesten moved forward to examine it himself.

Levan knew Hesten's marriage had been arranged, and he had not been overly happy with Nicie at first sight. But marriage was work, as he knew all too well, and their marriage was successful. Perhaps between them, they could finalize a list of qualities to evaluate the ladies, ticking off each one as he met them.

"I see all good points here, Levan," Hesten said as he rubbed his chin. "Obedience is very important in a wife. I would move that up. And beauty is, of course, a priority. You want to be attracted to your new bride, to hold affection for her and I would assume produce more heirs." He picked up a quill and scratched new numbers next to certain things.

"I have two heirs, already. That is not quite as important, but I know females enjoy having little ones about. Her appearance is important. Not just for me to find attractive, but the people must also fall in love with her to an extent." Public opinion was vital, Levan knew. Hesten agreed, and with a nod, they moved beauty to the top of the list, its importance undeniable. "I want to love her."

"I don't think love exists, sire."

Levan stopped and looked up at Hesten, his eyes casting a sidelong glance at him. "I hope you are wrong. Surely it must exist."

Ignoring Levan's comment, Hesten pointed to one of the words on ths list with a furrowed brow. "What does 'spirit' mean, if I may ask?"

Levan turned to Hesten and leaned against his desk, thinking of a way to describe the word. "I want a wife who has life behind her eyes. Someone who is not just living, but who is living life to its fullest. Spirit means a woman who loves to laugh, who is animated, who is lively." He paused. In a softer voice he said, "Veva was lovely. But she lacked spirit."

"If it means that much to you, sir, why not move it up on the list? Surely, being spirited as you say is more important than being intelligent or compassionate," Hesten pointed out.

"See? This is my dilemma. I cannot choose which is more important than any other thing. They are all important to me." Levan shook his head and folded his arms. This was proving to be harder than he expected. He continued to stare at the list, the words beginning to blur together. "Beauty, loyalty, intelligence, compassion, obedience, spirit, peacefulness, manners, patience, thoughtfulness, happiness," he said out loud.

"Why rank them at all, sire? Perhaps you will find one girl more attractive but she lacks compassion. Or maybe one will be highly spirited, but not as patient as you would like. Surely, one will possess each quality you desire. I have no doubt she will be amongst those who arrive in a few days' time, Levan. Have faith in your ability to choose the right mate and the right queen." Hesten clapped Levan on the shoulder and Levan nodded in approval.

"I hope you're right, Hesten. The perfect girl needs to arrive on the palace grounds on November first."

Hesten bowed. He was confident, almost to the point of knowing it as fact, that the king's perfect match was out there and destined to come into the palace. He had been training his sister Wilma for this position since the day Veva's crown had been removed. She had received messages each day about what the queen was to do, what her daily activities were, how to hold herself, and more. Wilma was the most beautiful girl he knew outside Veva, so he knew that would be no problem. She possessed a sharp mind, the product of extensive training, and her obedience was unwavering. Yes, Wilma would be crowned queen in a few short months. And then Hesten would begin his play for power.

"I'm certain the woman for you will be here," he told Levan. "In the meantime, allow me to draw your attention to the southern border of Viriland." He committed the king's list to memory before pulling a map out to discuss issues on the border.

Later that day, he wrote out a note to his sister and sent for a messenger.

This is Levan's list of most important attributes for the new queen to have. You must perfect every one and be prepared to display them when you meet him. He is very concerned about finding someone with spirit. Spirit is your ability to be lively, boisterous. And I will arrange for you to stumble upon a stray puppy or something while you're in his company. You can be compassionate and thoughtful to it.

With the note sent, he turned his attention to other palace matters. He had three new Palace Keepers to meet and show around. They would be added to the rotation while the fourteen ladies were in residence and then replace three men ready for retirement.

He rounded the corner and came face to face with three large men in uniform. "Good morning, men, and welcome to the palace. My name is Commander Hesten Egold, and I am King Levan's second in charge here in the palace and throughout Geoline. First, I will show you the grounds, and then you will be paired with a veteran of the palace for your formal training. Now, please introduce yourselves."

The first man, a strapping youth with copper hair, said in a stern voice, "Mickey Green, Commander." He gave a salute.

Hesten looked to the second man, the largest of the three with dark hair and skin, "Welsh Yardin, Commander." Hesten was impressed with the bass of the lad's voice.

The final man, with light blond hair and light eyes, looked the gruffest. "I am Carden Wallace. At your service, Commander." His voice was loud and his presence impressive. He was also the only one to give a proper salute. Hesten knew this one would take his job seriously.

"This way, men. Let me begin by showing you the Belin House. I'm sure you've heard of the Final Fourteen, as they're being called. This is where they shall live for their time here," Hesten said, leading the way to the back of the grounds.

CHAPTER 12

"If I'm not to tell anybody I'm a Follower of the Creed, I won't be able to bring my Testaments with me. How will I read it?" Esme asked Maurice the night before she was to leave.

The last several days had been tough on them both. Though Maurice's silent disapproval hung heavy like a shroud, he didn't challenge her decision to go to the palace. She had heard nothing more from Carden, and for that she was thankful. Sandrine had been over-the-moon happy Esme had been chosen, though Yasmin's excitement came with a certain amount of melancholy. She had not been one of the fourteen.

Now Esme packed her things. Even though she was told not to bring clothes, she brought a few items anyway. She had packed her dresses, her toiletries, and accessories. She wished she could take her desk but imagined one would be provided in her room.

But now Esme struggled with what to do about her Testaments. Her bags were bound to be searched by Palace Keepers or even the other ladies. It could not be with her.

"You'll have to do without it," Maurice said, finally. "I cannot think of a way for you to have it. You will have to tuck the Creed's Word into your heart. You know the words and verses of scripture; I have faith you will remember it."

"Will you pray for me, Maury?" Esme asked with tears in her eyes. She had been with him for fourteen long years. He was her only family, and the idea of leaving him, even for a short time, was like a physical ache, a dull throb in her chest.

Maurice sat next to her and pulled her close. He kissed her forehead the way a protective father might. "I pray for you daily, Cricket. Always remember the Eminence is with you. And if you have Him, you have me, for I live my life in Him." He grew quiet. Esme could tell he was deep in thought. "I wish you would stay."

They looked into each other's eyes. Their eyes, an identical shade of blue, locked in a moment of shared recognition. She had always loved that connection with him. Esme could feel her heart breaking. "I love you so much, Maurice. However, I have a strong inclination to do this. I don't know why. I not only want to go, but I have a sense of being guided to go. Please understand."

"I can't pretend to understand, Es. I just don't. But I do respect your decision. It doesn't mean I won't miss you, though. What will I do without you?" His eyes grew misty and he stood, moving to the opposite side of the room from her.

"You'll live. You'll finally not be stuck taking care of me," she said, laughing. She wanted nothing more than his happiness, and perhaps if she was out from under him, he would find somebody to love.

He turned to her. "I haven't taken care of you since you were twelve. Somewhere in there, the roles reversed and you started taking care of me," he said.

Esme stood and held out her hands to him. He took them willingly. "We've taken care of each other, Maurice. It's been wonderful. But I'm twenty-two. You're thirty-five. It's time for us both to grow up and find our own way in life."

"How did you get so intelligent?" He laid his forehead on hers and breathed her in.

"From you," she whispered. With a tender kiss to her hands and a curt nod, he departed, the only sound the soft click of the closing door behind him, leaving her in the quiet solitude of her room.

Esme sat on her bed and closed her bag, placing it on the floor. Slowly, she laid back. She thought she would not be able to sleep, but she her eyes closed and slept soundly through the night.

The next morning, she woke before the sun. Dressing in her pale purple dress, she then affixed her hair so it was out of her face but fell in soft waves down her back. With quiet and careful movements, she lifted her bag and carried it to the main area of her house.

"Did you mean to leave without saying goodbye?" Maurice asked, startling her.

Bringing a hand to her chest, she closed her eyes for a brief moment, overcome with emotion. "No, never. I'm just restless," she replied. "Do you want me to make you breakfast?" She wasn't sure what else to say. It was her way of saying she loved him.

"I think I'll manage. I'll take care of your chickens." His voice choked up.

Tears swam in her eyes. "Thank you. I appreciate it. I—"

"Go on," he said. "I will be in and around the palace, so while I may not see you, know I am always nearby." He pulled her into his arms, his embrace a comforting shelter against the world.

"I love you, Maurice. You're my only family." As Esme pulled away, she used the back of her hand to wipe the tears that streamed down her face.

"I love you too, Cricket. Please be careful," Maurice said as he picked up her bag and handed it over.

Esme nodded. With a creak, she opened the door and stepped through, the cold air rushing in to greet her. With a final look back at her cousin, she blew him a kiss and set forth for the palace. It was harder than she expected to leave him standing there, but he had been right. They would not be far apart. And in three months, she expected to return home.

It was only a few minutes' walk to the palace gate where she had been told to go. With her invitation in hand, she set off while the sun had barely peeked over the horizon.

Levan watched out the window. He had decided not to meet any of the incoming women until February, but that didn't mean he could not watch them enter the palace grounds. Of course, he still had three hours before they were set to arrive. It was only the ninth hour.

But, wait. What was this? The girl, her light purple coat billowing slightly in the breeze, approached the gate. She carried a small, worn yellow canvas bag, its straps digging slightly into her shoulders. This couldn't be one of the chosen women, who were expected to arrive in elegant carriages or on horseback. He was surprised to see someone approaching the palace steps, as he hadn't imagined anyone would arrive at such an early hour.

She conversed with the guard for a moment. Levan squinted and tried to determine who this might be. Her hair was barely visible under her hood, but it looked dark. This might be the one he had been so intrigued by—Esme. He put his hands to the window as if that would help him get a better look. His palms left condensation on the windows.

Then, in a swift and surprising movement, the woman's eyes lifted. She seemed to look directly at him. Levan thought they made eye contact. A gasp escaped his lips as he retreated from the window. She had piercing blue eyes. Could she see him from where he was? He was at a third story window—surely, he was not so plainly visible. He watched her look back at the guard and nod as he said something. As she turned her attention, he stepped back to the glass.

Levan watched Guy Hart jog up to the gate, his arms stretched open wide. This was indeed one of the hopefuls. Guy took the girl in a light embrace and made her laugh. The spark in her eyes was evident even from far away. She was the one with all the spirit as he had thought. He was jealous of Guy for the first time in the ten years he had known the man. Guy took her bag and led her down the path to the Belin House. They disappeared from view a moment later, leaving Levan watching after them.

"Your Grace?" came a voice from behind him. Embarrassed, Levan turned to see who had broken his thoughts.

There stood MacJames, his loyal valet and secretary, who bowed upon Levan's gaze. "Yes, MacJames?"

"The information you requested has come though, sir," the man said. "It is on your desk."

"Thank you. Make sure nobody disturbs me for the next hour, please."

"Yes, sir." MacJames bowed and left him.

With a final look out the window, he saw no further sign of Guy or the girl. Levan went to his desk and looked around the room before sitting. He knew nobody would walk in with MacJames outside the door, but he could never be too careful. The information was already there, ready for his review.

He read over the latest report on someone he was keeping close tabs on. To an untrained eye, it might look like an account of a country he wished to invade, and certainly there were those in existence. But this document was top secret. Hesten had no knowledge about it. Even MacJames did not know the entire story.

Everything looked to be in order. Things had been set to his specifications. The materials he had sent had been well received, and for that he was thankful. Levan knew nobody in Geoline, especially those in the palace, would understand what he was doing or why he was doing it. But that did not matter. What mattered was staying true to his word. And he intended to follow through.

CHAPTER 13

THE GIRL HAD COME early, just as Guy had suggested. This showed him she was moldable and determined—a perfect combination for the new queen. As he approached Esme at the gate, he held his hands out to her. "You took my advice. I'm so glad. I did not lie in saying you are my favorite. That is not something I said to any other girl coming here."

Esme nodded, a bright flash of excitement in her wide, blue eyes. Guy assessed her. Despite being from the heart of the city, a certain homespun quality was evident in her appearance. Her hands were calloused, her eyes held a certain quiet strength. She appeared so incredibly innocent and trusting. Her clothing was acceptable but not in the latest fashion with an older lavender dress that lacked the fullness many other ladies wore. Her youthfulness was striking, even more so considering she was among the youngest he expected to meet today. Maybe that accounted for her rustic look.

As they approached the house, Esme gasped. "It's so large," she said, her eyes sweeping the grand home.

"Fifteen rooms, a kitchen, and a common living area. It will be tight, but you should all be comfortable here," Guy said. "Being the first here, you have your choice of rooms. Mine is Room Five. It's tucked in the back and it's the largest. Not that I need the largest, but it keeps you ladies from fighting over it." He laughed out loud.

Esme giggled and the sound echoed through the empty halls. "Which room should I choose?" She followed him, her fingers trailing along the carefully sculpted and painted wall of the main living area, feeling the texture of the ancient wood beneath her touch. "This is so beautiful. The walls aren't white."

Indeed they were not. Guy knew the homes of Atelina were usually all whitewashed to keep things clean and easy. Colors outside the palace were muted as well. However, the moment you stepped onto the grounds, the world transformed. Vibrant colors and rich smells attacked the senses of those not used to it, as this girl obviously was not. The walls in Belin House were not terribly bold, but compared to white, it was a drastic change. The main living area boasted walls of sage green with paintings and wall hangings in every color imaginable. Guy saw the room through the eyes of someone unaccustomed to so much color.

"Just wait till you see the bedrooms. They're all in different colors as well. What's your favorite color? That might help you pick a room because they're all essentially the same," he told her. "Each room has a bed, a lounge chair, and a small desk with a straight-backed chair. That is all, unfortunately. The rooms are small, but you won't spend much time there. Most of your time will be here in the main living quarters."

Esme circled around, her eyes landing on everything and anything. "I love purple. And silver. They are my favorites."

"We have two purple rooms. One is Room Six, next to mine, and the other is Room Eleven," he said as he crossed his arms and watched her.

Guy felt a flutter in his chest as he saw the pure, radiant smile on her face. "Can I have the room next to yours? I've lived for fourteen years alone with my...father. I'm not used to so much female companionship," she admitted.

A smile touched Guy's lips as he told her how flattered he felt. "I would be delighted, Esme. Right this way. I expect others will arrive early in an attempt to make themselves look good, so please feel free to make yourself at home."

He opened the door labeled Room Six and allowed the girl in. She removed her coat and immediately hung it on the peg next to the door. Guy looked around the sparse room. A beautiful light amethyst hue coated the walls, while the bedspread, in the same shade, was piled high with soft, plush fabric. The desk was made of oak wood, and the lounge chair was a deep burgundy.

"You know what? I think Room Eight has a silver chair. Would it please you to trade chairs?" Guy offered.

"I don't want to create more work for you, Mr. Hart. Really, it's fine. The room is so lovely." She ran her hand along the bedspread.

Guy winked at Esme. "It would please me. Let me go get it." He picked up the burgundy chair and carried it to Room Eight. When he brought the silver lounge back to Esme's room, she was standing in the middle of the floor looking a lost.

"You are welcome to unpack, my dear. You have your own privacy room. Everybody does. It should cut down on any problems," Guy chuckled.

A knock sounded on the front door. Somebody else had arrived. Guy offered Esme a warm smile, and she waved him on with a bright, cheerful gesture. Hurrying to the door, he opened it to find Wilma Egold standing impatiently before him, with Hesten standing just as impatiently behind her.

"My dear Miss Wilma," Guy said, flashing the smile he knew made people feel at ease. He questioned whether or not that would work with these two.

"Guy," Hesten growled as he pushed through the door. "I assume we are first."

Guy felt Esme peek out her door without revealing herself. It brought him no small amount of satisfaction to tell him otherwise. "Actually, you are not. Another of the ladies arrived only a few moments ago. But you still get your choice of room, Wilma. Please come in."

Following her brother inside Wilma sniffed lightly as she looked around. Guy paused, his gaze lingering on Wilma's face, studying her expression and noticing that she appeared unimpressed. Her hair was blond and thick. She wore bangs that swept to the side of her chestnut eyes. She had high cheekbones like her brother, but her lips were lusciously full and pink. She looked innocent, much like Esme, but there was something behind that. Like innocence was only an illusion with this one.

Her skirts trailed behind her—they were so full. The cream color accentuated her tanned skin. She removed her cloak and held it out expectantly for Guy to take. *Oh yes, this one would create problems.* And her brother probably would as well.

"I want the best room," Wilma said as she circled the gathering room. "Which is the best?"

Guy resisted the urge to roll his eyes. "All the rooms are the same, my dear. So every woman desiring to be queen is treated fairly and equally, as it should be." He clapped his hands together, the sound echoing in the quiet house, and decided to show Wilma the best room—the one farthest from his own.

"You know, Wilma darling, I might suggest Room One to you. It is the first one. Right here in the front. It's done in a magnificent red. I think that's just the shade for you," he said, pointing to the room directly to their right.

"How hard was that?" Hesten barked. "Come, Wilma. Let us see if this room is suitable for the future Queen of Geoline."

"You two get comfortable and make sure this is the room for you. Let me fetch the other girl who has arrived. I hope you all will become the best of friends." With his back turned from the Egold siblings, Guy did indeed roll his eyes. He caught Esme watching him, her eyes sparkling with mirth as she fought back a laugh at his expression.

"Is that Hesten Egold? Is he not the king's second in command?" Esme asked quietly as Guy entered her room. Her eyes were as big as saucers.

"He is. And that is his younger sister, Wilma. I think Levan only allowed her in as a favor to Hesten." Guy took Esme's hand in his and heaved a big breath. "I won't lie to you. She will be nasty and one to watch out for. She and her brother will likely stop at nothing to ensure she gets the crown. I remember dealing with her before. But I must treat every woman as the future queen as much as it pains me."

"I understand," Esme said with a shy smile. "I will be as nice to her as I can stand."

"I can't imagine you being spiteful to any person," Guy said. "Shall we go meet them?"

ESME'S HEAD WAS SPINNING with all the names of the girls she had just met. Most ladies seemed genuinely pleasant though a few wore expressions of fear. Wilma and another girl, Darby, looked ready to crush their opponents with their icy glares. Darby came from Bloughton, not far from

Atelina. She had platinum-colored hair and tanned skin. Esme thought Darby portrayed a charming girl but hid a hyena inside.

That afternoon, they were given a banquet and an opportunity to become acquainted with each other. Esme was immediately drawn to the woman across the hall from her in Room Four. Geylis Calvin, a Myner native, possessed a kind heart and genuine spirit, evident in her warm smile and compassionate eyes. She had a crown of golden red hair that she wore up with ringlets cascading down her nape. Her eyes were almost turquoise. Just from the first day, Esme could tell they shared much in common. She was instantly warmed by the smile of her new friend.

She was also drawn to one of the girls from the rural areas of Geoline, Rhiann Partouk. Rhiann was from beyond Gwynberg in the mountain region of the nation. Being away from home for the first time, Rhiann seemed overwhelmed by the opulence and disarray of having fourteen girls confined in a space together. Rhiann's sobs echoed as her father left, but Esme was beside her, offering a comforting presence and a warm embrace. Rhiann had tiny corkscrew curls the color of honey and skin that looked like caramel. Esme thought she was one of the most beautiful women she had ever seen.

The initial days were a flurry of encounters and reintroductions with the ladies and acquainting themselves with Guy and the multitude of servants who frequented the place, all while adapting to the newly structured routine Guy had created.

"We will spend this next week on our wardrobe. You are now wards of the palace and must dress accordingly," Guy told them in a morning meeting. "This afternoon, a team of seamstresses will measure you one by one and make you seven outfits. Four day outfits, two formal, and the last is to be your choice. It can be as whimsical or as unadorned as you wish it to be. Stylists will choose colors on all but the last outfit, but you are guaranteed to look like...well, like the queens of a nation."

"What are we to do while waiting?" This came from a petite girl named Lynna who had already established herself as the outspoken one of the group.

"You are free to do as you wish. But you must stay in the house or in the gardens immediately around the house. There's a natural border, and I expect you each to stay within it or risk reprimand," Guy warned. "We will start with Alina, please."

"Ugh, I hate waiting," grumbled a girl named Zelda. She continued to expressing her utter hatred for the tedious process of waiting. Nothing but complaints had come from her mouth since the moment she stepped over the threshold. She huffed away to her room.

"I don't mind waiting," Alina said quietly. Esme learned Alina came from a poor family, and they nominated her in hopes she would win and elevate her family's wealth.

"No, darling, you are first," Guy said, ushering her closer. "Right this way."

When it was her turn, Esme was pleased with the six choices made for her already. The colors and styles had all been flattering and far nicer than anything she had ever worn before. The stylist finally asked what she would like for her self-chosen outfit, but Esme did not know what else to pick.

"May I see Guy before choosing?" Someone was immediately dispatched to retrieve him, and upon his arrival, he entered the room with a dramatic flourish. Esme whispered to him, "What would King Levan prefer me to have?"

"What do you mean?" Guy seemed confused. "You can choose any color or design you prefer."

She licked her lips, and took Guy's hands in hers. "I know that. But if I am to be the queen and please Levan, I need to know what his preferences are. What is his favorite color?"

Guy grinned from ear to ear. "Smart move, my darling. Levan happens to love royal blue." He raised an eyebrow as he thought. "And while he sees the full skirts as feminine, he's not a fan of all the excess. He enjoys skin, so bare arms would be highly attractive to him."

"Thank you, Guy," she whispered.

"Anything for you, Chérie." From the outer room, a call of his name summoned him, and with haste, he ran to help another of the ladies.

"I have decided. I would like the outfit to be royal blue," Esme said to the dressmakers with certainty. "The top should have uncovered shoulders and arms, but still with straps and a square neckline. Can you make the skirt in a kerchief style so it is full but not bulky?"

The designer and stylist conferred for a moment. The designer sketched something on her pad and showed Esme. "Like this?" The skirt was full, the kerchief design creating soft ripples, but it would not be bulky at all—perfect. Esme hoped it would suit Levan's preferences.

The stylist showed her a few fabric options in royal blue and suggested one with a subtle shimmer to it.

"Yes. Exactly," Esme said, pleased with everything. "Thank you so much for your help."

Both looked shocked at her words of thanks. "Why, you are most welcome."

She patted the hand of the one who had measured her and left the fitting area so Zelda could finally take her turn. In the common area, the girls who had already been fitted were comparing notes on what the designers said for them.

Lynna had chosen black for her personal choice, thinking it would bring out the paleness of her hair. Esme worried it would make her appear as if she was in mourning. Geylis said she opted for a dusty golden color she hoped would show off her hair. Alina had been too afraid to make a choice and let the designers do it for her. They picked a muted blue dress that was far too simple. Esme thought the poor girl would blend right in with the background.

"What did you choose?" Wilma asked Esme. Wilma hadn't yet visited the designers, and Esme suspected she was researching everyone's color palettes to choose a contrasting design.

Esme smiled demurely and sat beside Geylis. "I asked for a blue dress without many frills," she said. She did not want to give away too many details about her special dress.

"I think I'll ask for pink. A bold pink like that flower," Wilma said, pointing to a bright pink peony. Then she covered her mouth. "Drat. But I called it! I called the color. Nobody else can pick it."

Esme didn't think anyone would purposely choose such a shockingly bright pink dress; it was almost offensively vibrant. That color would make anyone stand out like a sore thumb in a sea of softer colors.

CHAPTER 14

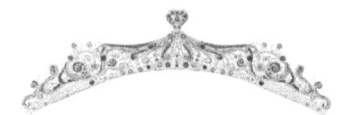

"One week in and one girl has departed for home already, sir," Guy reported to Levan. This time Guy accepted Levan's offer to sit.

"Truly? What made her leave? Who has departed?" Levan turned to face Guy. Why would someone want to leave the lap of luxury he offered? The queen's varlet looked haggard. He had eleven more weeks of this; he could not be so worn out already.

"A young lady from the countryside named Opal. She was quite homesick, Your Grace. I do not feel she was here on her own accord, if I may be so blunt." Guy coughed into his fisted hand and looked anywhere but at Levan.

Levan shook his head. He feared some of the ladies had been forced into applying or accepting his invitation purely as a way to advance the family. "I am sorry to hear it. How do the others fare?"

"Wonderfully, sire. Their personalities are really beginning to shine through now that they've adjusted to being here," Guy told him.

Levan allowed himself to chuckle. "And I suppose that is a good thing for some of the ladies, and not so good for others." A hearty huff and a loud laugh from Guy prompted Levan to join in, the sound of their laughter filling the air. "Do any make trouble?"

Guy scratched his lightly-whiskered chin. "No, sir, not at the moment. There are a few I plan to keep close watch of, but most of them are pleasant as summer rain."

Summer rain? Levan thought. As long as everybody was getting on fine, he wasn't too worried. "I thank you for the update. Make sure they are pampered but not spoiled too much."

Guy stood. "Yes, sire." He bowed and departed from Levan's office. As his footsteps echoed down the hall, Levan relaxed back into his chair.

The peaceful atmosphere evaporated as Hesten stormed into the room. "You tolerate too much, Levan," he fumed. Hesten paced in front of Levan's desk, arms crossed over his chest with one hand rubbing his chin as he stewed.

"Do I now?" Levan asked, raising an eyebrow. "Just what might I over tolerate, Hesten?" It was unlike his commander to question Levan's way of doing things. Usually, he accepted his orders, even if Levan knew Hesten disagreed. Judging by his adverse response, it was clear someone upset him.

"These...these Creed Followers." Hesten's long duster coat flew out behind him as he swept around to face Levan. "They are obstinate, disobedient, and have no respect for authority."

Levan knew there were a number of people in Atelina and throughout the country who followed what they called the Creed and their Eminence. Every one he'd met before had been gentle, compassionate souls, each one radiating a quiet kindness. They always lived in peace. "They make up but a small fraction of the people here in the city—in the country, really, and I have never had problems with them. But tell me, how have they offended you?"

"One man in particular, Levan. But he's a leader among those Creed Followers here in Atelina. And they are more numerous than you think within our borders. But outside Geoline—that is where the real threat is. They are all a threat." Hesten slammed his fist on the desk between them, causing Levan to jump.

Levan's ears perked up. Was there really a threat? No news had reached him. But if there was any chance of an uprising from outside Geoline that might gain popularity within their walls, Levan needed to investigate. "Where is this uprising?"

"Cartrelle. Creed Followers account for nearly three quarters of their countrymen. They're growing in numbers across every country in Europe. And here in Geoline, the number is close to one hundred thousand, they've doubled in the past twenty years," Hesten said. "Your Grace, I think it might be best to eradicate our country of these menaces before they pose a true threat beyond our control."

Levan unrolled the map to his left. He knew the layout of Cartrelle, which was roughly double the size of Geoline. If most of their people were Followers of this Creed, this Eminence, they could easily infiltrate his borders. "I shall look into this at once, Hesten."

Cartrelle, the land on Geoline's western border, was generally a peaceful nation. They were much more conservative than Geoline, but that did not mean they were not planning something. Raina Auburn, the ruling monarch of Cartrelle, was a quiet and secretive sort. Levan became suspicious. Perhaps it was time to send some scouts to their neighbors. Besides, he would love to expand his borders, and this might be a way to get into Tentakay.

That afternoon, Levan gathered his top informants and dispatched them to Cartrelle to see if Hesten's accusations had any merit. Although Cartrellans were typically passive, he wanted to remain vigilant and prepared. He instructed them to infiltrate the faith-based group and see if they had any plans to come into Geoline with or without the government's knowledge or assistance.

At the very least, this would provide something to keep Levan's mind off the beautiful women residing in his backyard. He thought about them entirely too much. Perhaps the familiar comfort of Lester and Lennox's company would help alleviate his anxiety regarding the palace's female visitors.

A CRASH FROM OUTSIDE told Esme someone was creeping around the grounds. She put her book down and ventured outside. Despite it being November, the weather was surprisingly warm, so she left her coat behind. She cautiously walked around the clearing. There were thick bushes against the walls of the house as high as the windows, but behind the house was a courtyard and a small meadow surrounded by a copse of trees. It was a picturesque little place with the last of autumn's leaves clinging to branches one more day. But nerves overshadowed her awe as she searched for intruders.

Another rustle from the trees gave her a start, and she turned to find the source. "Who's there? Come out," Esme ordered. She spun in a slow circle, not wanting to be caught off guard.

Two little mop-topped children emerged from behind a large tree, catching her by surprise. The larger boy stood tall and proud with shaggy ash-colored hair and green eyes. He was wholly unafraid. His younger companion, with a crown of chestnut curls, appeared more shy and skittish; he stayed behind the larger child.

Seeing the children made Esme sigh in relief. They could not hurt her. She wondered where they had come from. She went a few steps closer to them and stooped down. "And who might you two be?" The older could not have been more than six or seven years old, his brother she guessed to be four. And now that she was closer, she could see they bore a strong resemblance to one another.

"I am Lester, heir to the throne of Geoline," the tow-headed boy announced as he puffed his chest with pride. Then he pointed to his brother. "This is Lennox. He's an heir, too."

King Levan's children. Her gaze swept across the surroundings, seeking out a figure who was in charge of the children. Seeing nobody, she wondered if speaking with the boys was allowed. She knew they were not supposed to meet the king until he called for each girl, but nobody mentioned meeting his children.

"Who are you?" The younger boy stepped closer to her, and Esme dropped to her knees so she was on the same level as him. "You have hair like my momma." He sniffed and wiped his nose with the back of his hand.

Esme wanted to reach out to comfort the boy, who looked like he might cry at any moment, but she refrained. "My name is Esme. I'm a visitor here at the palace. And you're right, Lennox, I do have hair like your mother. She is a very pretty lady, so I thank you for the compliment."

Lennox came a step closer, close enough that Esme could smell the mix of dirt and little boy on him. It suddenly reminded her of her brother Aaren, who had been only four when the illness claimed his life. Esme quickly blinked back tears but could not tear herself away from the child. Her heart hammered in her chest How she wanted to reach out to these poor children.

Instead, she cleared her throat. "You know what, Lennox? I had a little brother about your age once. His name was Aaren. But he's gone now, and I miss him so very much," she said, sensing a tear trickle down her cheek. "I bet you miss your mother, too, don't you?"

With those words, the child flung himself into her arms, almost knocking her over. "Yes," he cried as he wailed into her shoulder. Stunned, Esme could only wrap her own arms around his little body and cry along with him. Before she knew it, Lester had come over and was patting them both on their backs, murmuring words of comfort to them.

It took several minutes, but when she noticed Lennox's sobs grew quiet, Esme pulled him back and looked at him. She handed him the corner of her skirt to wipe his cheeks. "Feel better?"

He nodded, "Yes. A little. Do you feel better?" He wiped his nose along his sleeve.

At least the shirt is green, she thought.

"I do. Thank you for letting me cry with you. That was very nice of you, Lennox. And Lester, thank you for being so comforting. I appreciate it," she said, giving a heartfelt smile to the older boy.

"You are welcome, Miss," he looked over his shoulder. "Come on, Lennox, we had better return before we are missed."

"Bye, lady." Lennox waved a pudgy hand at her and stepped back to his brother.

Then, as suddenly as they had appeared, the two boys ran back into the woods, leaving Esme behind, sitting in the middle of the clearing alone. She pulled her knees up to her chest and made sure her skirt covered everything before resting her head. In an instant, she realized the significance of her being there and took a few moments to gather her thoughts.

The winner would not only gain the crown and title of queen, but also the responsibility of caring for a lonely husband and two emotionally fragile sons. It was more than a king and a kingdom. It was a family. Something Esme always longed for.

L<small>EVAN HAD FOLLOWED THE</small> boys through the trees, not realizing where they were leading him. Lester, his take-charge eldest son, marched through the trees with a battle cry on his lips. Lennox chased after, still unable to keep up with his older brother.

Like the boys, Levan had heard a female voice call for whoever was hiding to come out. He stayed hidden while his boys bravely revealed their position. He watched the exchange between them and the girl until he heard the name that had been haunting his dreams—Esme. This was the girl. Silently, he drew closer and hid behind her in the trees.

As he watched, he was shocked to see his younger son fall into her arms, sobbing. He could not see her face, but the way her shoulders moved told Levan she cried along with him. She rocked his four-year-old son for several minutes, and Lester, newly seven, attempted to ease both their troubles. Soon they parted, and the boys ran back off in the direction of the main palace.

But Levan was entranced. Here was the woman who had captured his thoughts from the first time he saw her picture. He could see the gentle nature and loving spirit in her face, but now to see it in person—he felt the urge to go to her. She curled up into a tiny package, sitting in the middle of a meadow. She looked like a portrait, even from behind. He slowly crept to where he could see her face. Yes, she had been crying—he could see the red rimming her eyes. What caused her to cry with Lennox? Levan wanted to comfort her, to wipe the stains from her cheeks.

He could not, though. He could not approach her until it was time to formally meet her. He should not even be watching her as he was doing now.

Blast it! He was king. He could do anything he wanted, couldn't he? He knew the boys would call for him in a few minutes, so his time was limited, but he could not tear his eyes off the beauty before him. Esme. He backed away slowly, knowing he had to leave but not wanting to stop watching. When the trees obscured his view, Levan finally turned and went in search of his children.

As a Palace Keeper, he had been tasked with seeing to safety of the king and his whelps. He followed them into the wooded area in silence, observing. He saw Esme with the king's sons, noted the king's own attention to Esme, and he did not like what he saw. Esme could not help being compassionate, though he had never known she'd had a brother. She had told him her family died, but she never once said that included a younger brother.

Levan was smitten, that much was obvious. He could hardly take his eyes off her, even when his sons had gone back into the woods to search for him. Levan stayed behind and watched her like a lovesick puppy. The Keeper could see the longing to approach her in Levan's eyes, but he had stayed hidden. That was a good thing.

Anybody would be smitten with Esme. Not only was she kind and generous, she was gorgeous as well. Her smile alone could launch a thousand ships. One laugh from her lips would enrapture an entire continent. If she were to become the queen, she would be the people's queen.

Too bad she was meant to be *his* queen. As jealousy rose in the Palace Keeper, he could feel its toxic tendrils tightening around his heart. Normally he would try to repress it, but on this day, he welcomed it. He wanted nothing to get in the way of his being with Esme, least of all the king of Geoline. If he couldn't be with Esme, nobody could.

As Levan finally backed away from the clearing, he followed the monarch. It was his duty after all. His promotion to Palace Keeper had wonderful timing. Now he could keep his eyes on Esme and get paid for it. Carden Wallace knew things would finally fall into place.

CHAPTER 15

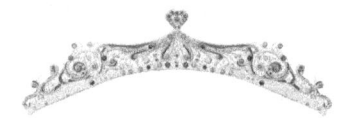

ALMOST A MONTH HAD passed since Esme arrived at the palace. She could hardly believe she was one third of the way through her time in training. Soon she would be presented before King Levan and have the chance to win him over. The ladies were learning all about palace life and diplomacy, about how to be a queen. But no one told them much about Levan himself. In their quiet time, Esme snuck into Guy's room to quiz him on everything about Levan and his sons. She wondered if anyone was educating the king on them as well.

There was a reason behind her questions, though. Day by day, Esme's feeling that she and Levan were meant to be together deepened into a profound conviction. Naturally, all the girls in the house believed she would be the chosen one, but Esme believed the Eminence was calling her to this position. Who could argue with that? Every day in her prayers, she asked to understand Levan and his family, and she prayed the Eminence would help her to follow the path set before her.

Each night after the sun dipped below the horizon but before their nighttime routine, Esme walked outside in the courtyard. Despite the cooler temperatures, she enjoyed the exercise and fresh air, especially on nights when Darby or Wilma fought, or Lynna bellowed for something. It gave her the chance for a little solitude in a place with so little of it. She was beginning to wear a path in the lush carpet of grass as she circled the edge of the meadow and diagonally across.

A shiver of déjà vu ran down Esme's spine as the whispering rustle of leaves in the crisp autumn air made her acutely aware of her surroundings. It was dark beyond the paved stones of the courtyard, so she could not see, but she could sense eyes fixated on her. Her heart thudded in her chest, and she drew her coat tighter.

Suddenly, a man materialized from behind the tree, his eyes hidden in shadow, and he didn't utter a word. He was large, but his form was familiar. The long overcoat flared as he came closer, revealing shiny black shoes and the familiar green of a uniformed guard. She had seen the Palace Keepers patrolling the grounds, but most stayed away from Belin House. Esme wasn't sure if she should be concerned or relieved at his presence.

Then a low voice spoke to her. A familiar voice. "Hello, Esme. I've been waiting for you."

Her breath hitched in her throat as shock completely overwhelmed her senses. "Carden? I don't understand. What are you doing here?" Esme asked, her voice high pitched but soft. She looked around to be sure nobody saw them conversing. "How long have you been here?"

"I've been here about as long as you. I've been watching your patterns," he said, stopping short of the lamplight so his face and blond hair were still hidden. But Esme knew his shape all too well. "I tried to tell you. Right before you came here. I said I had news I wanted to share. This was it. I was promoted to Palace Keeper. You, though, did not tell me you put in the application to do this. Giving yourself to the king like this—I can't believe Maurice allowed it."

A wave of fury washed over Esme, making her blood boil with anger. How dare he? "I do not have to explain myself to you, Carden. There is no relationship between us, and there hasn't been for months. I put in the application after I first ended things with you. And I have not given myself to the king. I haven't even met him." Her fists clenched beneath her crossed arms, a simmering rage holding her rooted in place, ready to explode.

"You may not have met him, but you met the children. And Levan... He was watching the entire thing," Carden sneered, finally stepping into the lamplight.

The heat in her veins ran cold. "What are you talking about? How did you know I met the children?"

Carden circled her, his forest green uniform hugged his body, making him look larger than he had been before. Esme had never been scared of Carden, but fear crept into her conscious. She whirled around to see him, her silver skirt fanning out like a bell. She pulled her coat tighter in the winter breeze, or perhaps it was because of Carden's icy stare.

"I was watching. I've been watching since you first arrived. I went to your house the morning you got the invitation to come here. I wanted to tell you before I came to the palace that I had been given this position," he said. He slipped back into the shadows and his face was again obscured. "When I discovered you were coming here, I thought this could be my chance to win you over. We can leave, Esme. We can have our life together."

"You cannot be serious in this, Carden. I'm here to see if King Levan and I... If I might be the one chosen. I no longer wish to see you. Ever." Esme made a move to go back to the house, but Carden stepped in front of her, blocking her path. She tried to get around him, but he anticipated her, quickly seizing her arm with a cold, firm grasp. "Please, Carden. Don't do this. Let me go."

"I don't want to," he said, a snarled smile coming over his lips.

Esme saw the pain in his eyes, but she was not sure why he was so obsessed with her. Their courtship had been brief, and it had been obvious to her they were not well matched.

She needed to change her tactic, she realized. Running away would not work, he was too strong. Perhaps if she didn't make it look like she was trying to escape from him, he would let her pass. With a deep breath, she spoke in soft, reassuring tones, hoping to soothe. "I'm not going far, Carden. Just inside the house. It's dark and growing colder. I need to go in. I will be missed, and they will look for me in a minute. And you will be missed from your post. It's not safe for us to meet out here."

After a moment, his face softened. As tension eased from his body, a peculiar half-smile slowly formed on his face. "Oh. Yes, you're right. Go back inside the house. I will be watching, and I will be in touch again." He moved as if to embrace her, but Esme managed to get past him without his touching her.

At a safe distance, she whispered under her breath, "Not if I can help it." With quick steps, she entered the house and proceeded directly to Guy.

Winded by the encounter and escape, Esme huffed as she found her mentor. He caught her as she flew into his arms. "What is it, Chérie? What has happened to make you so flushed?" His grip on her shoulders tightened, a sharp line creasing the skin between his eyes as he focused on her.

"Out— Outside," she stumbled over her words. "A Palace Keeper." A shudder ran through her body.

Guy touched her arms and examined her clothing. "Did he scare you? Did he touch you?"

Nodding, she said, "He scared me. But I know him. We...he courted me a few times last year. I ended our relationship long before coming here to the palace and without knowing he had been made a Palace Keeper." She took a deep breath. "He said he's been watching me and following me. He told me things I've done in the past few weeks. He said he wants me to run away with him. I am scared of what he might do, Guy." With a choked sob, tears spilled down her cheeks, salty and hot against her skin.

Guy ushered her into his room quickly. "Oh, Esme, do not cry, darling. We will take care of this. Do you...do you want to go with him?"

Could he really be asking her this? But Esme realized Guy was giving her a graceful exit, a chance to choose Carden over the king if she really wanted to rekindle that romance. She had never been completely sure about Carden, and now she knew why. The Creed intended her to be here, at the palace, doing her utmost to understand a lonely king.

Esme looked at the unwavering generosity in Guy's eyes. "No. I told Mau—my father—before I left that I felt like I needed to come here. I truly want to meet Levan and see if perhaps there is some attraction and affection between us. I do not want to be anywhere else."

"Good. I am glad. I would be most unhappy to lose you, darling," Guy said, handing her a tissue. "Do you think this Palace Keeper will try anything underhanded?" When Esme nodded, he sucked in a breath. "Very well. Then we will need to take action. What is his name?"

"Carden. Carden Wallace."

CARDEN MET THE TWO thieves behind the wall of the palace rubbish depository. It was the most discreet place he could think of where nobody would notice them. They wouldn't have wanted to meet with a Palace Keeper, but he kept his identity a secret and stayed in the shadows. All it took was money and the right words to convince the criminals to carry out his plan—kill King Levan if Esme was chosen.

He had not been sure it was the right thing to do, but after getting up the nerve to approach Esme, he knew he his thinking was correct. She was trapped. She told him she *had* to go back inside the house, not that she *wanted* to go back in. She said they could not be seen together, which meant she wanted to be with him but was scared. Her breath had been fast and her eyes skittish. Something terrifying had left her shaken, and he, ever the gallant and dashing hero, would be there to rescue her from her fear. Carden knew he had to save her no matter what.

"Levan will begin meeting these harlots in February," Carden said to the two men in hushed tones. "My understanding is he will marry one of them on March first. If he chooses Esme Gustoff—and *only* Esme Gustoff—Levan Haras is not to make it to the wedding night."

"What's it with this particular girl?" asked the taller of the two, a hulking man called Billiam. "What if he picks someone else?"

There was no need for him to provide an explanation to those he considered beneath him. Staying in the shadow of a large tree, he repeated the deal. "If he wants someone else, you do nothing. Keep the money, but harm no one. If Esme is his choice, do not touch her. But Levan must die. This gives you more than two months to figure out how to get it done so you are not caught."

"What if we are caught?" This came from Terres, the muscle of the duo.

"Then you don't know me. You've never met me." Carden looked around for extra measure. Darkness enveloped them, and there was no sound in the night air.

"We do not know your name, nor what your face looks like," said Billiam. He stepped closer to Carden but was quickly pulled back by Terres.

"All the better," Carden said, licking his lips. He had been talking to them for too long. "Make sure your plans are good. Levan may not have met her, but he's had his eye on the raven-haired girl already. The odds are in her favor. I shall not contact you again unless you fail. You don't want that."

"Yes, sir," Billiam said. He stood straight, his overly tall body swayed. "You can count on us."

The would-be assassins slowly crept away from Carden. Billiam turned left and disappeared. Terres counted to fifty then took off straight, just as they planned. Carden turned and went back where he came from, covering his tracks as we went. He swept his large footprints from the path, even though they were unlikely to survive until March.

Maurice walked slowly up the path to Belin House where his cousin and twelve others would reside for two more months. He did not want to appear over eager. He followed Dinald Waters, the Minister of Propaganda, to do a write-up on the ladies in residence. The people of Atelina had been hovering at the gates, hoping to catch a glimpse of the Final Fourteen, even though now it was only thirteen. Maurice had the idea of writing about them for the public, and everybody loved it. It had been the only way Maurice could think of to see Esme without drawing attention to their relationship.

Guy Hart opened the door to the house, where all thirteen girls who remained sat in a semicircle around the room. Maurice spotted Esme at once. In a sea of women with blond and brown hair, even with a redhead in the crowd, Esme stood out with her black hair and bright blue eyes. If possible, Maurice thought she looked even more radiant now than a month prior; her smile seemed brighter, her skin more luminous.

Upon seeing him, Esme's face lit up. She smiled wide, her eyes shining with longing to get up and run to Maurice, yet she held herself back. He was relieved she kept herself in check. She held herself with an air of regality: back straight, neck elongated, hands folded neatly in her lap. Her outfit was bright red, a color nobody outside of the palace ever wore. Bright colors were only allowed inside the walls, an unspoken rule Maurice had never understood. They were for royalty—or those vying to be royal, he thought. While all the ladies before him wore vivid colors, Esme was the only one in red. Most of the others wore blues, greens, and pinks. They were all lovely, but they did not stand out like his cousin. Perhaps that was only his bias.

Guy ushered the scribes in and turned to the women before him. "Ladies, here is your surprise. We are conducting a question and answer session to be written up about you. This way, the people of Geoline can familiarize themselves with you and catch a glimpse into who our next queen might be. And your families would likely enjoy hearing of your escapades here in the palace."

All the ladies squealed in delight and chattered amongst themselves while Maurice set up a small desk and readied his ink and quill. Dinald spoke in hushed tones with Mr. Hart before settling himself off to the side. Esme talked calmly with two others ladies, one a redhead with a lovely smile and the other a wide-eyed beauty with wild curls. Maurice noted she had been given a prime position among the ladies. She was comfortably perched on a gray wingback chair closest to Guy. Her friends took up two-thirds of a simple gold couch. The other seat on the couch was occupied by a girl with blond hair and a pout; he recognized her as Wilma Egold right away. Nobody spoke to her.

"Who is asking the questions?" A small, but obviously feisty, girl asked from the back row. "How does this work?"

Guy stood before them and clapped his hands together. "Excellent questions, Lynna. I have a whole list of questions from the citizens of Geoline. Mostly from Atelina, but some from other areas. Atelinians are hungry for a glimpse of you all. The questions cover anything from your personal preferences to what it's like here at the palace to how you hope to win Levan's affection. I will choose certain girls to answer particular questions, but you all may take turns answering anything you would like."

Maurice purposely allowed a few sheets of parchment to float off the desk, and he was glad they landed where he aimed—Esme's feet. As he shuffled around the desk and crouched to pick them up, he saw a smile creep onto her face.

"Excuse me, miss," he said, trying to hide a guilty, knowing smile.

"Of course. Thank you for coming to talk to us," she said. Then she made a bold move. She extended her hand to him. "My name is Esme."

Feeling tears might come to his eyes, Maurice looked down at her black-heeled shoes. "Maurice, miss. It's a pleasure." As they shook hands, Maurice thought he could feel a month's worth of hugs and easy laughs transfer to him.

It was then he realized she was not just surviving here. She was thriving. The privileged place she held next to Guy Hart clearly showed she was one of his favorites. Several hopefuls, eager to speak with his charming cousin, leaned over each other, their whispers and smiles creating a buzz of excitement around her. Maybe Esme had been right. Maybe she had been called by her faith in the Creed to come to the palace. Even if she did not win the title of queen, she might be here to aid the one who would be chosen.

IT HAD BEEN A shock to see Maurice stride into the house after not seeing him for a month. Leave it up to her cousin to find a way to see her without anybody being the wiser. She thought it silly to introduce herself to her own cousin, but it was the only way Esme could think of to make some sort of physical contact with him. She didn't know how much she missed him until now.

With instructions from Guy and a quick check that the scribe could hear everybody, they began the interview session. Each girl had been given a special seat, and Esme knew she was next to Guy for a reason. He tried not to make his favor obvious, but at times he could not help it.

Guy took his seat next to her. Maurice dipped his quill into the pot of ink and poised it over the papers before him. Esme had seen Maurice in action several times, but now she relished the experience. When he gave the go ahead, Guy jumped into action.

"All right, girls. We will take this slow so the scribe can record everything we say. Choose your words carefully," he said, flashing the smile that could get him anything he wanted. "Before you answer, please say your name so he can write it down. Don't worry about spelling; he has a list. Are we ready?"

The girls all nodded and giggled. Esme's gaze was fixed on Guy, though the corner of her eye caught glimpses of Maurice beside him, his presence a silent pull.

"This first question I'll direct to the beautiful Rhiann to start," he continued. "How does Atelina and the palace compare to your home?"

Rhiann was taken aback, her eyes wide. She suppressed a giggle. "Well, I am from a tiny place past Gwynberg called Clintscale. It's mostly farmland—the houses are much more spread apart. But much like Atelina, the people are incredibly friendly and inclined to help someone in need. Being here inside the palace walls, we don't have a chance to get out into the city much, so it's hard to compare the city from my rural home." She looked back to Guy who asked if Darby would care to answer.

Darby was seated across from Esme, so she had a front row view for Darby's hair flip and response. "Frankton is larger and older than Atelina, of course, but it's very similar," she said. "All the people are lovely, and I look forward to getting to see more of Atelina and meeting the people here." Esme could hear the smile plastered on Darby's face.

"Wonderful," Guy replied. He carefully watched Maurice, making sure every detail of the answer was accurately recorded. When Maurice looked up, Guy continued. "Our next question I'll direct to Esme. What are the other finalists like?"

Esme looked around nervously. "This is the best group of ladies, truly. I have made what I hope will be lifelong friendships with some of the other house residents, regardless of the outcome. We are still getting to know each other, of course, but everybody has been marvelous and generous. I look forward to learning more with them and about them."

"Anybody else?" Guy asked.

Zelda chimed in. "The other ladies are nice and all, but I am not a fan of waiting for everybody to arrive at the table in order to eat or have our meetings. I admit I'm from a small family where I never had to wait for others. So while I like everybody, my patience is seriously being tried here."

The other girls giggled nervously and a few nodded. Esme was also from a small family and not used to waiting on so many others, but it certainly did not bother her the way it did Zelda. But Esme realized Zelda had no patience in her body at all.

"Her name?" Dinald called out from his place in the back.

"I'm Zelda Amarckus," she replied. Maurice nodded as he took it down.

Many questions were addressed, each girl responding to at least one, as directed by Guy. He was diplomatic about it, which he needed to be in his position.

When Guy got to the last question, he posed it to Esme again. "Esme, can you tell us what the best thing about being here so far has been?"

She beamed at his question. She would say meeting Lester and Lennox had been a highlight, but she knew she could not mention that. "There have been so many, and yet we still have two months together as a group," she said as she looked around. "We have learned so much about our wonderful country, about how to best serve the people. But I would have to say the best part has been making these wonderful friends. Even if I am not chosen, and I realize there is a small chance of being chosen, I have made friends. I have met ladies from all over I would have never met otherwise. This has been an amazing experience so far."

"There you have it. I hope that's enough to work with," Guy said once Maurice finished his scribbling.

"More than enough," Maurice said as he laid his quill down. He flexed his hand and shook it out. Esme knew it could get cramped easily if he had to write a lot in a short amount of time like this.

The other ladies immediately stood and milled about. Esme remained seated, watching her cousin as he carefully capped his ink and rolled up the parchments to transport back to his office. She wasn't sure when she would see him again.

"This is an excellent way to ingratiate ourselves to the people," Wilma pointed out. "Will we be doing more of these?"

Dinald answered, "If this one gets good reviews, we will come back in a few weeks for another one." All the girls nodded with excitement.

"Why are you still sitting?" Geylis crossed her arms and raised an eyebrow as she stood before Esme.

Startled, Esme blinked and looked at her friend. "I'm sorry. I'm intrigued at the inner workings of the palace and the palace reporters. It's quite interesting."

Geylis sat back next to her and watched as well. She whispered to Esme, "It is too bad I did not make the acquaintance of that man before all this. He's quite handsome, and he seems confident in what he does."

It took a moment, but Esme realized Geylis was talking about Maurice. Esme slowly turned her head towards Geylis, her jaw slightly slack. "What are you saying?"

"I'm not saying anything, Esme." Geylis covered her giggle with her hand. "Just that if I had met that man before I applied to come here, maybe I would not have applied."

Just then, Maurice looked up at them. Esme lit up and motioned toward Geylis with her wide eyes and smiled, hoping he would get what she meant. Maurice's attention shifted from her to her redheaded friend, his curiosity piqued. Geylis' cheeks turned crimson, and she quickly averted her gaze to the ground. Maurice must have understood her meaning, for when Geylis blushed, he did as well and went back to what he had been doing.

CHAPTER 16

BEFORE LEVAN KNEW IT, February was upon them. The winter had been mild so far, which he expected. It was unusual for much snow to fall, a rare occurrence he sincerely hoped wouldn't happen this year, disrupting the quiet rhythm of the town. It always caused a panic in the people, who only saw it every few years. Levan had spent part of his youth in Norway learning diplomatic customs with his cousin, who was now King Germaine after marrying the former king's daughter. The northerly experience left a distaste for snow in his mouth, and he never cared for it after that.

But what Levan was most concerned with now was the daunting task of sorting through the women who had spent the past three months learning everything about him, about being a queen, and about life in the public eye. He wondered if any were up to the task. The updates he received periodically gave him some concern. A number of them seemed genuine, gentle, and caring. But a few only had status and power in mind, and that scared him. He knew he needed to avoid choosing one of those girls. The consequences of a wrong choice were too great to bear.

As the time progressed, Levan rearranged his priorities from what he had initially listed. After seeing Lennox's passionate outburst with the one finalist, Esme, he realized finding a mother for his children needed to be one of his main goals. The way he saw it, Levan had three goals that needed to be accomplished with one woman: a wife, a mother, and a queen. In that order. He feared some of his choices only saw the crown and not the family that came with it.

He was obligated to give each woman his undivided attention for a day. He left the order in which he met them up to Guy, but he knew he would need to meet the raven-haired girl before he could ever make a decision. Tomorrow would be his first encounter with one of the ladies who had been living on his land but remained out of reach thus far.

Of course, the first woman Guy arranged a meeting with was Hesten's sister, Wilma. Levan looked at her miniature once again. At twenty-two years of age, Wilma had accomplished much. She was a successful pianist and painter. With her family name and confidence, she had a way of instantly becoming the center of attention everywhere she went. It seemed Hesten's sister was much like her brother: self-confident, entitled, and a little arrogant.

Wilma carefully selected the most exquisite things imaginable for her time with Levan. The most elaborate meals, a private showing of a traditional Tejanian dance from a traveling troupe, and some time alone in the form of a private ride through the city's streets. While Levan had an appreciation for the finer things in life, it was not how he would choose to spend his day. It sounded more like work.

He was supposed to meet Wilma on a third-floor balcony of the main palace just before noon. When he arrived, he noticed a table for two was set up, decked out in the most intricate dining ware he had ever seen. A feast was laid out, making Levan wonder if he would be able to eat his evening meal later. As he looked over the display, Hesten appeared in the doorway.

"My good King Levan, I hope you don't mind the interruption, especially when you see I have brought you a beautiful gift." At that moment, a stunning young woman emerged from behind the French doors. "Your Grace, may I present to you my sister Wilma?"

Her ash blonde locks were swept into an elaborate updo with her bangs framing her face, making her look sweet and innocent. But then Levan noticed her green dress, and all thoughts of innocence disappeared. The top was so low cut it bordered on obscene, showing the line of her ample cleavage, making Levan divert his eyes. The material around her waist was sheer so he could see her skin and the skirt was so full nobody could get close to her. For that, Levan was thankful. Levan found her clothing, or lack thereof, shocking and disgraceful.

Guy had asked permission for the ladies to choose some pieces of gold and jewelry from the vault for their special day, and Levan obliged. Wilma was decked out in an extraordinary amount of jewels; there were diamonds hanging from her neck, gold bracelets stacked up on her arms, even gold chains circling her middle. Levan had to suppress a scowl at how atrocious she looked below the neck.

Bowing, Levan greeted the first of the candidates and hoped the rest wouldn't be so obscenely decorated. "Wilma, it is a pleasure to meet you. Again, it would seem. Though the last time I saw you, you were much younger and not nearly as...luminous as you are now." He wasn't sure what else to say, so he kissed her offered hand.

"I hope you two enjoy the day she has planned," Hesten said with an approving smile. The man's wide grin and almost manic nodding made Levan want to roll his eyes; it felt like an aggressive display of agreement. "Do not worry about anything today, sir, I have it under control." With that, he slipped from the terrace and disappeared.

Wilma batted her eyelashes at Levan and pushed her arms together to show her chest off. "Your Grace, it is a pleasure to be with you today." She took his hand and led him to the table. "I hope to show you I have exactly what is needed to be the one and only queen of this fine land. And I plan for you to see that I have matured. Considerably."

I couldn't miss it if I tried.

A servant stepped forward and filled their silver rimmed glasses with water as they sat. Levan requested a glass of wine and asked if Wilma also wanted some. She readily accepted. They ate lobster, tender beef, savory vegetables, and more. Levan had not eaten so much since the celebration he had thrown more than six months ago. The one that had cost him a loveless but content life with Veva.

"Levan, I chose this location for our midday meal so you and I might survey the beauty of Atelina together from the height of the treetops. I hope over the course of this day you will see that helping you rule over Geoline is my number one priority. Ask me anything, I know all about how our government works." She flashed a toothy smile at him.

The urge to roll his eyes was so powerful, he could practically feel the muscles in his face twitching. He finished chewing slowly before he responded. "Oh really? Then what are your thoughts on absolute monarchy like we have, versus something of a democracy, like they use in Tentakay?" Levan leaned on one elbow and waited for her response.

Without hesitation, Wilma lit up. "I think the absolute monarchy is far superior to a democracy. Too many people making decisions makes it hard for any one decision to be made," she said proudly.

Levan nodded. "And your thoughts on children?"

Now Wilma blinked and gave Levan a blank stare. Obviously, children had not factored in at all with this girl. "Children? In the government? As a monarch?"

With a laugh, Levan clarified, "No, in your family."

Her face contorted with a furrowed brow as she hastily sipped from her wine glass. "I think they are fine to have. I'd give you all you wanted, but that has no business in a discussion about the government." After taking another sip of her wine, she added, "And I would assume any children I did bear as queen would be the next heirs of Geoline."

Wilma was a beautiful girl underneath all the gaudy presentation. But her drive to power was just as gaudy. Unfortunately, he found her completely unattractive and couldn't imagine a power-hungry woman raising his children.

He spent the rest of the day with Wilma doing her utmost to play the perfect hostess, pointing out all her finest features, and trying to convince him she was worthy. By the end of the day, Levan was exhausted, and he fell into bed that night feeling he accomplished nothing except crossing Wilma Egold off his list. At least he could say he gave Hesten's younger sister a chance. Now he would have to explain that to Hesten.

Esme watched day after day as queen hopefuls made their way from the Belin House to the main palace. And she watched as they returned, certain they would be the one Levan chose for his wife. They had been prepared and preened as much as possible, and Esme waited day in and day out for Guy to tell her it was her turn.

Before her, though, went her dear friend Geylis. Esme was certain Levan would like the beautiful woman from Myner, a coastal city north of Atelina. Geylis's red hair gleamed and her sun-kissed skin nearly glowed before she went. Geylis shared with Esme her plan for a day with Levan: fine dining and a tour of Atelina's history museums.

While Esme thought her friend had a wonderful chance of being well liked by the king, she also thought her friend might better enjoy the attentions of Maurice. In the two additional times he had come to the house to interview Guy and the ladies, Geylis and Maurice had nearly tripped over each other several times and often lavished silent attention upon each other. Esme could see it plainly, but she hoped the others were not so aware.

When Geylis returned that evening, she said Levan had been inattentive if not a little bored. And she said he barely ate any of the seafood she requested. She also said she did not feel like Levan was the right man for her, but she stated it with such a tranquil smile, Esme wasn't sure what to think.

The next day, Rhiann took her turn. Her beautiful curls had been hand-combed, and her tawny skin had been moisturized until it became as smooth as silk. Her plans also included lavish meals, something Esme noticed to be a trend among the women. Rhiann also requested King Levan give her a personal tour of the palace and that they visit the Atelina Zoo with the children.

Esme knew involving the children would mean a lot to Levan. Guy told her as much himself. And while Esme was happy Rhiann would get the chance to impress both Levan and the children, she was a little envious she had not been the first to request seeing Lester and Lennox. And she did wish to see them again. Rhiann would do well with them, she thought, as she happened to be the oldest of five children.

When Rhiann returned, it was in a fit of tears. Lennox had been quick to point out that Rhiann was not his mother. Levan had hardly eaten the menu she prepared, and she herself had tripped on a rug while walking through the palace, causing her to limp the rest of the day. She cried into Esme's arms that she would not be chosen and that her family was counting on her.

Day after day ladies went out and came back. Some feeling encouraged, others feeling let down like Rhiann. Esme listened to each of their accounts and formulated her own plans for her day with the king.

Finally, Esme received the news that her turn would come the following day. Guy saved her until the end. "Don't you know the old saying? Save the best for last." Guy said as he popped into her room. "Do you know what you will wear?"

She paced her room and picked at her fingernails before shoving her hands behind her. "Yes, the royal blue you helped me with the first week. You did say it was his favorite color?" A nervous energy filled her as she treaded back and forth.

"Yes, darling, it is. And how about your plans for the day?" Guy sat in her lounge chair, the silver one he had traded out for her. He was the picture of calm in the midst of her inner chaos.

Esme leaned on her bedpost and ran her hand over her face. "Everybody has done big, elaborate meals, haven't they?" Guy nodded. "Then I shall do something simple. For lunch, have whatever was Levan's favorite childhood meal. Something simple. With cake—chocolate. And be sure there is enough for Lester and Lennox as well. I wish them to accompany us, as chaperones. We shall make it a picnic. In the afternoon, I would like us all to fly kites."

Guy was furiously jotting down notes. "And after that?" Esme watched the little crease between his eyes grow.

After that? What else could she do that had not already been done? She wracked her brain, begging the Eminence to give her the perfect idea. "I know!" She giddily explained the rest of her plan, checking each thing with Guy to be sure Levan would approve.

"Now," Guy said. "Jewels. You've seen what's available, I know. What do you want to wear?"

Esme still could not decide on the accessories she should use. She wanted to look regal, but not overdone the way Wilma and Helene had. Finally, she tapped her chin and looked at her mentor. "What would Levan's mother have chosen?"

A brilliant smile emerged from his lips and he scrunched his nose. "I knew I chose well in deciding on you. If Levan does not announce you as his bride, I shall expire at once. There were two pieces Carlotta always enjoyed wearing, and I think you shall love them as well. I'll be right back."

The next day, Esme donned the bright royal blue dress she had specifically designed with this day in mind. The top had a square neck that showed her collar off without cutting too low, and it flared out right at her natural waist. The skirt itself was designed in a kerchief style so it appeared fuller than it was and it didn't weigh heavily on her. Her hair was down, curled lightly at the ends, with a braid haloing around her head. Holding it in place was a small silver headband with sapphires in it. It had been a favorite of former Queen Carlotta, Levan's mother. Esme also wore a silver and ruby brooch on her top, another of Carlotta's favorite pieces.

Compared to the other ladies vying for the king's attention, Esme was severely underdone. Her skirts were not as full, her jewelry not as plentiful, her makeup not as heavy. But she still felt like herself, a simple girl who grew up in the shadow of the palace, raising her chickens and tending her garden—both things she missed.

Guy led her out into the courtyard and up to the main palace. He told her of a spot just beyond the palace walls with an excellent hill for kite flying and picnicking. She waited near the gate for Levan to arrive.

While she waited, she prayed. It was the same prayer she had uttered under her breath for three months. "Eminence, please be with me. Let me find favor in Your eyes first. Let my actions and thoughts please You. I am certain You have never left my side, even here. So I ask that You continue to be with me. Be with Levan, the sovereign leader of this mighty nation. Dearest Eminence, if it is Your will, let him find favor with me the way You have. Allow Levan's heart to be open to me. You have brought me here for a reason; I am ready to see that through. Amen."

After a few moments, Levan came around the corner, his face a mask of irritation, shoulders slumped. When his eyes landed on her, however, his entire face lit up, and a glimmer of a smile graced his lips. His dark blond hair curled ever so slightly at the ends, and his ice blue eyes spoke volumes. He wore a royal blue overcoat with dark blue slacks. The shirt underneath was the color of wheat, closely matching his hair. But more impressive than his clothing was the relief he wore the moment he saw her.

"Miss Esme?" he asked as he stepped closer.

Esme's breath hitched as she reminded herself to breath. "Your Grace," she said, sweeping into a deep bow. "I thank you for joining me this day. I am sure you have been well exhausted by all the other ladies."

Levan kissed her hand, but after releasing it, he reached out and touched the brooch affixed to her collar. "I have not seen this in some time. My mother loved it." As he examined her for other adornments, he spotted the headband. "And this as well. She would wear the headband all the time. She said it made her feel pretty. Not royal, just pretty."

Esme giggled. "I would have to agree with your mother. It makes me feel pretty as well. I am not royal, so I dare not dress or act as one. But I am a woman and appreciate pretty things."

She noted a twinkle in Levan's eye. "What have you planned for us today, Miss Esme?"

"As soon as our chaperones arrive, I have planned for us to enjoy a picnic on this warm winter day." Indeed, for the middle of February, the temperatures were high and the sun warmed Esme's face.

"Chaperones? Out of thirteen women, nobody has yet insisted on a chaperone," Levan said, confused.

Just then, Lester and Lennox came bursting through the trees, their faces flushed with excitement, their tutor trailing far behind. "These are our chaperones. If you don't mind." She winked up at Levan. A bold move, but one she was comfortable doing so. She bent down to the children, crouching under her skirt. "My name is Esme. I thought you might like to join us for a picnic and maybe fly kites. How does that sound?"

"It's you!" Lennox jumped into the air, fully trusting that Esme would catch him. And she did, hugging him tight the way she had when she first met them. "I thought maybe you had been a ghost since we never saw you again."

Esme looked up to Levan, waiting for his reaction. But instead of anger, she saw a man who clearly loved his children and wanted their happiness. His face was calm, content.

The group made their way up the hill, and Lester helped his father set out the blanket for them to sit on. Esme got right on the ground and handed out sandwiches.

"You don't mind sitting on the ground?" Lester was amazed. He took a bite of his sandwich and chewed loudly.

"Not at all. I grew up not far from here, right in the heart of Atelina. And I have a garden at home where I get down in the dirt and dig and grow plants and vegetables and fruit," she said, missing the patch of grass Maurice had let her turn into her garden.

"Are there worms?" Lennox asked mid-bite. His dark brown curls glinted in the sun's light.

"Yes, there are. Big, fat, slimy ones." They all fell into a fit of giggles.

Esme realized she had not heard anything from the king and turned to him. "Is everything to your liking? I asked that your favorites be made."

Levan was sitting with his legs stretched out in front of him, one hand behind him supporting his weight. He was gleefully eating his sandwich. "I have not had a peanut butter and strawberry jam sandwich in years. Well before I ever became the head of a country." He grinned though the motion of his jaw.

After eating, Esme produced two matching kites. The young boys were overjoyed with the idea of putting off their afternoon lessons to spend time with their father. After helping the boys get the kites in the air, Levan led Esme off to speak with her in private.

"I have been waiting to meet you, Esme," he admitted. If she wasn't mistaken, a blush dusted his cheeks, and he seemed a little shy. "Ever since I first saw your picture, something drew me to you. And then in the courtyard. I have to confess to you, I was watching when the boys approached you and Lennox cried on your shoulder."

Carden had told her as much, but she would not reveal that to Levan right now. She only nodded in understanding. Levan continued. "You were so gentle with him, and he has been...different...since." His voice trailed off. "I am glad to have met you at last, Esme." He added her name, and it sounded like heaven on his lips.

Esme felt a deep conviction, a certainty in her bones, that the Eminence had handpicked her for the Final Fourteen.

"I am glad, too, Your Highness," she said, her voice breathy. A blush spread across her cheeks in response to his intense gaze.

An hour later, the tutor returned to retrieve the boys. Esme got down on the ground and thanked them both. "I had a lovely time. I hope I can meet you again one day."

Lennox, ever the young child, posed the question, "Will you be our new mother?"

Esme blanched, unsure what to say. Unwilling to look to their father, she fumbled. "Oh, Lennox. I do like you and your family very much. You are quite the gentleman. Right now, let's be friends. If anything more is to come from it, we will have to wait and see. Besides, I know nobody can replace your mother, even if she loves you a whole bunch. Can we be friends?"

"That sounds like a fine idea," Levan said from behind his sons. The boys bound off with their tutor chasing them, trying to give them a nature lesson as they went.

Esme stood and looked at her hands. "I'm sorry. I hope that answer was sufficient. I was unsure what to say in response."

"It was a perfect answer, Esme," Levan said. She felt him step closer. Looking up, he was right before her. "What else did you have in mind for today? There is still time before the evening meal."

"If you're still comfortable with the temperature outside, I would like to sit and talk with you. I understand this may not be the most exciting afternoon you've had in the last few weeks, but..." She stopped short.

Taking her hand, Levan encouraged her. "But what?"

With a shy smile she confessed her thoughts. "I was thinking if I hope to become your wife, I should get to know the man. Not just the facts given to us. Our lessons did not include that your favorite color is royal blue."

Levan held her arm out to see her outfit. "And yet you knew it anyway."

"I asked Guy what color would please you the most. And I asked for your favorite childhood meal to be prepared for the midday meal. That was also not included in the lessons. I want to get to know the man behind the crown. Ruling the nation, to me, comes secondary to...to ruling my heart." Esme looked into his eyes, the blue looked as light as icicles yet were as warm as a summer day. She knew her cheeks were heated pink, but she could not look away.

"And do I?" He looked at her intently.

"Do you what?" She knew what, but didn't dare assume that was what he meant. Her breath hitched in her throat.

A low, gravelly voice replied inches from her ear. "Rule your heart?"

She breathed. Everything in her body screamed yes. But she knew she could not make it known so fast. Twelve others would also make the claim that he ruled their hearts. So instead she said, "You might. One day."

Sitting back on the blanket, Esme asked him questions about growing up, how he wanted his children to grow up, his hopes for the future. She could tell he was a powerful man who did not give up control easily.

He enjoyed his control and showing it off. But behind that was a man who would do anything for his children and who desperately wanted and needed to be loved. Might she be the one to provide that and possibly point him toward the One who loved them all more than life itself?

CHAPTER 17

As the air grew colder, the pair packed up their basket and Levan carried it down the hill. If he had been charmed by Esme from just seeing her picture, now he was head over heels for her. Levan considered demanding that she marry him but thought better of it. It should be a decision they both made. Though she did seem to know everything about him. And while he had learned some things about her, it was not nearly enough.

"Did you have plans for us this evening as well, Esme?" He asked with his eyebrow raised, hoping she had something in store.

She peeked at him from the corners of her eyes. "I thought I would leave it up to you. After hearing many of the others say they planned huge, luxurious meals and outings for you, I thought you might be tired of those. Hence the sandwiches and kites. But if you would like for me to stay with you, I would love to experience any of your current favorites."

Her eyes were like pools that hypnotized him. Although he was thrilled, he stayed composed instead of celebrating wildly. "I would be delighted to have our chef prepare my favorite meal for you. But I must warn you, it's an ancient recipe and not very healthful. But it is assuredly delicious."

Thinking for a moment, he added, "We can dine in my favorite room—the library."

"You have your own library?" Esme laughed. "I have always wanted to see one in person. I have heard of their wonders. Does it have a lot of books?" Before he could answer, she waved her hands. "No, don't tell me. I want to be surprised. I would love to have your not healthful meal with you."

Back inside the palace, Levan handed the picnic basket and blanket to a waiting servant. He issued instructions for the chef about what dishes to prepare, and then led Esme to the library. As they walked down the halls, he watched her as she took everything in. Many of the other women had not been impressed with the palace, but Esme seemed to appreciate every tapestry and vase she passed. It gave Levan a new appreciation for the things he saw every day.

"Where did all these come from?" she marveled as they passed a painting of a beautiful young woman.

He stopped beside her and studied the fine lines, the individually painted hairs, the attention to detail. "Someone had it commissioned years ago."

Esme reached a hand out as if to touch the decades-old paint, but she withdrew and looked at Levan with a blush. "Who is she?"

"I—I don't know." He truly was stumped. He passed that portrait hundreds of times but never considered who it was. "I've never asked. I would wager MacJames or Marcutin knows. We can ask them."

Though she smiled and nodded slightly, Levan could see her face fall when he didn't know the subject of the portrait. He resolved to have each picture labeled with both the subject and artist's names. He should be invested in the arts like France and England, after all.

The library was a small room, but it was his favorite. It smelled musty and old, and he had to keep it fairly dark. But Levan had a feeling Esme would love the library. As they walked, he asked, "Do you think we need a chaperone for this portion of our day?"

Looking around at the guards posted down the halls, Esme answered, "I have a feeling you are always being chaperoned, Your Grace. Whether you want to be or not." She was an astute girl, Levan thought. Naturally, someone watched him at all times for his safety and the security of the country as a whole.

He stopped outside a door labeled "Library," and grinned. "I think you sh-shall like this room. And while we dine, I want to pepper you with as many questions as you did me earlier."

He opened the door and led her inside. Esme gasped upon seeing all of the books adorning the shelves. It was a modest collection, but there they were with red, blue, black, and green spines lined up side by side. Hundreds of ancient volumes and newer texts were spread across the shelves of the room.

"Look at them all. Have you read each one?" she squealed. Esme dashed to the closest wall and held her hand out, her fingers gently touching the spines. She seemed to be absorbing the very essence of the book as she inhaled deeply. Her excitement energized him. "I could spend all day here."

"I had a feeling you would appreciate this more than most," he said with a hearty laugh. "It's rare to find a woman who can read, let alone one who enjoys it. You should take one with you."

"Oh, I do enjoy it. Thank you so much for showing these to me. I adore them." But then she abruptly halted, pivoted on her heels, and fixed her wide, fearful eyes on him. "But I could never take one, even just to borrow."

"Why ever not? You look like you want to." Levan fell back into one of the overstuffed chaises nearby and waved his hand dismissively. "Pick whichever one you would like. Don't worry about cost."

Esme slowly stepped toward him, her eyes down. "It's not that I don't appreciate the offer. Truly, it's grand. I'm not worthy of such a gift, and I don't want it to look like I'm only here for status and riches."

"Are you not? Why are you here then?"

She bit her lip, and Levan wondered what it tasted like. When she looked up, she finally spoke. "While those things are surely nice, it's not as important as joy and love. Do you see? It is hard to explain. I am looking for the things that fulfill me...here," she said, laying her hand across her heart.

"Did you find it before you came here?" Levan sat up, his heart picking up speed.

With a shake of her head, she replied, "No. I was content but not fulfilled."

"And here at the palace? In Belin House?" Levan rose and approached Esme, his hand so near hers that he could feel the warmth of her skin, a shiver running down his spine.

"It is my daily hope that this place, and the people in it, will bring me that fulfillment," she said, shifting her weight toward him. Her words were slow and deliberate. "That's why I came here. I felt drawn to this place. To you. Maybe...maybe you are my fulfillment." She reached her hand out and took his, slowly placing it over her heart.

THE POWER THAT SURGED over him in that moment was instantaneous and incredible. He could feel her heartbeat through the thin material of her dress, but it wasn't just that. It seemed as if it beat only for him. Levan could sense that. The blood rushing through Esme's veins did so with the purpose of loving him and going through life with him. He wanted to live in that moment forever, feeling her heartbeat.

Levan stepped back, dizzy. "Esme. I-I think this—this is it."

Her face fell as she backed away from him and cold air swept between them. "Oh. I'm terribly sorry, sire. I did not mean to assume." Her cheeks flushed with embarrassment as she turned her eyes away from him and placed a hand over her face.

He caught her hand again and held it firmly, keeping her from getting further away. The air around them felt light and perfumed, and Levan was pretty sure he could hear music even though there were no musicians. He put his hand to her chin and made her look up at him. "No, Esme. I mean, I think you are it. I think you are the one I want. I could feel it as sure as I felt your heart beating."

With urgency, she hurried towards him, and he enveloped her in a warm embrace, effortlessly lifting her up. She was the one, he knew. He had known it from the beginning. As he set her back down on the floor, Levan could not help himself and he lowered his face and pressed his lips to hers. He had not taken such liberties with any of the other finalists, though a few offered that and more.

Her lips were full and warm. She pressed them against his, a mix of desire and uncertainty evident in her inexperienced kiss. Levan wrapped his arms around her and pulled her body in closer, and Esme immediately molded to him. Levan had never experienced such strong emotion when kissing another before.

When they broke apart, Levan could see Esme's chest heaving as she caught her breath. His own seemed to be caught up in his throat as well. He stared at her: her cascading black hair, her intoxicating blue eyes—she was perfect to behold and even more perfect from within. Levan believed this woman could be wife, mother, and queen rolled into one lovely package.

As his senses came back to him, there was a knock before the door opened. One of the kitchen maids came in wheeling a cart with their evening meal. The pair watched silently as she set it up on a small table.

As she bowed to them, Esme asked her name and thanked her. Levan had no idea what the woman's name was. Yes, Esme would make a wonderful queen.

Sitting at the small table, Esme inhaled. "Mmm, this smells wonderful. What is it?"

"It's chicken. Almost like roasted, but instead, it is coated with a breading, then deep fried in oils until it's cooked and crispy. I forget who introduced it to the court, but it's become a favorite." Levan picked up a drumstick and bit into it, showing Esme how it was done.

She giggled and picked up a piece as well, biting into the crisp outer skin. She savored the taste and declared it scrumptious. "Does it bother you that I am not of noble birth?" she asked.

"As a woman, you would inherit your husband's station. And I desire to become your husband, which elevates you to the highest of nobility," he said with a shrug. "So no, it does not matter."

"Did you have any other questions for me? My favorite color, perhaps?"

"What is your favorite color?" He hoped it was blue, like the shade of her eyes.

"Purple. All shades. And I really enjoy silver as well. Guy even traded out the chair in my room so I had a silver one instead of a red one," she said in amazement. "Wasn't that kind of him?"

"Indeed. How did he manage that without offending the person from whom he took it?" Levan took another bite of chicken. He wasn't surprised Guy had gone through lengths to make her happy. Levan wanted to make her happy as well.

"I was the first girl there, so nobody knew. Guy said I was his favorite. Won't he be elated? He's so pleasant and remarkable. He does his work very well," Esme said, nodding.

"Do you like it in Belin House?" He had walked through it before the ladies arrived. It was a small place, akin to a country cottage by his estimation, but he received reports saying the girls were comfortable.

"It's been an amazing experience. The house is huge and lovely. And I've enjoyed not just learning about Geoline and you," she said with a genuine smile, "but meeting the women from all over the country. It's not terribly far to get from here to places like Gwynberg, and yet I have never been there. I'm happy to have made two wonderful friends from other places."

Levan narrowed his eyes and felt certain he could figure out who they were. "Let me guess, Geylis a-and...Rhiann?" Out of all the girls, those two had been as kind as Esme.

Esme looked astonished. "Yes! They are wonderful friends." Her smile faltered. "I will miss them when this is all over."

"You can stay in touch. Maybe they will decide to stay in Atelina," Levan suggested.

"Rhiann has many younger siblings she must take care of. Her parents were counting on her being chosen so she could send help for their farm," Esme said, suddenly looking worried for her friend. "What will happen now?"

"We will help them, Esme. Anything you want," Levan promised. "What about Geylis?"

He had known of Rhiann's plight and desire to help her family. In fact, she mentioned her parents and their farm no less than ten times on their outing. Levan was certain he would not pick Rhiann, but he did want to provide aid to her family. While Geylis had been charming, it was clear from the get-go they would not be well suited to each other. He had seen the look of relief on her face when Guy retrieved her after their day together.

Esme grinned. "If it will not offend you, I think Geylis has her affections already aimed at another. She did nothing dishonest or underhanded, I assure you. But I have seen her blush madly in the direction of a certain man we have seen on the grounds. I think he returns the affection."

Levan laughed. It was a delightful gesture on her part to make sure he didn't feel slighted by the red-headed woman, showing her kindness and consideration. "I am not offended. I am happy she will not leave here lonely. Now, tell me about your family, Esme."

SHE FROZE. HER FAMILY? What should she tell him? Maurice made her promise not to tell anybody where she came from or who her family was. Did that now include the man she intended to marry? Esme took a long drink of her water, trying to seem cheery while her mind reeled. What should she say?

Levan spoke again before she could reply. "I confessed to seeing you interact with Lester and Lennox. While there, you mentioned you had a brother who was no longer l-living." Levan's eyes searched her own. His face was full of compassion and Esme felt her armor melting away.

"Yes," she sighed as she straightened her spine. She would tell the truth, but keep it carefully crafted. "My whole family is gone. When I was a little girl, a terrible illness hit my household. My sister caught it first and brought it back to the house. She was ten, I was eight, and my brother, Aaren, was only four years old. Soon our whole family had the illness. My parents actually died from it first. Hattie tried to care for us, but she was too weak. I still have nightmares of Aaren and I lying in bed, I was waiting for us to die. I held him as he took his last breath, and I stayed next to him, thinking I would take my own final breath soon enough."

Esme wiped away tears as she spoke. She never spoke of her family. Even Maurice did not mention them; he only comforted her when the nightmares came. She could still remember shivering, holding onto Aaren's cold body.

"But you lived," Levan said, interrupting her thoughts.

She gave him a small smile through the tears. "Yes, I did. I woke up one day, and my heath was restored. Everybody around thought our entire household was dead. They sent a..." she was about to say a preacher, but she dared not. "They sent a man in to check, and he found me sitting up dazed and confused. I was washed, my clothes burned, and I was nursed back to health. Shortly after that, my cousin came to get me. He adopted me as his own, and I have lived with him ever since."

Levan's face was tight and distressed. "I had no idea such a sickness came through Geoline. Was there no medication to help you?"

She shook her head. There was no way to tell him she was originally from Cartrelle—a place full of those who followed the Creed and Testaments and a country Levan and his father always wanted to conquer. It would be smart to stay quiet about that. "We tried several. None worked. At least not for them. I do not know why I was spared." Maurice always said the Eminence had a plan for her life and that was why she lived. Was this fulfilling that plan?

"I am so sorry for your loss. I, too, lost my parents. I was not as young as you, but it was still hard." Levan reached out his hand and laid it over her own.

"I remember it," Esme nodded. "It was not long after my own parents perished."

Levan cleared his throat. "What luck you had that a cousin was willing to take you in and bring you to the capital."

"He did not just bring me to Atelina all those years ago. He brought me to you," Esme said, a smile showing on her tear-stained face. Yes, this was part of the Eminence's plan. Coming to the capital. Living with Maurice. And now meeting the king.

Before Levan could respond, there was a loud knock on the door and a dark-haired man burst through. He was fuming about something, Esme could tell by his red-faced sputtering. "Your Grace, I am sorry to disrupt your evening, but I must have this addressed at once."

"What is so important, Hesten?" Levan looked exasperated. Esme had seen Hesten before, but he usually looked so calm. She had not recognized him in his agitated state. Levan looked at her with an apologetic glance. "I am sorry, Esme."

She shrugged and listened to Hesten carry on about a man who refused to show him respect. Realizing the conversation might take a few minutes, she excused herself and went to the shelves to look over the books.

There were so many books. Esme wondered if Maurice knew they were here. He turned her onto a love of reading from the moment he had taken her in. They poured over the few books they had as a way to forget their grief.

Maurice was the nephew of Esme's mother, Laurel. He had been born in Cartrelle, just like Esme, but had come to Geoline two years before taking Esme in. His mission had been to help set up home bases for Creed Followers in the faithless country. He had been naturalized as a citizen, changed his last name, and gotten a position as a scribe. Eventually, he was promoted to one of the head scribes and became one of the royal family's most trusted men.

Esme was overcome with emotions over missing both her family and Maurice. While she had been lucky enough to see him on occasion, she missed their daily banter. She wondered if he was eating right, if he was cleaning the dishes. Was he taking care of her chickens Lucky, Sunny, and Henny?

Then a hand was on her arm, making her jump. "Are you alright, darling? Did Hesten upset you?" It was Guy. He had come back to retrieve her and walked in on Hesten's angry rant, still going strong.

With a sigh, she looked over at where Levan and Hesten still stood deep in conversation. "Oh, no. He did not. I was just thinking about my family. I miss them so much," she said quietly.

Guy was not familiar with her whole story. He patted her hand and clucked over her for a minute. "I know. You will see them soon, though. Did everything go as well as you hoped?"

Esme crinkled her nose and nodded. "He said I was the one, Guy. And he felt my heartbeat. It was so intense and marvelous." She looked over to Levan, who was trying to wrap up things with Hesten. "I think I love him."

Guy turned her toward the two men standing in the middle of the room. He cleared his throat. "If you will excuse us, gentlemen, this young lady has a curfew." Both men turned toward them. Hesten looked nearly enraged.

Levan was somewhat calmer. "Hesten, there is nothing to be done tonight. As Guy pointed out, it is late. We can discuss this in the morning." He waited and Esme watched as Hesten stormed from the room his agitated voice trailing behind him. His sister was much like him, Esme noted.

Levan came across the room to them. "I apologize, Esme, for that callous interruption. Hesten is a passionate man." Levan looked to Guy the way a young man might look to a girl's father. "Is it really time for her to depart?"

"I'm afraid so. It's well past sunset, I'm afraid. All young ladies need their beauty sleep," Guy said, patting her hand.

Levan bowed before Esme and took her hands from Guy's, bringing her closer to him. "Guy, please make arrangements for a-all the other young women to return home. She is the one I choose. And see to it that Rhiann is well compensated for the twisted ankle she received while she was in my company," Levan winked at Esme. "Do not tell any of them who has been chosen. Esme will pack her things as well. Tomorrow after everybody else has left, put her up in the North wing of the palace. She will stay there until we wed on March first."

Guy bounced where he was. "Absolutely, Your Excellence. It will be as you wish."

Esme knew the minute they were away from Levan, her mentor would wrap her up in a huge embrace.

"I would like to continue our conversation, perhaps tomorrow afternoon? Until then, Esme, and always, my heart will go with you," Levan declared. He squeezed her hands, guiding her forward for a light kiss on her cheek.

"Levan?" she asked quietly, her voice almost inaudible. When he raised an eyebrow, she licked her lips and said with that small voice, "I choose you, too." He kissed her again, this time on the lips. It was more demanding than before, and it made Esme's heart skip a beat.

She felt like she nearly floated out of the palace on wings. She had done it! The little orphaned girl from Cartrelle would become a wife, mother, and reigning Queen of Geoline in two weeks. Esme thanked the Eminence above for his provision and leading. She knew it was Him and Him alone who orchestrated the path of her life.

CHAPTER 18

On the way back to Belin House, Guy quickly gave Esme a rundown of what would happen. She still felt as though she was floating, so the first order of business was to come down from the clouds.

"You need to not look quite so thrilled, my dear," he warned.

The smile on her face was hard to tuck away. "I think I shall be thrilled forever. I cannot believe he chose me."

"I told you," Guy reminded her, "You have been my favorite since day one. Feel free to look happy. Most of the girls did when they came back. But you really need to get your head out of the clouds."

Pausing, Esme focused on the crunch of each individual pebble beneath her thin slippers. Grounded. "So what do we need to do?"

Guy faced her and took her hands in his. "We go back in and you can be happy with how things have gone today. Share about your day, that's fine. But tell nobody he has chosen you. I can assure you, he has not said that to anybody else." He squeezed her hands.

"Before bed, I'll gather everyone and tell them they are to return home tomorrow and the chosen one will return to the palace in a few days' time.

But you, my future Queen, will be whisked up to the palace to set up your quarters. Maids will be assigned to you, and we will begin the preparations to make you Queen Esme of Geoline."

Butterflies whirled in Esme's stomach. "You make it sound so easy."

"Let's hope it goes as easily as it sounds," Guy replied with a roll of his eyes. "Let's get a move on."

Back inside the house, Guy clapped loudly. "Attention ladies! The last of you has had her chance to meet and woo the king. Please gather in the parlor as soon as possible so I can explain what's next."

Several girls came out of their rooms in their dressing gowns and shuffled into the parlor. Esme excused herself to change quickly out of her blue dress into something more comfortable and appropriate for their house meeting. She changed into a dressing gown and met the rest of the group, sitting next to Rhiann on a small chaise.

"How did it go?" Rhiann asked.

Esme reached out and gently squeezed her friend's hand, a small gesture of solidarity and affection. "It went well. I met the children and they are adorable."

"Ladies, I have good news and bad news," Guy announced. "The good news is everybody has had their time with King Levan. He truly enjoyed meeting each of you and rediscovering all that is beautiful about Geoline and Atelina. The bad news is our time together has come to a close."

The girls gasped, a chorus of sharp intakes of breath, echoing through the silent room. "What? What will we do now?"

"Ladies, please." Guy paused.

Wilma stood and put her hands on her hips. Her lips were pursed. "So? Who has he chosen?" Esme felt her heart speed up as she looked in her lap. She could not give it away.

Guy went to Wilma and took her hands, gently guiding her back into her seat. "If you will allow me to continue, Wilma." He pushed her back into her chair before he continued. "Only the king knows his decision, and it will not be announced right away. Everyone is to pack their things for their return journey tomorrow."

Esme sighed, but tried to keep it quiet. She wondered if Rhiann could hear her racing pulse, but then, perhaps everyone's pulse was racing.

Before girls could protest, he held up his hand. "Yes. Everyone. Pack all of your things, including your new dresses and anything else made specifically for you. I should have gathered borrowed jewels from everyone..." He surveyed the room, his eyes finally landing on Esme.

She quickly took the headband off and held it out. "The other piece is in my room," she said. "I'll get it when we finish here." Guy nodded.

"Carriages will begin arriving mid-morning to take you home. Those who traveled the furthest will be among the first to leave so you have the most daylight to travel by. I will come and say private goodbyes to each of you, but before that, know this has been an amazing few months, and I am so grateful to have met you all."

The sound of sniffles filled the room. Girls were crying, clutching their friends tightly, their sobs echoing through the air, a testament to the bonds they had formed. Geylis came over to where Esme and Rhiann sat and pulled a chair close. Esme reached out so she was holding each of their hands.

"I can't go home," Rhiann said, her voice small. "There's too many people in too small a space. My family can't afford to feed everyone." Tears, hot and heavy, rolled down her cheeks, leaving glistening tracks.

Esme wanted to help her friend, but she didn't know how. She couldn't tell her Levan would send her home with money to better her family's situation. But then an idea came to her. What if Rhiann were to become one of her ladies in waiting? It would elevate her station, keep her in the city, and she could be paid for her services. She would need to speak with Guy. Until then, she put her arm around the girl and tutted over her.

"I hate that we're all being sent back. I don't fool myself in thinking I'll be chosen, and I don't want to be, if I'm being honest," Geylis admitted. "I wonder if they could drop me off in the city? I want to stay here."

"Talk to Guy," Esme suggested. If Geylis didn't, she would—and make sure her friend was able to meet Maurice. She would love for her best friend to become her cousin.

As they made their way back to their rooms, shouting erupted from the other side of the house. "I'm not packing my things. He's choosing me."

"What would make you think that? He's going to pick me," came a heated reply.

Lynna and Wilma. Esme and the others rushed down the hall to where the two ladies stood outside their doors. Guy stood between them, trying to keep them away from one another.

"Ladies, please," Guy pleaded.

Lynna reached around Guy and grabbed Wilma's hair, yanking it. Wilma let out a high-pitched shriek, making Esme jump and take a hasty step back. Hands were everywhere as some girls tried to pull the fight apart. Before anyone knew it, a glint of silver flashed and Lynna shouted in victory.

There was blood on the floor. Blood and hair. Lynna had used a letter opener and sliced off a chunk of Wilma's hair, cutting her ear in the process. Wilma fell to the floor, her hands at her head, crying. Guy grabbed Lynna by the wrists and forced her back into her room.

"Someone get a doctor for her," he shouted over his shoulder. He took the letter opened from Lynna and shut her in her room as she continued to shout. One of the girls, her face pale with fright, ran towards the nearby guard, shouting desperately for a doctor.

Others rushed at Wilma, clucking over her and pressing linens to her ear where the blood was flowing. Esme looked away, the sight making her queasy. She realized her hand was being crushed and looked down to see Rhiann holding her for dear life.

Esme pulled Rhiann to her. "It will be fine. They'll take care of her. Come on." Tugging Rhiann's arm gently, she guided her back towards her room. "Let's start packing, hmm?"

The palace doctor was ushered to bandage Wilma. She shouted that Lynna and her entire family would be hung for what happened. Esme kept Rhiann busy packing her things and chattering.

"Who do you think Levan chose?" Rhiann asked.

"We'll find out. Perhaps it will be you," Esme replied, hating to lie to her friend.

"I don't think I'm cut out to be the queen. I'd be happy living in the palace as a scullery maid," Rhiann said, a sad smile on her face.

Esme folded a dress into Rhiann's trunk. "Nonsense. Though being a lady in waiting would be nice. A lady in waiting could enjoy the fineries of the castle, perhaps marry a nobleman or something."

"If I go back to the farm, my parents will marry me off to Fins Roarshank." Rhiann scrunched up her nose and shivered at the thought.

With a laugh, Esme asked, "And we don't like Fins Roarshank?"

"He's my father's age, he's missing teeth, and has buried three wives already," came the reply. It was no surprise Rhiann wanted nothing to do with marrying him.

Guy felt every bone in his body ache. He was too old to be breaking up fights between grown women. He couldn't believe Lynna had not only shorn off half of Wilma's hair but nearly sliced her ear off as well. What was supposed to be a night of tearful goodbyes turned into mopping up blood and blonde hairs from the stone floor.

The worst part would be telling Hesten about what happened. Much like his sister, he would demand revenge and want Lynna hanged for her crimes. While Guy agreed she would need to be reprimanded, she wouldn't have gone off the deep end if Wilma hadn't goaded her with cruel words that weren't true.

The hour neared midnight, and only a few lamps were still on. He knocked softly on Zelda's room and she bade him enter. "Are you ready to return home?"

"Will I be back?" she asked as she closed her trunk and sat on it. Her dark hair was pinned up, and she held her head high.

"I truly don't know," Guy replied. And he didn't. While he was aware she would not come back as their queen, she might revisit the city again. He gave her a hug and wished her all the best before exiting.

Then he found Alina's room and knocked. With a soft click, the door swung inward, revealing Alina, her face blotchy and red from crying, eyes swollen and glistening with unshed tears.

"What makes you cry, my pet?" Guy gathered the sensitive girl into his arms and patted her back.

"I don't know," she wailed as more tears came. "I want to go home to my momma. But I don't want to leave."

Guy hushed her gently, his hand on her arm, and guided her to her bed. "I know, little one, I know. Your momma will be so happy to see you. You've done so well here." In her three months at Belin House, Alina had gone from an undernourished waif to a filled in woman. Guy would hate to see her starving again when she got home.

One thing he wished he could do for all the girls was keep them living in the lap of luxury as they had been. Or at least ensure they had enough food on the table and new shoes each year. Surely, Levan was aware of each girl's station before coming to the palace. He would talk with him about compensating the families of the poorer girls.

Tucking Alina into her bed, Guy turned off the light and told her to sleep well. It would be her last night having a bed to herself.

With a final sweep to ensure all was well, he went back to his dimly lit room. The minute his head hit the pillow, he was fast asleep.

A sharp, insistent rapping on his door woke him far earlier than he wanted. "Guy Hart, open up at once." He recognized that voice. Hesten Egold.

Guy quickly moved outside to talk to Hesten, hoping he could appease the man without another scene. "I know why you're here—"

The man's face was red. Then again, it was always red. "Do you? My sister was maimed. Your queen has been attacked. That other girl tried to kill her. That's treason."

Guy took a deep breath, the crisp air filling his lungs before he slowly let it out. "Sir, it was not an attempt at murder, I assure you. Lynna was angry. It should not have happened—I agree—but it is being dealt with." He didn't have time to rehash everything with Hesten.

"She will be hanged! I accuse her of treason for attacking the queen," Hesten shouted. Guy could see some girls peek their heads out of windows.

"Hesten. Your sister is not the queen. It is not treason." He knew the man's stubborn glare meant his words would fall on deaf ears, but he tried reasoning with him anyway.

"She will be the queen in two weeks."

"You don't know that for certain," Guy rebuked. "Did Levan tell you he was choosing her?"

Now Hesten's face faltered. "Wilma said—"

"If you were to ask any of the ladies inside, they would all say Levan is going to choose them. They're all hopeful. Lynna will be dealt with. Your sister will recover. Nobody is going to hang." Guy motioned for a nearby guard, who quickly approached them.

"All the girls are going home today. Your sister included. She's still in the doctor's infirmary." To the guard he said, "Take the commander to his sister, please."

"I know the way," Hesten hissed before stalking off toward the palace. As he walked away, Guy heard him mutter, "My sister better be the one chosen."

What would his reaction be when he discovered Wilma was not chosen? Guy would need to make sure there was extra security all around Esme for several months until the Egolds got over the slight.

CHAPTER 19

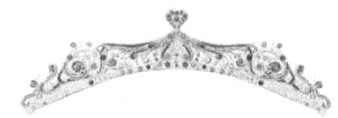

WHEN MAURICE HEARD ALL the hopefuls had been sent home and Esme had not returned, he knew she was the one chosen. Dread became an unbearable companion as the day wore on. Esme was a Creed Follower—she should not be associating with nonbelievers, let alone marrying them and helping them rule a nation.

Esme's words echoed in his mind, suggesting it might not have been Levan's decision but rather the Eminence's that led her. Might his Cricket, his little fighter girl, be the person their Eminence had sent to be queen? He knew if anyone could do it, she could. Esme was the most compassionate, caring person he had ever known.

The wedding was set to take place on March first. Maurice had not received a formal invitation. But then, he would not because he insisted Esme not reveal who she was to anybody. And for that, he was profoundly grateful, because his conflict with Hesten Egold had reached a dangerous boiling point.

Hesten was threatening Maurice, making Maurice glad Esme was nowhere near to be caught in the crossfire. While he always tried to maintain a pleasant and calm demeanor, Hesten's ridicule and abuse were hard to swallow. Maurice didn't know why Hesten hated Creed Followers so much, but it didn't matter in the long run. The only thing that mattered was the protection of his brethren.

While he had not been invited to the wedding, he would still be there, recording everything for posterity as one of the head scribes. Maurice was grateful he could stay out of sight because he knew he would cry at some point. He hoped the tears wouldn't soak his parchment. It was not every day his adopted daughter married the supreme ruler of a nation.

The prospect of his young cousin's reign and the Geoline people's response filled Maurice's thoughts. It had been almost nine months since Veva had been deposed, but the people had not forgotten. Several protested the way in which Levan went about finding a new bride. He had never said anything to Esme because he did not want to worry her, but Maurice did fear for her life. Both because of the people and her soon-to-be husband. If Levan could be rid of one wife so easily, ridding himself of another would be even easier.

But he had seen the look in Esme's eyes the last time he was inside the palace gates for the final group interview. While every girl, poised and elegant in their gowns, exuded grace and class, Esme glowed with an inner light that surpassed mere refinement. Her confidence, her assurance, was evident. Maurice wanted Esme to be happy above all else, and it seemed this was how it would be so.

He had also seen the look in a certain other lady's eyes. Maurice had taken notice of the woman next to Esme immediately, but as a queen hopeful, he knew he had no business even talking to her. Geylis Calvin was her name, and the minute he learned it, he knew he would never forget. After Esme's signal that he had caught Geylis's eye as well, Maurice found ways to casually walk past her. He chuckled to admit he had given her looks akin to those of an infatuated boy.

Perhaps now that Geylis was no longer at the palace, he could inquire after her. In an attempt to busy himself and keep his mind off Esme's impending nuptials, he wrote a letter to the fiery-haired beauty. He knew Geylis was from Myner, an ocean side city north of Atelina. It would take a few days to reach her, but he had to try.

Before he lost his nerve, he scrawled out a missive, asking if she remembered him and if she had any interest in seeing him. He was a kind man, respected in his community, who earned a comfortable living. Any non-noble woman would do well to make a life with him. He signed it and folded it closed, firmly sealing it. He would post the letter immediately.

He marched down the road, determined. But nothing could have surprised him more than seeing the very woman coming down the street, her eyes darting all over the place as they searched. His eyes widened when he saw her, and he stopped in his tracks.

"Miss Calvin? Geylis?" His voice caught in his throat. "Do you remember me? Maurice Gustoff."

A broad smile broke out on her face as she saw him. "Maurice, I am so glad to see you. I'm actually here looking for you. I heard you lived down this way." She played with the hem of her bronze-colored sleeve.

"Whoever told you that?" The urge to make contact with her tugged at him, yet he couldn't ignore the impropriety of it. He felt like a boy who fumbled over himself to impress a young lady.

She looped her arm through his effortlessly, the smooth contact surprising him. They walked slowly along the buildings. "Guy Hart did. When I told him I did not want to be chosen, he said he noticed the looks between us and wanted to make sure we crossed paths again. I'm not going back to Myner. I'm staying in Atelina."

Wonders never did cease. "Guy told you? Does—does he know who I am?"

She threw back her head in a throaty laugh. "Of course. You were at Belin House for those interviews. And you are a head scribe. Truth be told, my dear friend Esme also noticed the looks between us."

Maurice joined in the laughter. "Of course she did." His little cricket was always observant. He needed to tell her Esme was his cousin, but he preferred to do so in private.

"Where are you going, anyway?"

Holding up the letter, Maurice winked at Geylis. "I was on my way to mail this letter. To you, actually." Across the front of the paper it said *Geylis Calvin, Myner, Geoline.* "I had hopes there wasn't another Geylis Calvin in that area."

"I was the only," she replied. They walked a few more steps before she asked, "Can I read it?"

Heat crept up Maurice's neck, and he felt beads of sweat on his brow. "I suppose." He handed it to her, and she carefully opened it.

They stopped walking so she could read his words. Maurice tried to hold still and not fidget, but it was hard. He poured out his heart to her, his voice raw with honesty as he confessed his deep faith in the Creed. And he asked if she felt the same way and if she felt it strongly enough to return to Atelina and him.

"I do," she whispered. "I feel it too." The touch of Geylis' hand sent a shiver, thrilling and sharp, down his spine. "I was not raised a Creed Follower, but I would become one."

His heart soared. There was potential between them, and that was all he needed. "Where are you staying?"

"I was on my way to figure that out," she said with a shrug. "Guy was kind enough to hold my belongings until I found a place."

"Come, you can stay with Nermal and Sally Hobbes. They are leaders in our group. They'll be happy to have you." He felt a fresh wave of energy, invigorating him and sharpening his senses.

"Are you sure?" Her rosy lips stayed in a smile as her copper hair glinted in the sun.

He chuckled. "About staying there? Or about seeing what's between us?"

Geylis threw her arms around him. "About staying there. I'm sure about you."

"Let's go find out." They broke apart and rushed down the street to where the Hobbes family lived.

With arrangements made, Maurice and Geylis finally had a few moments of quiet. The Hobbeses knew Esme well and were aware she was inside the palace walls. He needed to tell Geylis the truth.

"There's one more thing you need to should be aware of. I hope it won't change any of this." After their hosts tactfully excused themselves, he sat with her, the soft glow of candlelight illuminating their faces.

Her eyes searched his. "Now you tell me something serious?" She straightened her back. "I'm ready."

"It's about Esme. She's my cousin. I'm her only family, and I've raised her since she was a small girl." Maurice steeled in the event Geylis changed her mind about him. He knew she and Esme were friends, but he wasn't sure how friendly they were.

"She's your cousin?" Geylis's voice was high and thin as she laughed. "I thought you were telling me bad news. This is the best news I've heard in, well, hours."

"Is it?"

She clapped her hands and bounced on her seat. "Yes. She's become my dearest friend, and I was so sad to leave her. Is she at your house? I would love to see her."

Maurice cleared his throat and quieted his voice. "She has not returned home. My biggest fear is that she's been chosen by Levan."

Soft, small hands took hold of his. "I had a feeling she would be the one. It was clear Guy favored her. I considered becoming a lady's maid to the new queen to stay in the city, but this is even better. If she's your cousin—" Geylis paused. "Funny, she never said she had been raised as a Creed Follower."

Maurice explained their situation, including how Hesten Egold had set his ire directly on Maurice and the other Followers. But she didn't shy away. In fact, it seemed to embolden her to learn more and become a Creed Follower herself.

WITH THE ATTACK ON Wilma, Hesten was certain Levan would have rushed to her side, but he had only wished her a speedy recovery. It became clear his sister had not been the one chosen and Hesten had watched for each of the other candidate's departure from the palace gates. Hesten's blood ran cold when he realized the raven-haired imp had never left and had been moved into the palace itself.

Wilma had been born to be a queen. She was regal, elegant, and she would do whatever Hesten told her to do to further their family's position in Geoline. The girl Levan had chosen, the simpering Esme, was too bright-eyed and innocent. The fact that she had a welcome smile and kind word for everyone who crossed her path made his blood boil. Servants should be treated as such.

Still, Hesten knew his place. He needed to appease the king and his queen-to-be in order to keep his place as Levan's second in command. The girl would never whisper political musings in the king's ear. But it was Hesten's job to do so.

In his own home, Hesten stepped over the children underfoot. "Nicie, why are they all over the place? Why can you not control them?"

Exasperated, his wife rolled her eyes at him from the veranda. "The governess went to visit her sister, so I have nobody to watch them. I cannot control them." She stayed where she was, paintbrush in hand. Nicie's life was a continuous cycle of painting landscapes and eating. Her back end had expanded from both.

"Father! Father look," shrieked his oldest child, Marhest, who came at Hesten with a toad in his hands. Joaquin toddled behind his older brother, just as covered in dirt.

Hesten recoiled as he held his hands up. "Stop right this minute. Take that creature back outside. Then both of you go to the nursery." He pointed his finger towards the veranda where Marhest and Joaquin sullenly marched. "Now, where is that youngest child? Is he into something as well?"

Nicie tilted her head for a moment, listening. "No. I think Bowey is still napping." She drew a thin line of blue on the canvas in front of her.

"Don't call him that childish nickname." Hesten hated it. Everybody called his youngest son Bowey, and it was undignified. Even the king called him Bowey. "You named him Bowment, call him that."

"What has you so upset?" Nicie finally put down the brush and held her arms out for her now-pouting boys. "Is this still about Wilma? Levan chose someone else, it will be fine. Wilma will receive several offers of marriage now that she's home and known as one of the Final Fourteen. Noblemen will be banging down the door asking for her hand."

That wasn't the point, but Hesten didn't have the time or the patience to explain the nuances to his irritatingly obtuse wife. He slid his boots on and walked to the door. "I'll be home late."

As he opened the door, he heard his wife mutter, "What else is new?"

Their life in the public eye was idyllic. They put on a pretty show for Levan, the castle staff, and everyone who saw them outside their home. But inside, Nicie turned into a spiteful woman. Hesten knew he didn't help matters, but he was the man of the house. It was her job to cater to him. Over the years, she had become spoiled and slovenly.

If only Veva were still around. She had been spoiled, sure, but she was meticulous about her appearance, always taking great care of herself. Hesten sorely missed the former Queen's influence on Nicie. He doubted the naive child stepping into the role would be as stately as Veva.

When he strode through the palace gates a few minutes later, his mood was no better. With the abundance of tasks at hand and Wilma lacking influence over the king, things became more challenging. There were things he needed Levan to do, things that benefitted him and his family. His brother in Tentakay, the cousins in Florence, they were all counting on him to come through and elevate his people throughout Europe.

Seeing Maurice Gustoff and a few other scribes standing inside the doorway turned his mood even more sour. Would he never be rid of this man? As he passed the group, the men turned toward him and a few bowed their heads in deference to him. Maurice did not bow his head. Ire rose throughout Hesten's body until it spewed out as hateful yelling at the group of insubordinates.

His feet planted just outside the group. "Why do you not bow your head, Gustoff? You are to bow before me." Spittle rained from his mouth down on the men before him.

The men around Maurice stepped back, leaving him vulnerable. Hesten would make an example of him. Instead of cowering, however, the man stood tall and raised his head higher. "I bow to no one, Commander Egold, save my Eminence and my king. You are neither."

The other men shuffled back a few more inches, leaving Maurice exposed. Hesten stepped closer and thrust his finger in Maurice's chest. "I will

see you and your people fall. You can bow to your Creed from the depths."
With that, Hesten spat on Maurice and turned on his heel, walking off.

It had been on his agenda to get Levan to sign some decrees into law. Maybe he needed to add something extra to it. An instrument to enable the mass execution of those who thought they were better than others and disregarded paying respect to their superiors.

CHAPTER 20
1 March 1537

Carden watched from afar. He stood guard at the doors of the hall where his Esme would marry the loathsome King Levan. Why would she willingly give herself to such a man? A man who would easily cast aside a previous wife for the sole reason of displeasing him? Levan would do the same with Esme when he grew tired of her—he felt certain.

Carden was nothing like Levan. He vowed to cherish Esme, her laughter and smiles would be in his heart forever.

Carden longed to dispose of the king before the bridal couple could exchange a single word, but tomorrow would have to do. A message from Terres informed him King Levan would no longer exist following tomorrow's banquet held in Esme's honor.

His upper lip twitched. Standing still was no easy task, and he was expected to stand perfectly still while guest entered the great hall. Moving was only allowed if he saw someone who looked suspicious or carried a weapon.

But Carden laughed on the inside. If someone attempted to assassinate the king, he would be delighted to offer assistance.

His lip twitched again. What if someone wasn't here to hurt Levan, but to hurt Esme instead? The thought made Carden sweaty. His eyes darted from person to person, their rich silks and jeweled finery a blur of color in the vast palace hall. He knew nothing of Veva's family. What if, out of bitterness and rage, they came to seek revenge and take it out on Esme? He now wanted to search each person who passed him. But he had to remain still.

GUY HELD OUT THE lace that hung from Esme's tiara. "Are you ready, darling?"

She was convinced his smile was larger than hers. Esme wished Maurice could be with her, but since he could not, Guy was a remarkable substitute. He spent the past two weeks fussing over everything wedding related and treating Esme the way a brother and friend should. They readied her in the room she had been occupying for the last few weeks. Maids—Rhiann included—bustled about, and the lilting song of birds mixed with the quartet somewhere below wafted up through her window.

"I think I am ready. You would know better than I," Esme teased.

She turned for one final look in the mirror. Her dress was silver. Not just silver in color, but actual spun silver that glinted in the light. It had capped sleeves dripping with crystals. Her midsection was covered in a layer of tulle that draped from one shoulder to the opposite hip. More crystals hung daintily from the silver skirt, which was not nearly as voluminous as recent fashion dictated. Instead it had many folds but fell straight from

Esme's hips. And lastly, the lace had been pulled through the tiara adorning her head, and it trailed several feet behind her.

Standing behind her, Guy sighed. Tears danced in his eyes. "You look like a bride, Chérie. And you look like a queen. The people will love you. Levan already loves you. Go with confidence, Esme."

Esme inclined her head and took his large, dark hands in hers. "Did you not want to marry, Guy?"

A single tear slipped down his cheek, glistening in the light. "I had my one true love, but it could never be." He dabbed a handkerchief to her eye before a tear could fall. "I am happy to live vicariously through you. I am like an uncle to Lester and Lennox, and I expect the same to be true for your children."

In such a short time, he had become so precious to her. She hugged him close. "Thank you, Guy. Thank you for everything."

"Don't thank me," he said, pulling back and looking her in the eye. "Thank the One who sent you here. The Eminence is the one who set everything into motion, darling."

Esme's eyes grew wide. "You know? And you are a...?" She searched his face for an answer.

"Of course. Why do you think you were my favorite? We may be few and far between, but we are here. And we support you, Queen Esme." His voice was a whisper.

Esme fought back even more tears as she hugged Guy again. How could she not have known? And how had he known she was among the Creed Followers? Oh, to have someone nearby to share her faith with was such a comforting and welcome relief.

"Now, go get married," he ordered.

They made their way down the stairs, the music growing louder as they went. The halls that were usually bustling and busy were void of people, save the few Palace Keepers who stood as silent sentries along the wall. At the doors of the grand hall, Esme stopped. She knew Levan and the boys were on the other side of the door. Maurice was on the other side. Perhaps even Geylis.

Music began, slow and serious. It was time. The notes carried to her ears, making her eager to start her life with Levan. The doors opened and hundreds of pairs of eyes turned to see her. But she focused on the eyes at the front of the aisle, for they were the only ones that mattered. She willed her heart to steady and her feet to carry her with confidence.

The ceremony would not be fashioned for Creed Followers, and for that Esme was disappointed. But in her mind, she would promise all the traditional promises to her husband and to the Eminence. The people of Geoline promised things only to man. They used rings out of habit rather than Creed teaching. But still, Esme looked forward to being vowed to Levan for the rest of her days.

She made her way up the aisle alone, feeling the intense gaze of hundreds of people fixated on her. Was she ready for this? She smiled nervously but then caught the eyes of the man standing before her. Her groom. Levan's usually steely expression was soft and light. Beside him stood his two little boys, proud to be next to their father to welcome her. They all wore matching suits with long, royal blue overcoats and silver pants to match her dress. Each had a simple white peach blossom tucked into the lapel.

Esme willed the threatening tears not to come forth. It would ruin the hard work her team had put in. She prayed for the Eminence to bless their marriage, to give their union purpose. And she asked that their marriage bear fruit in the form of more children to bring them joy.

And before she knew it, she was beside the man of her dreams. A judge from Levan's upper courts had been selected to recite the marriage contract and he began.

"We are here today to bear witness to the marriage of Levan Darbley Haras, Sovereign Ruler of Geoline, and Esme Amelia Gustoff of Atelina."

Esme was relieved she bore one of the most common surnames in Geoline. Nobody would think to link it with Maurice. She wondered where he might be in the crowd.

"Esme, you are entrusted with the life and well-being of Levan. Do you promise to love him, treat him as your true husband, and swear fidelity to only him for the rest of your days?" The older man adjusted his glasses as he looked to her for a reply.

"Yes, I dso promise," she said, looking only at Levan.

"And you Levan are being entrusted with the life and wellbeing of Esme. Do you promise to love her, treat her as your true wife, and swear fidelity to only her for the rest of your days?"

Levan's face broke into the biggest smile Esme had ever seen. "Yes, I do promise," Levan replied. Then quietly, to only her, he added, "Forever, my love."

She could feel her heart pounding in her chest, yearning to leap into his waiting arms, but she reminded herself to bide her time. The judge went on a little more about the marriage promise, the raising of children, and then touched on the duties of a wife to her husband and a husband to his wife. Esme barely heard what he said, she was lost in the expression of Levan before her.

"Levan, please give Esme a ring as a sign of your bond to her," the judge instructed. Levan produced a ring of platinum encrusted with diamonds and royal blue sapphires. He slipped it onto the third finger of her left hand. "Levan you are now bonded to Esme."

The judge once again adjusted his glasses and looked to Esme. "Esme, please give Levan a ring as a sign of your bond." Esme slipped the ring off her thumb to give to Levan. It was much larger than her own, but a matching platinum band, inlaid with four sapphires. She designed it so each sapphire represented one member of their family, the two of them and the two boys she was inheriting.

"You are now bonded to Levan," the judge told her. Then to the crowd he announced, "I declare this pair bonded and married in the eyes of the law and in the eyes of each person in this room. Let no person come between them. Now celebrate as they share a wedded kiss."

The crowd erupted into a cacophony of noise and cheers. Streamers and confetti rained down on everybody in celebration. Levan wrapped his arms around Esme, producing butterflies in her stomach. He pulled her against him and lowered his lips to hers. Esme was all too eager to return the kiss, enjoying the feel of his hands on her back and his ring on her finger. When they broke apart, Esme was so overjoyed she could not help but laugh.

Levan swept her up into his arms, carrying her back down the aisle. Lester and Lennox ran behind whooping and cheering. Esme's lace trailed behind them like a wispy cloud, and she giggled like a little girl. She felt safe and secure in Levan's arms as she breathed in his scent for the first time. The thought of falling into an all-consuming love had always held her back, as she feared being unable to escape it. Now she relished that feeling, that loss of control. Levan smelled like clean leather and cedar. He smelled like home.

Outside, Levan placed her back on the ground and kissed her again. Lester and Lennox jumped around them, still excited and cheering.

"Oh, Papa, are we a whole family now?" Lennox asked, tugging on his father's coat.

Levan scooped his younger son up in his arms. "Yes, Lennox, we are." He smiled at Esme and held out his hand for her. Together, they caught Lester between them and shared a family hug.

"Hooray, Momma!" Lennox bound from Levan to Esme, wrapping his chubby little arms around her neck. This time, Esme breathed in the scent of soap and strawberries. She would remember that smell for the rest of her life.

When Lennox let her go, she looked at Lester and whispered, "I know I cannot replace your mother. But do you think we can have our own special bond? I would like to try." Lester nodded and put his arms around her waist.

Just then, the chaos of the crowd came pouring out the double doors. People of every size, shape, and color came to the little group to congratulate them. They kissed Esme on the cheek, the hand, reached out to touch her dress. Questions came from all sides.

Esme covered Lennox with her arms to avoid his being knocked down, but they were quickly separated from Levan and Lester. Somebody knocked into them and stepped on her veil, yanking her head down.

Trying to ignore the scramble of people, Esme turned, looking for Levan's head above the crowd. He was nowhere to be seen. She turned again, feeling a panic rise in her throat. Lennox cried as more people bumped into them and reached out to touch them. He wrapped his arms tighter around her neck. Esme thought she had two options: curl up and wait for the crowd to tire and dissipate, or take action. And the crying child in her arms made her choice easy.

She lifted her head a little higher, craning to see where Levan might have gone. Not finding him, she decided to head back into the hall, against the crowd. "Hold on, darling," she said to Lennox.

He tightened his grip and peered out from his self-made cocoon. "Please move," she demanded of those around her. "I need to get through."

Her voice had not been loud, but it had been commanding. And they moved. With each person who shifted, she took a step forward, until there was a pathway before her leading back to the hall. With each step, Esme held her head higher, and the people stopped and watched. Protecting Lennox was her top priority, and she would not rest until they were well away from the mob around them.

Back in the hall, Guy found her. With a gentle hum, he buzzed around her before patting Lennox's back. "Oh, Chérie, what has happened? You look positively disconcerted. And look at your dress. Please, let me help."

Her jaw was tight and her arms grew weary from shielding the child, but she did not dare let him go. They moved away from the stares of people, Guy blocking any who tried to sneak a look.

"They scared him. And me," she told Guy. "Touching me and my dress, kissing my hands and cheeks. The people were pressing in on all sides. I had to get him away from there."

Lennox lifted his head and sniffed. "Someone pinched me." His curls were matted down, and his eyes were rimmed with pink.

"Is that what made you cry, little one? Where?" Esme smoothed her hand over his brow the way she remembered her mother doing when she was upset. Lennox pointed to his thigh. "Oh, I am so sorry, Lennox. I'm glad we got out of there."

They waited in their hiding spot a few moments before the imposing form of Levan appeared before them. "Th-there you are." He rushed to his new wife and son, filled with concern. Lester was attached to his side. "I didn't know what happened to you. When all the people came out, we got sep-parated. I could not find you." He pressed a kiss to both Esme and Lennox. "Someone said you demanded to be let through the throngs of people and started walking." He cracked a smile. "Wonderful job as the new queen, my darling. Is everything well now?"

"Lennox was pinched by someone. It made him cry," Esme said as she kissed the boy's forehead. "We were both scared."

Levan looked from Lennox to Lester to Esme. "There's nothing to be scared of now. We're together, and we shall always be that way."

CHAPTER 21

THAT AFTERNOON, THE NEWLY formed family gathered on the third floor of the palace for Esme's official crowning ceremony. Levan kept a close watch over all three members of his family. Getting separated from Esme and Lennox earlier had caused him much anxiety. He knew some were not happy with his taking a new queen, but he had not heard any plans to take action against him or his new bride. Still, Levan knew he could not be too careful.

He was incredibly proud of Esme. Like a true mother, she had known her child was scared and hurt, and she had taken charge. He wished he could have seen her in action, but he heard she stood tall and commanded the people to get out of her way. The crowd parted with her covering Lennox the way a protective mother fox would with her young. He wagered she looked regal and beautiful the entire time, even with her veil askew from someone stepping on it. Thankfully the pinch on Lennox was not serious, and he had gotten over the scare.

The balcony for the crowning ceremony overlooked the main courtyard of downtown Atelina. It seemed onlookers overtook every inch of the several acres. Levan made sure security was working hard to keep his family safe, and Palace Keepers were positioned all around them.

Once outside, the crowd cheered for several minutes. Levan and Esme waved to the people until the roar was just a murmur. Hesten went to the edge of the balcony and addressed the crowd first.

He raised his arms to command quiet. Levan smirked at Hesten's love for theatrics. "Ladies and gentlemen of Geoline. It is my greatest and most humble pleasure to present to you the royal rulers of Geoline, Levan and Esme Haras." He paused while Levan and Esme came forward to lively cheers. "May I also present Geoline's heirs, Lester and Lennox Haras."

More cheers. Levan could not help but to smile.

"On this day, our sovereign king has married the beautiful and intelligent Esme and now wishes to crown her Queen of Geoline. What say you, ladies and gentlemen?" Hesten smiled and looked at Levan.

The responding noise was deafening. Small children waved colorful banners from atop their father's strong shoulders. Bouquets of flowers flew toward the balcony, though none reached them. Levan was pleased the people accepted Esme. After all, she was one of their own.

Now Levan stepped forward. He clapped Hesten on the shoulder, shook his hand and waved to the mass of people before him. "My fellow people of Geoline. This is not my country. This is our country—our nation to nurture and help thrive. From among you, I have found a bride who is intelligent and beautiful and who grew up in the shadow of this palace. Esme has won my heart, and I hope she will also win yours. And now I would like to bestow upon her the title of Queen."

He looked over his shoulder to Esme, holding out his hand. She approached him and gave a deep curtsy, but her eyes never left his. Levan could not help but see the love deep inside. "Please kneel, so I may honor you," he said, as was custom. She kneeled at the stool placed before her and bowed her head. "As the king of this great nation, I crown you Queen Esme Haras of Geoline. From here on, you shall be my helpmate and my guide."

A crown of silver, nestled on a pillow of shimmering blue, was held out to him by Marcutin. The crown itself boasted five high points at the front, with several smaller ones completing the circle. It shone brilliantly in the warm sunshine. Levan nodded his head to Marcutin and lifted the crown off the pillow. The silver felt cool and heavy. He raised it high in the air, then gently laid it atop Esme's silky, raven hair. With the piece in place, she lifted her head and stood.

Taking her hand once again, Levan brought Esme forward and presented her to the people watching. She curtsied deeply to them, and they cried out their approval. Esme waved and blew kisses as Lester and Lennox came to stand before them. Levan was filled with pride.

The moment they were back in the palace, they exhaled and the sound echoed in the grand hall as they stretched their tense muscles. "I was so nervous," Esme giggled. "I feared the crown would fall off my head." She lowered her head as Guy removed the heavy headpiece and returned it to its pillow. MacJames did the same with Levan's own crown.

Guy handed the sapphire headband to Esme, and Levan watched as she delicately positioned it in her hair. "This is so much better. And like your mother, I feel beautiful with it on."

Levan admired her. Her cheeks were pink from the excitement, her eyes bright, and her lips a lush rose color. She was beautiful—jeweled headpiece or no. He was ready to be done with the public merriment and have a quiet moment with Esme alone.

As the excitement wore down, the children's tutor came and collected them. Guy ushered Esme to the bridal chamber to prepare. Levan was not sure what exactly she needed to do to prepare, but he was not in the mood to argue this day. He went into his office, put his feet up on his desk, and enjoyed a glass of wine while he replayed the day's events in his mind. It had been wonderfully successful.

THE NEXT MORNING, ESME slept well past sunrise. It was mid-morning before she sat up and got a true look at the room Levan occupied.

It was the largest bedroom she had ever seen in her life. It made the meeting room at Belin House look like a closet. The walls were not white as they were throughout other homes in Atelina, but a rich, warm blue that felt happy and comforting. The bedspread under her fingers was sage green with gold threads running through it. Huge landscape pictures hung on the walls beside giant tapestries, all surely antiques that were hundreds of years old.

Esme looked to the other side of the bed for Levan, but he was not there. She stood and wrapped a plush robe around her, cinching it at her waist. The floor was carpeted all around the bed, and the fibers felt wonderful between her bare toes. She took a moment and squished her feet around, enjoying the decadent sensation.

The door to her left opened and Levan came through, dressed in a crisp linen suit with a deep orange coat and wheat-colored pants. The shirt under the coat was a deep brown that made his blue eyes look almost white in contrast. His hair had been slicked back, making it appear darker than the its usual sandy blond. The moment he laid eyes on Esme, his stern expression softened and transformed into a lazy smile.

"My beautiful bride, I see you have awoken," he said, putting a hand to her cheek. "I shall call Guy for you." He moved away when she stopped him.

"Must you call him so soon?" She linked her fingers behind his neck and reached up on her tiptoes to give him a gentle kiss.

"Ah, my love, today is your day. Your bridal feast begins in two hours. You will need that time to prepare," he reminded her. "And I have a few things to accomplish on my own in that time." He picked her up and spun her around before stepping away.

Esme understood being married to the king would not be easy. His attentions would often be elsewhere. That had been part of Guy's lessons, so she tried to understand. The country came first. But that didn't mean Esme had to like it, just accept it. They had been married fewer than twenty-four hours, and she selfishly wanted a full day with only her husband.

Knowing there was no use in pouting, she put a smile on her face. "I will see you at the banquet then, Levan."

"I will meet you back here and escort you down to the hall. Guy has the schedule." He strode from the room without hesitation.

Esme sat back down on the edge of the bed. Her elation turned into deflation. Frustrated, she huffed twice before the door burst open and Guy bounded in, a whirlwind of joyful noise.

"Come along, Chérie. We must make haste back to your rooms so you can begin readying for your banquet." He took her hand in his and pulled her up, whisking her away to her own apartments on the other side of the wing.

Waiting for them was her dressmaker, hair stylist, and jeweler. An army of people clamored around her. In that moment, more than any other since she had walked through the palace gate, she wished for Maurice to be by her side once again in the quiet of their little home.

Almost two hours later, Maurice himself *was* brought to her side. Esme smiled as he approached her. How she wished she could embrace him. He wore his tan suit, the one she picked out for him the year before. He had come in to record her thoughts before the banquet. She had not realized before how often her words would be recorded for posterity. Every word counted here.

A quick, charming smile played on Maurice's lips as he entered; but, the smile vanished as he leaned in to her. "Esme, you must to listen to me. There is a conspiracy to murder Levan." He made a show of readying his quill and pulling up a fresh sheet of parchment.

This was not a funny joke. Her eyes searched her cousin's. "What do you mean?" These were not the first words she wanted coming from her cousin after her marriage.

He carefully wrote and nodded his head. After an excruciating moment, he looked up at her. "Two men, Billiam and Terres, are known thieves. I overheard them talking and they plan to poison your husband. I believe they have been set up to do it, but I do not know by whom."

Alarmed, Esme battled the overwhelming need to find Levan, a knot of anxiety tightening in her stomach. She needed more information. "When will this happen?"

A stranger walked past her and waved, Esme attempted a smile as if nothing was wrong. As if her cousin had not just said someone wanted to murder her husband. She kept her eyes averted from Maurice. It had to appear as if he was only asking her questions about her banquet.

"They said they planned to do it today, during the feast. They were hired on with the kitchen staff a few weeks ago. They said they will poison the food taken to Levan after the tasters have checked it," Maurice told her.

"How did you overhear this?" The taste of bile rose in Esme's throat. What if Maurice was implicated as an assassin?

She noticed Maurice's writing was unsteady as he took a deep breath and spoke slowly. "Fortunately for your husband, I am adept at being overlooked by most. They speak without checking their surroundings, but I do not think anybody else heard them."

Esme's hands shook as she tucked her hair behind her ear. "I will warn him." She longed to embrace her cousin and feel his comfort as she did as a child, but she could not. Nobody knew they were related, and she intended to keep her promise to Maurice by not telling anybody. "Thank you, Maury, for telling me. I miss you."

An ink-stained hand barely touched her shoulder as he looked her in the eye. "You love him?" Esme nodded. "Then I do this for you. The Eminence is with you always."

With that, he released her and packed up his scrolls of paper. He went over to Guy and they spoke in low tones. Both men looked over to Esme a few times, and she huffed in frustration. What were they doing? She needed to get to Levan immediately.

Finally, Guy led her back to the king's chambers where Levan waited for her.

He held out his hands and she rushed to him, her legs quaking with fear. Would Levan believe her? He had to believe her and take action quickly. She recalled the names of the two men, Terres and Billiam. Terres and Billiam.

"Are you ready, my queen?" Levan kissed her cheek, but when he noticed her wide-eyed expression, his smile fell. "What is it? Are you nervous?"

Esme took hold of Levan's sleeves. "Levan, please listen to me. I have heard there is a rumor that two assassins plan to poison you today at the banquet. Billiam and Terres are their names. They are thieves, hired to assassinate you. They have found work in the kitchen. Levan, you must stop them before anyone gets hurt."

Esme looked into the intense eyes of her husband, the man she loved. She prayed he would believe her. They had just married—he could not fall victim to their plotting!

"I have tasters who check all my food. Yours as well, actually," he replied, a thin smile on his lips.

Shaking her head, she placed her hands on either side of his face. "Please. They plan to poison it after the taster's test. You must get rid of them." Tears welled in her eyes, and she did not even try to hide them.

"Of course, my love. I will have it looked into at once." Levan motioned for a dark-haired Palace Keeper to come forward. "Billiam and Terres. They are working in the kitchens and apparently plan to poison the food. See what you can find. If nothing else, dismiss them immediately."

The green-clad guard bowed. "Yes, Your Grace." He departed from them quickly.

Levan smoothed her hair and pulled her close to his chest. "There now. Nothing to worry about. It will be taken care of. Now, where did you hear this rumor?"

Esme glanced over to Maurice who had accompanied the group over to the king's apartments. "Maurice, the scribe over there. He was not sure you would believe him," she said timidly.

"And you believe him?" Levan followed her gaze to the man who had raised her. Despite Maurice's past friendly encounters with the king, Esme wasn't sure if Levan would believe the words of a scribe.

Nodding, Esme replied, "Yes. I do." She had trusted him with her life for years.

"I've always found him to be a trustworthy man. He's never wronged me before. If there is foul play afoot, we shall know it soon enough," Levan said, kissing her forehead.

CHAPTER 22

How had they been found out? In some way, they must have made a blunder and leaked information to someone. As Carden walked the hall, he kept an eye out for anyone coming his way in case the two thieves decided to share a Palace Keeper had been behind the whole thing. Thankfully, he never revealed his name to them. He hoped they were done away with before any serious questioning took place.

Thirty minutes prior, he had been pulled into a group of Palace Keepers rushing for the kitchen. Before he knew it, Billiam and Terres had been cornered and searched at length. Sure enough, the guard searching them came up with a small vial from Billiam's shoe. Terres looked directly at him for an instant, but since they had never seen his face, there was no way he could be identified. It was to his benefit that all Palace Keepers were similar in size.

The two would-be assassins were carried off to the holding jail, and Carden was told to return to his original post. Hopefully, getting caught red-handed would prevent a trial that could expose him as the mastermind behind the plot to assassinate King Levan. They would be dead before the end of the night.

Carden smacked his hand on the table in front of him. How had they been so careless? How had they allowed themselves to be caught? He should have known better than to trust two bumbling thieves with such serious work. He paid them almost a year's wages only for them to get caught. He wondered if he could get it back somehow.

As it was, he knew Esme spent the wedding night with the king. Carden was disgusted, but he trusted it would only have been one night. He could forgive her one night. Then with Levan gone, Carden would come to rescue her and they would be together. They way it was meant to be.

There had to be a way to get rid of Levan. Carden looked around. The hall for Esme's bridal banquet was filled to capacity with well-wishers, dignitaries, and several guards making sure nothing complicated the day for the royal couple. He would be caught right away if he did anything.

Or... If he did shoot King Levan from right in the middle of the room, there were several people standing around with guns. All the Palace Keepers looked the same. Same haircut, same uniform, same issued hat that sat low on their brow, blocking their hair and eye color. If he shot, he could claim it was someone else who ran the other way. It just might work.

He needed to be closer to Levan to get a clear shot. He moved forward while staying against the walls of the room. He approached one door that made a good exit and looked toward Levan. As Levan whispered to Esme, the pair laughed together. Carden heard the blood rushing in his ears. Esme would be in the way, he realized. He moved again, nodding to those who greeted him as he went.

In a different area, Carden believed he had a perfect opportunity to shoot the pompous king and make a swift exit through a side door. Esme might be smattered in blood, but it would wash off. A thorough but brief circle to scout out where other Palace Keepers stood revealed three others close by but not paying him attention. He could easily pinpoint one of them as the murderer.

Licking his lips, Carden slowly and casually pulled his gun from its holster. Keeping it low so he didn't garner attention, he lined it up as best as he knew how. He had been well trained with a gun and rarely missed his shot.

One. He closed his eyes, willing Levan to stay still.

Two. He put his finger on the trigger.

Three.

CHAPTER 23

Esme stood in surprise as the ricochet of a bullet echoed through the room and a group of men fell to the ground. She quickly put her hand to her heart and laid the other on Levan's arm.

Levan also jumped. His eyes searched hers as his hands went to her shoulders. "What happened? Are you well?" He ignored the commotion while waiting for her reply.

Gulping, Esme nodded and shakily returned to her seat. "Yes, yes, it just scared me. You are not—are you—" She could not finish the question as her voice dried up.

Levan nodded, cupping her chin in his hand. "I am fine, Esme. I need to go check what happened. Stay right here." He stood to his full height and waved his hand. Guy was immediately at Esme's side. Esme glanced at where the children were, glad they were being well distracted from the uproar across the room.

Esme took Guy's hand as he guided behind the high-backed chair to take cover. She didn't argue when he pulled her down to a crouching position. "What happened? Was that a gunshot?"

Guy's almond-shaped eyes looked into hers, and he smiled for her sake. "I believe so, my lady. I also believe three or four Palace Keepers took the shooter down before he had a chance to really take aim. They are well trained, Chérie."

Esme sighed in relief, wiping her brow with an unsteady hand. The crowd was still in chaos. She couldn't see Levan, but she saw the commotion in the center of the room. Four guards had a man in their grasp. But Esme struggled for breath upon seeing who it was they held. Carden.

"No." She stood and yelled before realizing she did so. The hall went silent, and all eyes turned toward her. She broke free from Guy and rushed to Levan's side.

Levan caught her as she approached, not letting her go any further. "Do you know this man?" His stare was intense, almost angry.

"Yes. I have known Carden for years. We grew up in the same neighborhood together," she said to her husband. "He would not have done this. Carden, please tell me this was not you." Tears welled in her eyes, stinging and hot, as she saw the man with shackles already in place.

Nostrils flaring, Levan looked from Esme to the captured man. "How well do you know him?" Levan fumed.

Jealousy now reared its ugly head. Esme realized he took her outburst as a sign of loyalty to Carden and not him. Esme prayed she could clear things up quickly.

She leaned close to her husband. "I know him well enough. He tried very hard to win my affections last year to no avail. I turned him down. He did not take my rejection well, and he even approached me while I was staying in the Belin House. I told Guy at that time Mr. Wallace had scared me."

Spots danced before her eyes, and she felt light-headed. "While I hate to think of someone I know doing this, I don't doubt his capability to shoot at you or me," Esme admitted.

The anger Levan directed at her subsided a little, and a small smile came on his lips. But then he turned back toward Carden, grabbing him by the lapels. "What have you to say for yourself?"

Carden's eyes skipped over Levan and the other guards, landing firmly on Esme. His voice rang throughout the hall. "I did this for you, Esme. To free you from him. Billiam and Terres, they failed. I believed I couldn't fail. But I guess I did. I'm sorry, Esme. I love you." His face fell, and he hung his head in shame.

Levan did not let go of him, but he turned toward Esme and glared at her. "You...you needed to be free of me?"

A surge of unexpected terror filled Esme. She needed to reassure her husband she had not been part of this plot. Tears spilled over her cheeks as she lowered herself to her knees before the king. "I would never want to be free from you, Levan. I just pledged my life to you, and I did so willingly. I love you with my whole being. Guy can attest to what I said a moment ago. Carden Wallace approached me and asked me to accompany him away from Atelina. I told him no. Guy then made sure the Keepers rotation was changed to keep Mr. Wallace away from me."

She could suffer the same fate as Veva for this, Esme realized. The unforgiving floor made her knees ache, but she kept herself lowered and submissive to her husband.

Levan tore his gaze away from Esme and turned his attention back to Carden. "Carden Wallace, you are no longer a Palace Keeper or a Keeper of any kind. You shall spend the next fifty years in the walls of our highest security prison after your ears are cut off, your hands mangled, and your knees twisted. If you are still alive in fifty years, your case will be revisited. But expect no mercy if my family is still in command. Killing you would be too swift a punishment. You will live in agony the rest of your days."

Then his attention returned to Esme. He placed one finger under her chin and tilted her head up so she was looking at him. In a calm, quiet voice, he said, "I believe you, Esme. Stand."

Getting to her feet, Esme curtsied. "I am beholden to you, my king. Please, can we try to enjoy the rest of the banquet? I would prefer to put this behind us, my love." She led him back to the table where their empty, high-backed chairs sat askew. Part of her wanted to look back at Carden and express some sort of compassion, but she knew better than to do that in front of Levan. She kept her back to him as the Palace Keepers led one of their own to await transport in the jail.

That night, Esme recounted the evening's drama. How easily she could have lost her life with Carden's foolishness. She had ended things with him, and had he understood at that point—or so she thought. What happened to make him so obsessed and possessive of her? Thankfully, Guy testified to Levan on her behalf she indeed had warned him about Carden approaching her in the courtyard. That helped calm Levan further, but he was still sulking over the idea of Esme spending any amount of time with Carden before she had come to the palace.

As they prepared for bed in their dressing gowns, Levan was oddly quiet. It worried Esme. "Levan, sweetheart, please I knew him before you had begun the search for a bride. You—you were still married," she lowered his eyes to avoid his gaze. "To Veva."

LEVAN SAT IN AN overstuffed red chair in his bedroom, a liquor-filled glass hung limply from his hand. With a knitted brow, he looked toward the fireplace where flames danced. "It bothers me to know you ever looked at another man. No matter how long ago, Esme."

"From the moment I heard you were ready to take a bride, I had no doubt I was made for you and you alone." She knelt before him on the plush carpet and put her hands over her heart. "Something in here told me we were meant to be together, you and me. I adore you, Levan. When everything happened last year, with her, I could sense something. I knew you were not comfortable taking her away from your children, and you felt forced to take action. Nobody understood that I could see that in you."

"You could t-tell that?" He looked into her eyes. Esme nodded. "I didn't think anybody in Geoline would sympathize with my position. I felt like a mons...monster. Yes, I punish—and even execute—those who commit heinous acts. But Veva did not deserve it. And while I did not love her, she was the mother of my children, and we had an understanding between us."

Esme looked at him and laid her hands on the sides of his face. "And for that, I am sorry. Truly. Though I hate to think that without it happening, I would not have had to opportunity to become your wife, to love you as I do."

Levan wondered if he should tell her what had really happened with Veva. But no, now was not the time. They were exhausted from all the excitement of the day. Two assassinations attempts within a few hours was a new record for Levan. And surely the first for Esme. After all, this was only her second day as queen.

Hesten had requested an audience with him before the day's excitement, but the idea of sitting with Hesten for hours on end made Levan's head hurt. It would have to wait until the morrow. Levan was aware of the nature of meeting: these Creed Followers Hesten had such a problem with. Lately, they were all Hesten could talk about.

But then, Levan chuckled to himself, *I supposed Esme was the only thing on my mind lately and I probably talked about her overmuch as well.* Levan had not experienced any problem with the Followers in Geoline, and his informants had not given him any grounds to invade the Cartrelleites to the west. Surely Hesten would understand waiting till morning.

Esme started to leave for her own bedchamber, but Levan stopped her and held onto her hand lightly. "You should stay here tonight. For safety." He winked. "Get settled in. Hesten wanted to speak with me, but I'll tell him it will have to wait." Once Esme nodded, Levan excused himself to rearrange the meeting.

He found Hesten in his office, waiting not so patiently. "There you are, Sire. I was afraid you had forgotten about me," Hesten remarked. "Let's get down to business, shall we?" The man practically jumped toward the desk and made a grab for the papers waiting there.

A headache formed behind Levan's eyes. The man's bloodlust was too much for him at times. "Hesten, you are a l-loyal advisor and an excellent leader. But I'm afraid I am not up for this lively dis-discussion tonight. I'm exhausted; my wife is scared. Why don't we reconvene tomorrow when we've all rested? Besides, I'm sure you want to get home to Nicie and those precious children. I bet the baby is getting bigger every day."

Hesten rolled his eyes. Levan knew Hesten appreciated his wife, but he loved power. Levan could sympathize. He had felt the same way when married to Veva. She was there because she was supposed to be there, not because he loved her. But Esme... She captured his heart, and that meant more than all the land and money Levan could imagine.

Hesten nearly pouted. "Tomorrow?" There was a certain whine to his voice that reminded Levan of his children when they didn't get their way.

"Of course. Esme and the children need me to calm their fears right now. It's not every day one of the Palace Keepers tries to shoot you." Levan scratched the stubble on his chin. How had that Keeper gotten so high in the ranks if he was that unstable? "Before I go, Hesten, jot down a note that the standards for becoming a Palace Keeper need to be more rigorous.

"I thought you were not working tonight, Your Grace," Hesten said with a scowl. "If you have time for this..."

"No, no. Just make a note for tomorrow. I need to discover how that unstable man got to be a Keeper in the first place. We obviously have a flaw in our process somewhere." Levan waited for Hesten to take the note then opened the door for him. "Do you plan to stay the night in my office?"

Hesten followed him like a scolded puppy—with his tail between his legs. Levan hadn't realized until now the extent to which Hesten's desires for control were so consuming. It made him doubly glad he had not chosen Wilma as his wife.

Back in his room, he found Esme lazily turning pages in a book. Her eyes were heavy, but she turned each page absently. She wore a silver night robe with aubergine piping along the edges. Her makeup had been removed, showing only the true beauty of the woman he married.

"You are the most beautiful woman I have ever seen," he whispered to her as he kissed her exposed neck.

She giggled as he kissed her. "Do you think? Even compared to when my hair is done so elaborately and I have all those cosmetics on?" Esme put the book down and turned to him.

"Especially without it. While you are lovely when you're done up and dressed in your finery, I much prefer you looking as you do now. Simple, natural beauty. Not only do I prefer it, I find my affection for you is doubled—no tripled—like this." He took her hand and helped her to stand.

Taking a step back, he looked at his bride who smiled at him without reservation. He could see the love in her eyes, bottomless like azure pools whose depths could never be known. A slight blush crept up her neck and into her cheeks as he stared at her. She did not speak, nor did she try to hide herself. Esme simply allowed him to caress her with his eyes while she looked at him herself.

"What do you think, Queen Esme? What do you make of all this thus far?"

"I cannot begin to say, King Levan. I have certainly experienced more excitement than I'm used to. But it's worth it to be with Lennox and Lester. And you," she said, stepping toward him. "The only thing I miss is my garden. It's the beginning of planting season, and I long to see things grow and blossom."

Levan took her into his arms. She was a perfect fit. "Then you shall have your garden. Tell Guy tomorrow what you need, and it will be ready by week's end. In the meantime, I am hoping to soon see you grow and blossom on your own." He laid a hand protectively over her middle, imagining it would soon expand with their child. With two boys underfoot, a baby girl would be the perfect addition.

"Tomorrow, bah," Hesten said to himself, kicking a stray rock as he walked toward the palace gates. He continued muttering to himself. "That prissy little biddie is all he cares about these days. If only he had decided upon Wilma. I could have his ear both in the boardroom and the bedroom. Wilma would have seen to it that Levan did everything I wanted." He cursed Esme under his breath.

Footsteps behind him silenced Hesten. He did not need anybody walking near him thinking him mad for talking to himself or accusing him of treason for talking poorly of the new queen. He slowed his step to allow the other person to pass.

"Hesten, lovely March evening isn't it?"

Drat. Maurice Gustoff.

A grimace came across Hesten's face. "Why must you always be so cheery? Have we not had this discussion before?"

"I find no reason not to be cheery," Maurice said. "Even though tonight did not go as planned for the new queen, she is a lovely girl, and I hope our king will be happy with her."

"He'd have been happier with my sister," Hesten hissed, his arms crossed. "She should have been made queen instead of that juvenile girl he chose."

Maurice furrowed his brow and licked his lips. "I don't think you should speak of Queen Esme in that manner, Hesten. She deserves your respect."

Hesten's already sour mood became even worse. "Respect? Do you have no respect for a man in my position, Gustoff? Do you not realize I am second in command in this entire country? And who are you? You are nothing. You are lower than nothing." Hesten spit as he screamed, his voice becoming hoarse. Heat radiated from him as his chest heaved.

For his part, Maurice stood there and took the verbal beating. Hesten thought the man was incredibly weak. Could he not defend himself? Would he not even try? Enraged that Maurice did not retaliate, Hesten struck out at him, and his fist found purchase in Maurice's jaw.

"You aren't even a man, Gustoff. Get up and fight like a man," Hesten bellowed as the scribe cowered at his feet. "Or, or maybe you should stay on the ground and bow down to me. Treat me with the respect I deserve. But just you wait. You and all your Creed Followers. When I am finished with you, you will wonder where your Eminence went."

Maurice stayed on the ground, silent. Hesten stormed off toward home, the feeling of rage abating after the physical exertion.

CHAPTER 24

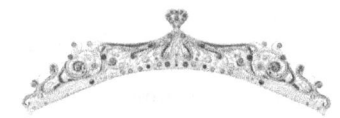

Two months had passed since their wedding, and Levan knew he couldn't delay any longer; it was time to tell Esme the truth. He had not yet told her because he was afraid it would make her run—or at least turn from him. But it was something he believed he needed to do, and after her confession of understanding his position a few months before, it was the right thing to do. He could no longer hide this secret from her.

As he felt her stir beside him, Levan spoke quietly. "Are you awake?" He reached for her and caressed her arm.

She shifted and placed her head on his shoulder. "Yes, I'm awake." Her arm wrapped around his middle, and he closed his eyes from the comfort she brought.

"Esme, there is something I need to speak with you about. It is incredibly important but also not something easily explained." He sighed and wished she would be understanding. He feared Esme would not be receptive to what he needed to tell her.

Craning her neck to see his face, she looked concerned. "What's wrong, my king? You can reveal anything to me."

The weight of the secret pressed down on him, making a sudden announcement impossible. Showing her was the only way. "Will you travel with me to Bristow? On official business?" There was no way to see her face given their positions, but Levan wondered what her reaction was.

He could feel her breath in and out. "Of course. I'm happy to accompany you wherever you need. Is there something pertinent you need to see to?" Her voice was steady, unassuming.

Could she feel his heart rate quicken under her head? "There's something I need to show you. It's of the utmost importance because I want to be truthful with you."

Esme's body stiffened, but Levan had to commend her for keeping her voice level. "Whenever you would like, I will be ready."

"Be ready in an hour." With that, Levan pulled the bell that signaled their staff to enter the room.

It was a three-hour journey south to Bristow. This was one of the poorer regions of Geoline, governed by a few minor lords. But it was also where a maximum-security prison stood, home to some of the country's worst enemies. As they passed through the gate, Esme's eyes widened upon seeing men in shackles and guards with whips at the ready.

"Where are we, Levan?" Her voice was a whisper, and she shrunk away from the carriage window.

"Stay here a moment," he commanded as he took leave of their carriage. He went to the head guard and told him the reason for their visit. Levan requested four armed Keepers with them at all times for safety. He returned to the carriage and held his hand out for Esme to step down.

Worry lines formed between Esme's eyes. She took his hand and carefully stepped down, her chest rising and falling rapidly as tears formed in her eyes. "My king, my love, have I offended you?"

It dawned on him Esme thought she was being banished to the prison. He pulled her close and tried to ease her fears. "No, no. You have done nothing wrong, my darling. I am bringing you here to see a prisoner, not to deliver you to a terrible fate." She relaxed into him. "Do not fret, Esme. I need you to see someone."

She gasped and pulled back. "It's not Carden Wallace, is it?"

With a snort, he shook his head. "Hardly. He will never concern you again." His face grew somber. "Come. Please stay quiet, and do not speak until I give you permission. It's for our safety."

A single nod was her reply. Guarded by four Keepers, they made their way down damp and chilly halls. Finally, they climbed two flights of stairs to a small room with several small covered slots at eye level. Each slot was only large enough for one person to see through. This was the spy chamber.

It was something Levan's grandfather had installed as a way to overhear what his enemies said and see them as they paced their cell. From high above, they could see the cell inhabitants without being seen in return. As long as they were silent, there was no way anyone would know of their presence.

One guard took a stand next to the slot in question while the other three fanned out around Levan and Esme. With complete silence, the guard uncovered the slot and took a preliminary peek. He nodded to Levan.

Taking her hand, he brought her to the stairwell, away from anyone who might overhear them. Levan knew his expression was serious based on the fear in Esme's eyes, but it was for her benefit. "I'm going to show you something that will likely upset you. Do not speak until we get back outside, do you understand?" When she pressed her lips together and nodded, he pulled her forward.

He looked first, peering down into the chamber. An overstuffed bed with fine linens askew sat along an inside corner. Beside it was a modesty screen so the occupant could change clothing and perform bodily functions in private. A table with two chairs sat in the middle of the room, used for both writing and meals. Books were currently stacked upon it. And the person in question leaned over a book, reading.

The head of dark hair rose slightly and looked to the lone window high up on the opposite wall. It was large enough to allow light in for reading during midday but inaccessible for the prisoner. The head lowered again to concentrate on the book.

Levan beckoned Esme forward. He pressed his finger to his lips, reminding her to be silent. She nodded, though her brows furrowed. Standing back, he allowed Esme to look into the room. The glint of her eyes revealed they took in everything below, including the person. She looked back to him with question in her eyes. He gestured with his chin to keep looking.

The sound of a knock came from below and Levan could tell the door opened. He heard the voice of a gruff woman call out, "Tea time, madam."

The voice, familiar to Levan, came through the slot. "Thank you, Gertie." It was just as he had last heard it.

Esme's back straightened, and she stumbled away from the viewing window. Her hand clamped over her mouth, her eyes were wide with fear. She shook her head when Levan attempted to approach her, turned to the stairwell, and fled.

CHAPTER 25

THE STAIRWELL WAS NARROW but not too steep as Esme ran all the way to the bottom, Levan hot on her heels. She assumed the guards followed him, but she did not care.

Veva was alive. Veva, who was believed to be executed, was residing in this miserable prison. Hot tears burned Esme's eyes and cheeks. The taste of bile rushed up her throat, and she forced it back down. It couldn't be true.

As soon as Esme hit the bottom step and fresh air washed over her, she turned and retched into a corner.

After a few moments, she regained her composure and stood again. Levan reached to her, but she jerked away. "How? How can this be? I thought she had been executed."

When Levan moved closer to Esme again, she skirted away from him. "Please, Esme, listen to me. You know I never loved Veva, but she was still my wife and the mother of Lester and Lennox. I could not allow her to be killed for a slight transgression. I could never live with myself if the children thought I had killed their mother. I know in England Princess Elizabeth thinks her father is a monster for having Anne beheaded. I do not want that. I do not want my children to loathe me."

By this time, tears flowed freely down Esme's cheeks. "I do understand that, Levan. But you married me, claiming to be free to marry again. And here, I see your wife very much alive in this place. I cannot be married to you if you are already married."

Esme's face was red and stained with wet streaks. Why had he told her? This ruined everything between them. They were not married in the eyes of the Creed if his first wife was still alive. Breathing became difficult and Esme gulped in air.

Levan commanded one of the guards to help her, and a strong hand took hold of her elbow, holding her up. Someone found a stool and placed it before her, the Keeper helping her to sit. Levan knelt before her.

"Veva and I are not married anymore. I divorced her, like Henry did with the first Catherine." He did not touch her, but she could feel the heat radiating from his body. "I have hated hiding this from you. That is why I brought you here."

"I must admit the rumors of your ruthlessness swirl outside the palace gates," she said in a cold tone. Someone thrust a skein before her, and she greedily drank from it. Feeling quenched and a little calmer, she finally glanced at her husband. "I never wanted to—I never did—believe them. But I am unsure of what to think at the moment."

"Please let me explain." With a creased brow, he took a deep breath, and Esme knew he was willing to move the world for her.

She could barely look at him, but she tried as he knelt before her. "When Veva refused to come to me wearing her jewels, I did not understand why. Hesten had gone himself to ask her to put them on so I could display the wealth of our wonderful nation. I admit I was trying to brag to someone I did not care for. I said I could fund a war with her jewels alone, and I wanted her to display my wealth. But she refused. My first thought was to tell the crowd she had fallen ill or was indisposed, but then Hesten announced she was being disobedient.

"Much of the crowd was already heavy into the drink, and they began causing a ruckus. The next thing I knew, everyone was chanting for Veva to no longer be Queen. I was backed into a corner." Esme finally looked at Levan who was now staring off into space and shaking his head, a tear on his cheek. This was not common knowledge.

"I tried to think, but it all happened so quickly. I gave Veva an hour to say goodbye to the children then she was locked in the jail. But I worked quickly that night with Guy and MacJames to get her out of the palace and as far away as possible. Guy went with her and helped her get set up here. It is small, and she has a companion, Gertie. Veva goes by the name Eva here, so they don't quite know who she is. She receives updates every month on the children. In turn, I get updates on her and what she's doing. She is guarded at all times."

Esme closed her eyes and felt the wetness of her lashes on her cheek. "What about the execution?"

"Everyone was told it was done. And outside the three of us, and now you, everybody believes her dead," he said. "Even Hesten thinks she was executed."

"So you're not still married to her?" Esme's mind was reeling. How could this have happened? She loved him so much—how could he betray her like this?

"No, I'm not. The minute her crown was removed from her head, she was no longer queen and no longer my wife. And to make sure, MacJames had legal papers drawn up, which we both signed that very night. She readily agreed to sign, but that's not a surprise given the alternative. Divorce may not be popular outside of England, but sometimes these things are necessary if you want to protect someone you care about. I can show you the document if you like."

He scooted closer to Esme, the dirt rubbing into his clothing. "No matter how I felt, she brought my sons into this world. And because of her misdeed, she will never see them again, which she told me is a terrible fate. But she and I are no longer married."

Esme wiped the tears from her face. "Why didn't you tell me this before?"

"It is not easy to say my first wife is still alive and living in a prison cell," Levan said with a semi-laugh. "I didn't know how to tell you, but I knew I needed to. Please forgive me. I swear to you I don't visit her. I don't long for her. I could not kill her for simply being herself—any more than I could kill you for being you. And I love you. I would do anything for you, Esme. Please believe me."

"I want to, Levan, I do," she said, finally placing her hands on his stubbly cheeks. She caressed the rough skin and looked into his beautiful eyes. How could she deny him anything? "Can we go home?"

Immediately, hands came out to help them both to their feet. Esme had nearly forgotten they were surrounded by guards at a prison. They both stood, and Levan gave the order to ready the horses for the return journey.

Inside the comfort of the carriage, Esme took several steadying breaths. This would take getting used to. It was one thing knowing Levan had been married before, but he was not the widower she thought him to be. Veva was alive. But she was no longer a part of the family. She was no longer married to Levan or acting as the mother of the boys.

"I love you," she finally whispered to her husband as tears gathered in the corners of her eyes.

"And I love you. With everything I have," he said as he leaned in to kiss her. "Are you angry with me?"

Shaking her head, she responded, "No. I understand your reasoning. I just wish... I don't know. Do you remember how you felt when you found out Carden Wallace and I had been associated long before you met me? I have a similar sensation to that. A little jealous, even though I know I have no reason to be."

Levan nuzzled his face into her neck, and Esme breathed in his hair. He was heavenly. "I adore you, Esme. You, Lester, and Lennox, you are my world. More important than anything else."

Esme smiled and kissed her husband. "I'm so glad to hear that. Thank you for telling me the truth."

"No secrets. I promise you, Esme. There shall not be any secrets between us now or ever again."

A smile crossed her face, and she hoped it looked more genuine than it felt. "Of course not," she whispered back to him.

Panic filled her. Here was Levan, revealing a grave secret to her while she kept the core of her life a secret from him. Esme longed to reveal her faith to her husband. She wanted to pray with him each morning after they woke but lay in bed. And the children—oh how she wished she could share the news of the Creed with Lester and Lennox. But she had promised Maurice. And he said things that are different are destroyed. She had a hard time believing Levan would ever harm her—after all, he had just shown her a very much alive Veva. But fear of the unknown kept her from telling him the truth. She prayed the Eminence would protect her if her secret was ever discovered.

As they journeyed back to Atelina, Esme noticed Levan's gaze drop to her mid-section. "How are you feeling today, darling? Is everything well with you?" He asked frequently in hopes she would announce she was carrying a child.

Alas, today would not be that day. "Levan, I am perfectly fine. We've just gotten married. Give it time. Besides, I want to enjoy you and you alone before my body expands beyond all recognition." She laughed, trying to turn her mind from her secret to the family Levan wanted to start with her.

"I cannot wait to see your belly swell. I shall love you all the more," he promised her.

Esme's heart was near to bursting. She had truly been blessed with a husband who adored her and whom she adored in return.

PART II

CHAPTER 26
SPRING 1538

"It is so hard to believe we've been wed for two years," Esme said, laying her head on Levan's chest as they lounged in their quarters. "It seems like yesterday we gave our vows to one another."

"You are right. I treasure every day with you," Levan replied, running his hand down her hair. He squeezed her tight and kissed her forehead. "I wish we would have a child, though."

A chill came over her, and goosebumps rose on her arms. "I know. But we are still young and we have the boys. I love you so much."

"I love you too," he parroted back to her, but Esme could tell his heart wasn't in it. He was disappointed in her lack of producing more heirs.

But it wasn't all about having children for Esme. In the two years she spent as queen, Esme had grown exponentially. And she felt Levan had as well. His philanthropic activities had come a long way. With Esme's garden, they established a free food bank for anyone in need. Based on the example in Atelina, cities like Harmon, Bruchlin, and Gwynberg began providing free food banks.

Personally, Esme had become close with Lester and Lennox. She loved mothering them but never let them forget Veva loved them as well. She was especially attached to Lennox, now almost seven years old. He happily called her Momma and loved to walk through the gardens with her, helping her tend to the plants. Lester had taken a shine to the chickens and had grown into an animal lover.

Esme did long for children who were part Levan and part herself. Any woman would. From the time they were married, Levan had been insistent on providing her a child to grow and nurture in her own womb. Esme cried and prayed for a baby, both to satisfy her own heart and that of her husband. But in two years of marriage, Esme's prayers had been answered with a firm no.

She tried not to dwell on it. She had plenty of things occupying her time. She loved to play with the boys, she hosted many social and charitable luncheons or other functions, she had Yasmin and Sandrine over often, and she insisted on digging in her own garden—much to Guy's dismay. She traveled across Geoline with Levan and Hesten, meeting people and seeing the landscape of their country. But Esme knew the people in the city were beginning to talk about her barrenness. Why could she not provide another child for the king? Or perhaps their marriage was not true. Rumors were spreading everywhere, and she had at least a few clues that some of them had originated with Hesten.

There was a mutual dislike between her and Hesten. Not that she hadn't tried to like him. He was an important component of the smooth running of the government. She understood that. And she had done her utmost to be polite and cordial to the man. But it seemed he would have nothing of it.

He was brash, rude, and temperamental. Everybody knew it and apparently ignored it. He was Levan's second in command and closest associate. She did not call him Levan's best friend because she never did see them do things good friends might do. For his part, Hesten thought she had stolen the title from his sister and considered her to be spoiled. He barely tolerated her and ignored her most of the time, which was perfectly fine with Esme.

She sighed. She missed Maurice. She saw him on occasion as he bustled around inside the palace walls, and she always stopped to speak with him, though it was always brief and they never touched. She missed his hugs and their long talks. She wanted to tell him everything going on in her life. And not just what was put out as public knowledge.

Maurice and Geylis married the previous year. Because everyone knew of her generous nature and her friendship with Geylis, nobody thought it was odd when Esme insisted on hosting a party for her friend and her new husband. She visited with Geylis once a month now that she lived in Atelina, and she loved every minute of their time together.

"Are you well, my love?" Levan asked, looking down at her. "That was a mighty big sigh for being so happy about two years of wedded bliss."

She pulled back and looked at Levan, horrified. "Oh, no, that sigh was not about you. No, you are perfection, my darling. I was thinking about my family. I miss them terribly. I wish I had my mother to talk to. Maybe she would have answers about why I cannot conceive."

Then she thought of something she had not considered before. "Levan, what if—what if that illness that took my family's lives also took away my ability to have children? We must call the physician right away and have him run every test to see." Fear and guilt welled in her chest, making her panic.

Putting his hands on her shoulders, Levan tried to calm her down. "Esme, my little s-star, stop this. Y-you call me perfection, but it is you who are perfect. I have two beautiful sons and a beautiful wife who loves those children as if she birthed them herself. It will happen. Have faith in yourself."

But it was not faith in herself Esme needed. It was faith in the Creed and Eminence who had put her in such a high position. He would have to be the one to bless her and help her conceive a child. She wished she could tell Levan she was a followed the Creed. She was Queen now, what could it hurt? Then she thought of Veva. *She* thought it could not hurt to disobey Levan and look what happened to her.

So instead of telling her husband to have faith in the one and only Eminence, she merely nodded and smiled weakly at him.

"I have a meeting with Hesten this morning, but after that, the rest of the day is yours. Do you have something wonderful planned for us?" Levan kissed her on the tip of her nose.

She did indeed have plans for them. A picnic lunch with the children, just as they had done on their first outing together, then a private showing of Levan's favorite play to be performed by the royal players. In the evening, she asked the chef to bring a meal back to their bedroom so they could relax and dine in privacy. She told Levan of her plans, and he was pleased.

"I will go meet with Hesten at once so I may return to you all the sooner." With that, Levan got himself ready for his meeting, leaving Esme in his wake, lulled by the thought of spending the rest of her life with such a wonderful man.

LEVAN STRODE INTO HIS office ready to get the meeting over with. He had places to be and a family waiting for him. Besides, it had been the same story with Hesten for years now: whenever there was spare money and time, he pushed for an invasion of Cartrelle. But thus far, Levan had been given no concrete proof an invasion would be beneficial to him. They had already wasted resources sending troops to watch the constant stand-off between Tentakay and Viriland.

As usual, Hesten was already in Levan's office, sipping tea while he paced the floor. "Have you worn a groove into that spot with all your pacing, Hesten? Honestly, you worry more than somebody's grandmother."

Hesten put the tea cup down and thrust papers in Levan's face. "Look at this. Do you see this? This is the perfect reason to finally invade Cartrelle. And surely, I do not have to mention the fact that having that land under your control would give you access to the ocean from the north, the Ippi River to your west, and Hosworth River below. You'd be—"

Levan interrupted, yanking the papers from Hesten's hand. "Just let me look at what you have, Egold. I am familiar with what borders our land and theirs. That has not changed."

Levan studied the images in front of him. Cartrellen protesters were cursing Levan, saying everyone in Geoline was going to hell. Levan knew it was in the Creed, their hallowed book, but he did not subscribe to their myths. The people were angry, but they were not invading his country.

"People disagree with me all the time, Hesten. I don't see where this merits us attacking an otherwise peaceful people," he argued. Hesten must have more than this to show him. He checked the clock on the mantle to see if it was time to meet Esme. It was not.

"Look at this, Your Grace," Hesten said, bringing the next page to the top. It had charts and copies of Cartrellen documents. "Proof that Queen Raina intends to invade us and turn Geoline into a nation of Creed Followers. It will be a religious takeover."

"Dated December 1537, just a few months ago," Levan read. Sure enough, the documents laid out plans for the Creed Followers of Geoline to rise up and fight against the king and his people. And they would be aided by Queen Raina and the Cartrellens. "Unbelievable. Where did you get this, Hesten?"

A wicked smile curled up on Hesten's lips. "I have my ways, sir," he said. "But even if you do not wage war on Cartrelle itself, you can take matters into your own hands now and annihilate every Follower within our borders. That would show anybody else that we—that *you*—will have no mercy on these beastly people and their so-called Creed and Eminence. I will even provide the funds to help you be rid of these vermin, sir."

Levan nodded. If his people's safety was at stake, Levan agreed. "I see no other way, Hesten. If this is indeed true, these people need to be stopped. Draw up the documents to arrest every Creed Follower in Geoline."

With a flourish, Hesten brought up an already completed document. "All it needs is your signature, Your Highness."

Reading it over, Levan thought everything was in order. Today was March first; the arrest of all Followers would take place on April first. He signed it, eager to be on his way to meet Esme and the children.

THE NEXT DAY, NEWS slithered out of closed doors throughout the palace. King Levan had signed an edict calling for the arrest of all Creed Followers in Geoline. Maurice hurried home to Geylis, trying to appear as normal as possible. She accepted the life of a Creed Follower while they had first been together, but it was still new to her. What would her reaction be? He had to tell her.

"Geylis, there is news from the palace. It's not official yet, but it's bad news," he said, shaking his head in disbelief.

His beautiful wife was folding laundry, but she stopped and looked to him. "What troubles you, Maurice?"

He looked at his bride of only a year. How could he tell her they would all be arrested within a month? How could he tell her that her closest friend's husband—the very man she had competed for herself—decided they were now second-class citizens and no longer allowed within their borders? The news was slowing leaking out of the castle and would be public soon. He wondered how fast it would travel to Cartrelle and Queen Raina. Would she come help them? What would happen?

"Maury? What's wrong? What's happened?" Geylis's face fell as she looked at Maurice. "You look like you've seen a ghost. Is Esme all right?"

"Not for long. None of us are safe for long," he said as he sat. Dizziness came over him. He had to do something. "The king has issued a proclamation calling for the arrest of all Creed Followers. We are to be removed from Geoline as a whole. How could he do this?"

"I just... I don't understand," Geylis said, tears welling in her eyes. She sat next to him and put her hands in his.

Maurice met his wife's gaze as his mind raced. He suddenly realized exactly what had happened. "I do. Levan has been deceived and lied to by the man he trusts the most. Hesten. I guarantee Hesten is behind this."

Geylis threw her arms around Maurice. He buried his head in her shoulder and they both wept. Maurice struggled with how to protect not only his wife but Esme as well. She obviously had followed his instructions from years ago and never told Levan she was a Follower of the Creed.

She will have to now. It was the only way to save them—not just the three of them but the thousands of people in Geoline who were Followers. Last he heard, there were almost one hundred thousand of them, mostly in rural areas and along the border with Cartrelle. But there were also larger factions inside the cities, especially Atelina. And now a very important one was within the walls of the palace even as Levan signed the decree.

"I must go to her, Geylis. Esme is the only one who can save us. She must talk Levan into reversing the order," Maurice proclaimed. "Send messages to every faithful Follower you know. Tell them to start praying for the Eminence to hear us and for Esme to be able to put a halt to this genocide."

Horror filled Geylis' face. "Genocide? Do you think he means to kill us all?"

Maurice stood and nodded. "I do. Not Levan. Not knowingly, at least. But Hesten? Absolutely. We won't let that happen, though." With that, he put on his coat and sped out the door, heading for the palace gates.

CHAPTER 27

THE IMPOSING GATES LOOMED before Maurice, their iron bars denying him access to the palace grounds. A gruff Palace Keeper stood guard, blocking him from entering.

"I'm sorry, sir, but without proper identification you cannot enter," the Keeper said.

"But I come in through these gates daily. I'm Maurice Gustoff. I am a scribe. I spend every day inside that gate," he argued.

"I am sorry, but without your credentials, you may not pass this gate," the man reiterated.

"Can I send a note to Her Grace the queen?" Maurice ran his hand through his hair, not knowing what to do now.

The green-clad man crossed his arms and peered down at Maurice. "No."

Distressed, Maurice grabbed onto the gate and rattled it. If he could not gain entrance, he would entice someone—anyone—to come out. "Let me in! I must see Queen Esme!"

When the Keeper pulled him free from the ironwork, Maurice ripped his shirt open and cried out like a madman. He knew it would draw attention. He carried on for as long as he could, and when he could scream no more, he laid himself out before the gate so anybody who wished to go through would be required to step over him. He continued to ask for Queen Esme.

WHILE ESME TENDED TO her garden, Guy took a leisurely stroll through it. Now that spring approached, she was insistent on planting all sorts of little seeds and talking to them as if they were human. As he moved beyond the garden and into a large courtyard, he noticed a commotion by the gate.

"You must move, sir," a Palace Keeper insisted with a booming voice. Guy inched closer, trying to catch a glimpse of the person being denied entrance.

Then Guy saw him: a man in ripped clothing lying prostrate on the ground in front of the gate. It must be some sort of protest. What was there to protest? The weather was good, things were peaceful—there was no recession in sight. Guy stepped closer to get a better look.

"I insist on seeing the queen," the man demanded.

A jolt hit Guy's heart. This required his immediate attention. If the man wanted to see Esme this badly, he needed to investigate. Guy was flabbergasted to see the scribe Maurice Gustoff looking so disheveled and sprawled before the gate.

"Mr. Gustoff?" Guy asked aloud, wondering if he identified the man properly.

The protester tilted his head up and shielded his eyes. "Mr. Hart! Please, please! I need to speak with the queen immediately."

"I'll go at once," Guy promised. He ran as fast as he could to the garden area where Esme counted out her seeds for the spring plant.

Smiling, Esme was oblivious of the ruckus going on at the gate just for her. "Guy, what makes you run so quickly?"

He huffed at the exertion but quickly said, "The scribe Maurice Gustoff is at the gate. They will not let him in, but he says he needs to see you at once."

Esme sat up and took notice. "Maurice? Why? What has happened?" Guy could see concern etched on her face.

"I don't know, but he is covered in dirt and his clothing is ripped. He's lying in front of the gate so all who try to pass through must step over him. Something must be gravely wrong," Guy admitted.

In a single, swift motion, she stood and moved toward him, her hands reaching out to take his. "Please, go to him at once. Ask him what has happened for him to behave in such a manner. And take him some clean clothes, please."

Guy departed, again running across the palazzo toward the front gate. He stopped in the laundry for a fresh shirt and tucked it into his own coat. Maurice was still on the ground, now with three guards standing over him. He slowed to a hasty walk as he approached the group.

"Excuse me, gentlemen, I bring a message from Queen Esme for this man." The Keepers, knowing who he was, parted and stepped back. Guy got on his knees and bent down to the man. "Mr. Gustoff, Queen Esme sent me to ask you what is going on to make you behave so. She also sent this shirt for you and asks that you put it on instead of this ripped garment."

"I shall do no such thing. Not until something is done about the edict," Maurice seethed.

"Edict? I know nothing about an edict," Guy admitted.

Maurice told him everything. About the order signed by Levan himself calling for the arrest and destruction of all the Creed Followers in Geoline.

How he was certain Hesten was behind it. "It was whispered from the halls as I worked this morning. Did you not hear of it?"

The news rattled Guy. No, they had not heard any such news. "The queen's chambers can be isolated, I'm afraid." The Palace Keepers were still within earshot, so he knew he had to speak carefully. "I am so sorry, and I am sure Queen Esme will sympathize. What made you think she could help you?"

Of course, Guy was aware this man had married Esme's friend Geylis, but surely she could have come to speak to Esme herself. Maurice's actions were quite peculiar.

Guy knew Esme believed in the Eminence, just like he did. The notion of what Maurice was proposing appalled him. Would he and Esme be a part of this edict? Their identity as Followers remained unknown. How did Maurice know the queen was one? From Guy's understanding, she hadn't even mentioned it to Geylis.

"I know she can. Please." Maurice pulled on Guy's lapels and got closer to him. When the Keepers stepped forward, Guy waved them off. Maurice whispered in his ear, "Nobody is safe. She is the only one who can save us."

A chill ran down Guy's spine as Maurice released him. He helped Maurice stand and watched a moment as the man stumbled away from the gate.

Before returning to the queen's quarters, he walked through the halls, stopping to talk to everyone he encountered. Sure enough, several people told him the king had signed an edict from Hesten to get rid of the people they now called "sheep"—the Followers.

Esme paced back and forth while she waited for Guy to return. Had something happened to Maurice? Had something happened to Geylis?

Why would her cousin carry on so dramatically? She knew he would never act so ghastly without reason. She wrung her hands and checked for Guy again.

Finally he rounded the corner. Esme had to fight impending tears to speak. "Oh, Guy, please. What did Maurice say?"

"I fear it's grave news." He sat and placed his head in his hands. Never had Esme seen him so downtrodden.

Her heart rate accelerated, and Esme feared she would faint. "Please, Guy."

He filled her in on what was going on. The rumors, the end of Creed Followers in Geoline. There was no way her husband would do such a thing. He was a reasonable man, and the Followers were peaceful.

A few minutes later, Rhiann came into the room with a piece of paper in her hand. "An edict, my lady. I was told to bring it right to you as it may affect your staff." She handed the piece of parchment over.

Sure enough, it was an edict announcing all Followers of the Creed would be removed from Geoline on April first. It didn't specify how that would be accomplished, but after two years, she knew what it meant. Death.

Her eyes scanned to the bottom of the paper. It had been signed by Levan, but she knew Hesten was behind it. There were tens of thousands of Followers just in Atelina; she could not imagine how many there were in all. It would decimate entire villages.

"Maurice said you would know what to do, that you had to put a stop to this," Guy told her. He stepped closer to her, "Esme, would this include...us?"

Tears swam in her eyes. "Of course it does, Guy. We are among them, are we not?" She wiped her wet cheeks with the hem of her sleeve.

"Why did Maurice come to you, Chérie? What makes him think you are the answer?"

She looked him in the eyes and did the one thing Maurice had told her never to do. "Because Maurice Gustoff is the one who raised me. He is my adoptive father and my cousin, and he is a leader amongst city Believers."

Before Guy could react, Esme continued. "You must go back to him. Tell him I fear I cannot do this. While he does not voice it, I can tell Levan has grown weary with me because I have not given him more children. I fear I have failed him. This would only displease him further. And we are all aware of the consequences when Veva angered him. He would not take it well to learn I have withheld something like this from him for so long."

An ache came over Esme that nearly took her breath away. Before Guy could leave, she called out. "Guy? When you find Maurice bring him to me right away." He nodded and turned on his heel.

She needed to speak to her cousin without the intermediary. Back to pacing, Esme prayed for direction. She felt like she had asked for little from Him over the years, and she admitted in her prayer that saving the Followers was more important than giving her a child.

How her perspective changed in a few moments. An hour ago, she had been planting cucumber and watermelon seeds tenderly and praying for a tiny seed to bear fruit within her body just as these would bear fruit in the summer. And now it looked as though she would not be around to see it. But of course, Levan would not let anything happen to her. She would not be arrested and executed with the others, would she?

Her thoughts turned to Veva. It was likely the former queen never thought Levan would have her dethroned and imprisoned either. Esme wiped away tears as they came, but she did not try to stop them.

Finally, Guy rounded the corner with Maurice on his heels. Esme threw herself on her cousin and clung to him. It was the first time she was able to hold him tight in over two years, and what a horrid reason to be able to do so. When she released him, she searched his blue eyes for answers.

"Maurice, I don't understand. How could my husband have done this?" She wiped her tear-stained cheek and took a steadying breath.

"I think Levan is just a pawn in this game, Cricket," Maurice started. Then he looked at Guy with suspicion.

"Guy can be trusted with our very lives, Maury. He is one of us." She smiled at her assistant. "Praise the Eminence that He sent a Follower to be by my side through everything."

"I'm glad of it," Maurice said to Guy. "Levan signed the decree blindly, I believe. Hesten is the one behind all this. And I think it's my fault. I am the reason all the Followers will be abolished." He looked at Esme with utter grief.

Pulling him to a bench under a portico, she sat him down. She shook her head, partly in disbelief and partly to let Maurice know it was not his fault. "How could this be your doing? Surely, you have done nothing wrong. If you had broken the law, you would have been arrested. Why would Hesten want to punish thousands of people because of you alone?"

"Hesten has always hated me. It's never been a secret. I believe he is jealous of my jovial nature. He sees the Eminence's light radiate through me and he can't stand it. I'm sure you have noticed he is full of darkness inside. So, he took a natural dislike to me from the beginning. He started off calling me names and berating me years ago. In the Testaments, we are called to turn the other cheek according to the words of the Disciples. So, I ignored him and continued allowing the light to shine through me."

Maurice paused and sighed, closing his eyes. "When you were married, Es, something in Hesten snapped. He knew I was a believer in the Eminence, and one night, he not only mocked me, but he struck me."

Esme's hand flew to her mouth. "No! Maurice, why did you not tell me?"

"How? How could I tell you what had happened? And at that point, it was done. Hesten degraded your name, and I defended you. He hit me so hard I fell. And when I stayed down instead of fighting back, he ran away. He broke my jaw. The good thing about it was Geylis nursed me back to health. That was when we fell in love."

Esme took Maurice's hand in hers. "I had no idea. I am so sorry. And while I'm glad you found Geylis in the ordeal, I still don't see how this would lead Hesten to want us all gone."

"For the past two years, his hatred for me has only grown. While he has not touched me again, he has spewed his ignorance and bias everywhere he can. He promised me some months ago he would get rid of me and everyone like me. I took it as an empty threat. But now I see it was not."

"How am I to help, then? I can't make Hesten like you and suddenly believe in the Creed," Esme said. She felt like a little girl drowning in a large pond. How could there be any way out?

"You must go to Levan. Tell him everything. Tell him who you are, where you come from. He loves you—perhaps he will rescind the order," Maurice said. "You are our only chance." Hope shone in his eyes.

Esme sighed and shook her head. "I fear I cannot to go Levan. While he says he is not unhappy with me, I know he longs for another child, and I have not been able to provide one. His distance from me grows every day. Some nights, he doesn't even sleep in our bed. And going to him—revealing everything—might mean a death sentence for me anyway. Two years ago, we promised each other that we would have no secrets between us. And here I am with a secret larger than life."

Esme's gaze swept from her cousin to her right-hand man. She trusted these two men with her life. They would protect her, wouldn't they? "Surely, he would not include me with all the others. Won't I be safe here?" She wanted—no, she needed—reassurance. Neither man had it.

As he stood, Maurice's gaze bore into her, filled with contempt. "I assure you this, cousin: just because you are married to the ruler of this land, you are not exempt from this punishment and cruelty. If you are silent now, our people will be saved some other way. But you, Esme, you and your family will perish. The very day this man came to our door to say you had been selected, you told me you had a conviction to come here. That *something* drew you in. Perhaps you were chosen for this time. Perhaps you were placed here by the Creed and Eminence to save us all."

His expression scared her. His notion scared her even more. It was true: Esme had been drawn to Levan. She believed the Eminence had a purpose for leading her to the palace. But she thought it was to bring love and joy to Levan and to mother Lester and Lennox. Never had she thought she would save an entire group of people from exile and most likely death. But if this was what she had been chosen for, so be it.

A lump formed in her throat, and she swallowed it down. What could she do? She needed time to think and pray. "I'll do it. I will go to Levan. But Maurice, I need support. Please, I beg you. Please send word throughout Atelina to all the Followers. I need them to fast for three days and three nights. And pray with everything you have. All my people here shall do the same. In three days, I will approach Levan and hopefully have a solution for us all." She shook her head. She wasn't sure she could do it, but she would do her best. Then she added, "Maurice, I tell you this now. I love you. Always know that. And if I should meet my fate, know I will see you and welcome you at the gates of Heaven."

Maurice bent down and kissed her forehead. "The Creed and Eminence is on your side, Cricket. You cannot fail in His eyes. But if He is willing, I will see your smiling face in a month's time right here in the city. I will go now and begin spreading the news."

They embraced, and Maurice took a hasty leave. Esme looked to Guy. "We have our work cut out for us. Prepare my finest clothing, ready my hairdresser and other attendants. In the morning, we begin the preparations for me to make history."

CHAPTER 28

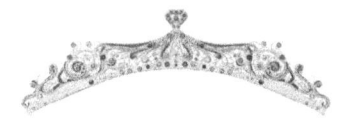

Hesten checked the calendar on his desk. In twenty-seven days, all the Creed Followers in Geoline would be rounded up and arrested. He knew they numbered near one hundred thousand. Levan had no idea they were so numerous. He probably thought they were a faction closer to ten or twenty thousand. But it did not matter. Soon they would be a group of nothing.

While he walked around in near glee, he noticed Levan was somewhat more sullen. He hoped the king was not changing his mind on the matter. Cornering him in the hall, Hesten questioned Levan. "Sire, you look distressed. Is something bothering you?"

"Actually, Hesten, I was wondering what is to be done with all these Creed Followers once they are arrested. Shall we put them to work? Exile them? I hear some places are sending their exiles to the Americas." Levan scratched the stubble on his cheek.

Hesten was glad Levan had not taken the time to read the entire edict he prepared. And the people received a less detailed one. He, in fact, did have plans for all those people. The adults would be killed. The children would be sold off as slaves in other countries, if they survived.

"Do not worry about that, Your Grace. I have a plan all worked out," he said in his most soothing voice as he clapped Levan on the back. "We will be rid of people who do not respect your position as head of this country, and you will be back to having complete reign. There is no losing side, here, Levan."

Playing into Levan's ego always worked. Next to himself, Hesten didn't know anyone who loved power more than Levan.

"You make a convincing argument. Let us sit. It's time for court to convene," Levan said, turning toward his place at the head of the hall.

Court was the gathering where the people of Geoline had the opportunity to present their grievances to the king. Some thought they were owed money or that they didn't owe money. Some had issues with shopkeepers or merchants; others were neighborly spats. A judge heard all cases first, and only particularly difficult cases, or those from nobility, came before Levan and Hesten. Hesten prided himself on being the one sitting beside Levan for the dealings.

While it was easily three times longer than it was wide, it was not a narrow room. Benches lined the walls where royal staff members made arrangements with those who had come before the king. Sometimes, ladies would sit and do their needlework while they watched. It was always a hub of activity. A scribe sat on one of the benches with a small, portable desk in front of him, making note of everything that happened.

Hesten joined the king on his right side, sitting in a chair only slightly smaller than Levan's. Levan's chair was upholstered in a bold royal blue color, while his own was fashioned in burgundy. *Still a regal color,* Hesten argued to himself as people pleaded their cases before Levan. He was still in a position of honor, second in command of a nation. He looked at Levan. Perhaps one day he could be first. But one step at a time, he remembered.

"Your thoughts, Hesten?" Levan interrupted his thoughts, which were not on the case being argued before them. All eyes were now on him. He wouldn't sweat it, though. He was a smart man.

Hesten looked at the parties standing before them. One, a man dressed in lavish clothing who looked to be wealthy. The other appeared to be nothing more than a shop boy, his clothes dingy and his hair unkempt. "I believe I would side with the gentleman over the boy, Your Grace."

Naturally. Who would side with a poor shop boy?

Levan apparently. "Really? I was rather inclined the other direction. This man cannot come into a store and take items without paying." Levan turned away from Hesten and addressed the pair before him. "Despite what Mr. Egold thinks, Mr. McNew, you were extended credit, and now you must pay or be labeled a thief and go to jail. You have taken advantage of the kindness granted to you. And I shall tack on an additional fee of twenty percent for this lad's troubles. Marcutin, help these two make arrangements."

Marcutin came forward and led the two away. Hesten felt a fool. He should have been paying attention.

"Mind elsewhere, Hesten?" Levan asked under his breath. He thought he heard a bit of amusement in Levan's tone.

"My apologies, Your Grace. It will not happen again," Hesten said, feeling his olive skin burn with his wounded pride.

As the hall doors opened again, Hesten's eyes widened in shock at the unexpected figure who entered the room.

ESME TOOK A DEEP breath. Guy straightened her coronation crown on her head and fluffed her skirt out behind her. The silver crown weighed more than she remembered, though maybe it was the purpose with which she wore it that weighed on her. She had chosen an elaborate dress of royal blue with a plunging neckline. The dress bore a ten-foot train of lace, all royal blue. Levan's favorite color. Everything had been piped and accented in silver thread so the dress shimmered in the light.

The air seemed heavy as Esme and her entire staff, weakened by three days of fasting, prepared her for this occasion. Her hunger was so severe she feared she might collapse, especially with the added burden of what was unfolding. But she had resolve. For three days they had fasted and prayed. Every time a hunger pang hit her, she prayed for the Eminence to guide her. Every minute had been filled with prayer, and Esme even taught her staff how to pray. If nothing else, even in the face of death, three of the ladies on her staff had accepted the Creed as their own faith. For that, she counted everything a victory.

When she was ready, she nodded carefully to Guy. "Pray, Guy. Pray with all you have. I don't know what is before me, but I have faith the Eminence is with me. I go to Levan now, and if I perish, I perish." He nodded in return and kissed her on the cheek.

He opened the door for her, stepped in front of her, and called out for everybody in the hall to hear. "Esme, Queen of Geoline, here to see His Grace the Sovereign King." His voice was strong as he enunciated every word clear as a bell.

Guy stepped out of her way, and Esme immediately saw Levan. Her husband's posture straightened, and he looked uncertain, even from the great distance between them. Esme put her shoulders back before taking her first step toward him. She heard the people around her whispering, a buzz of voices rising like the roar of a river after the rain. She took another step, then another. Slowly. She had to pace herself. She wanted to run, but she knew she needed to make a memorable entrance.

And an entrance she had made. Hesten sat beside her husband, his face twisted in a grimace, but she made a deliberate effort to ignore him. Her gaze was fixed solely on Levan. He wore a coat of emerald green. It was a striking color on his skin, and it made him easy to focus on. Esme prayed. She prayed so hard she thought she might cry. She prayed Levan would be receptive to her, that he would hear her, and that he would free her people from the fate Hesten had delivered upon them. And, she prayed that, when everything was said and done, Levan would still love her.

Just a few more steps. Each one echoed in the hall. Now that she was close, the people had gone silent, waiting to hear what she would say. She longed to lick her lips but had been trained not to when in the company of others. Her throat felt parched, but she reminded herself she would be fine.

One more step. The silence was deafening. All eyes were on her, but she could only see one thing. She looked at Levan then lowered her eyes and sunk into a deep curtsy. As she rose, Levan stood, his arms outstretched to her.

"Queen Esme, my most beautiful wife, what brings you to the hall today?" He smiled at her and kissed her cheek. "What have I done to deserve such an honor, my lady? Anything you ask will be granted to you."

Esme wanted to blurt everything out right then. Especially if she would be given anything she asked. But no, she knew this was not the place or the method to make her request.

She raised her chin and spoke with clarity. "If it pleases you, Sovereign Lord of Geoline, I ask that you come to a private banquet I have prepared for you tonight. It is for only you and Commander Egold to enjoy as a celebration of your rule."

A sly smile crossed Levan's face, and he took her hands in his. "Is that all you ask?"

She fought the urge to sigh. "That is all I ask of you, my lord." Esme wanted to wrap her arms around her husband, to beg him for mercy. But instead, she smiled demurely, and her face hurt with the physical exertion.

"Well, Hesten? Do you accept this noble offer of a banquet for us?" Levan turned to Hesten while still holding Esme's hands.

Hesten, vile creature that he was, stood and gave a sweeping bow. "I would be most delighted, sire. I thank you, madam, for your invitation." He returned to his seat but kept his eye on her. Esme could tell he was suspicious.

"We shall be there, my most gracious queen," Levan announced with a laugh. He winked at her, but she only nodded back.

"I thank you, Your Highness," she said with a smaller curtsy. "And I look forward to seeing you tonight."

With that, she made an excruciatingly slow turn and deliberately walked back up the hall, leaving Levan looking after her. She took a long, deep breath as the whispers of others rose to meet her. *What is she doing? What is going on?*

At the end of the hall, Guy shut the door after her, and she nearly collapsed onto a nearby bench. Immediately, her hairdresser removed the heavy crown, and Esme felt relief. Guy knelt beside her, offering her a roll slathered in butter.

"We can eat now, yes?" Guy asked. Esme looked at him and laughed. She took the roll and bit into it.

"Yes, tell everyone they may eat again," she replied. With that, a tray of buttered rolls appeared before them all, and everybody took one, eager to end their hunger. She hoped the Followers had been fasting and praying with her and that they were now enjoying a nourishing meal.

Step one was complete. She had gone before Levan and made her request without issue. Now she needed to make sure the banquet was the most opulent one Hesten had ever seen. She wanted that dog eating out of her hand before she stated her case.

CHAPTER 29

RHIANN ESCORTED LEVAN AND Hesten to a small room just off the kitchen. Levan recalled playing in the room as a child, and he wondered if Lester and Lennox knew of it. That was not important at this moment, however. What was important was that he and Hesten had been so formally invited to this feast. He wasn't sure exactly what—or who—they were honoring, but they awaited entrance.

The sound of Rhiann's three knocks echoed through the silence, and in response, the door slowly swung open, revealing a warm and inviting interior. She stepped aside with a curtsy to allow them through. Inside the door, Levan saw Guy and one of the kitchen maids bowing. The sound of silence met his ears. Levan thought his wife would have her favorite music playing for a festive occasion. This must not be a festive occasion, he concluded.

A round table was set up for them with naught but three chairs. Each place was set with the palace's finest china, gold table dressings, and a goblet of red wine.

Esme sat at the place farthest from them, in the corner of the room. As she stood at their entrance, Levan's eyes followed her every movement, captivated by her graceful curtsy. She wore the headband she loved so much, the one that had been his mother's. She also wore a dress of ice blue that looked dazzling against her pale skin and black tresses. A stunning necklace made of silver and aquamarine encircled her throat and chest. She held her hands out for them, and Levan noticed a matching cuff bracelet winding up her right arm. She was spectacular.

"Sovereign King and Commander Egold, I welcome you," she said with a tight smile.

Levan approached her left side and lifted her hand. He kissed her wedding ring while gazing into her eyes, making sure she took notice of his action. Then he turned her hand over and kissed her palm. Esme's eyes grew wider, and she tried to mask a larger smile.

On her right came Hesten, who took her proffered hand. He kissed the back of it and offered her a curt bow. "I am most grateful for an invitation to such a beautiful party with such a beautiful hostess, my queen." Levan almost rolled his eyes. Hesten was a master with words.

Esme nodded in response. "Please sit. Our first course awaits us," she said, motioning to the seats. "Guy, please tell Zane we are waiting." Guy Hart nodded and disappeared, only to arrive again followed by three young men who placed bowls of soup before them.

Throughout the meal, one of the young men served each of them, eagerly taking their empty plates and bowls, serving each course, and refilling their wine when needed. Being served such lavish dishes, Levan couldn't think of another occasion where he had been so indulgent. He thought surely he would not eat again for a week.

After the last course was finished, the three lads did not return. Guy even made a silent exit. Levan was certain something was going on with his wife. His mind raced with what it might be. Was she finally with child? But why invite Egold for such an announcement? Was she ill? Did she know of some security threat?

He couldn't take the suspense any longer. "Esme, this was a most filling and tasteful meal, my love. Tell me, and anything you want will be yours," he said, feeling slightly intoxicated by the wine and full on the food. "What do you desire?"

Esme lowered her lashes to him. "If I find favor in your eyes, my husband and my ruler, I ask that you and Hesten return tomorrow night for another feast. And then I shall tell you my request."

"What do you think, Hesten?" Levan asked, wagging his eyebrow to the commander.

Hesten was thrilled and a little drunk. He raised his glass and extended it toward Esme. "By all means, Sire, I heartily accept."

Levan stood and bent down to kiss his wife. "We shall be here tomorrow, then. And I will grant your request."

Esme only smiled. The door opened, and Guy stood with MacJames to escort the men out.

THAT NIGHT, LEVAN COULD not sleep. Curiosity gnawed at him, leaving him restless, as he pondered Esme's intentions. He dared not ask her once they were alone. She had made quite the production out of the evening meal and obviously wanted Hesten included for some reason. He could wait to find out what she wanted. But since he could not sleep, he had gone into his office for some bookkeeping.

Looking over the annals reminded him of the banquet he had thrown in Esme's honor, and he recalled the attempt two thieves made on his life. He quickly scanned the page for their names. Billiam and Terres, that was it. They had been executed, he read. Good. What had happened with the man who caught them? Levan looked. He was surprised to see it had been Maurice Gustoff who uncovered their plan. How had he forgotten? He looked to see if anything had been done to award Maurice but saw no record of it. He would rectify that in the morning.

Hesten went home that night full of pride. He had been asked to a private banquet with the King and Queen. Surely, that meant something. Hesten sensed Esme had prepared something extraordinary for him, and he couldn't help but wonder what it could be.

At home, he put his feet up and demanded that his wife Nicie rub his feet. She was pregnant yet again, this time hoping for a daughter. Hesten was proud of his three sons—one more than Levan had. And perhaps another was on the way. Esme, for all her beauty, had yet to give Levan a child in two years of marriage. He knew Levan should have married Wilma.

Still, Nicie was a good wife who did her best to please him. Her eyes were her most beautiful attribute with their stunning hazel color. Her body had always been soft, which Hesten had liked, but now it was more doughy, even when not expecting a child. Her unwavering dedication to him was evident. She was willing to cater to his every desire, even massaging his tired feet after his extravagant feasts.

While Nicie kneaded her fingers into his feet, he animatedly recounted the story of the evening's events. From the wine to the dessert, and Esme's odd request that they return again the next night.

"Everybody was talking about her grand entrance into the hall earlier," Nicie said, her voice straining as she ground her knuckle into the arch of his foot. "People thought perhaps she was going to announce another heir was on the way, this time from her."

Hesten shook his head. "I thought of that. Then why invite me? Besides, her waist was tiny." He looked to Nicie's expanding middle and frowned. "No, I think this definitely has something to do with me. She kept glancing my way at the table. Perhaps she wants to honor me. Regardless, I am right where I want to be in this world."

Nicie sat his lap and kissed him. "I'm so glad, Hesten. Everything is going your way." She laid his hand on her mid-section and he felt his offspring twist inside her. He tried to ignore her weight on him, but she was heavy.

Shifting her off his lap, he stood and turned to her. "Don't I know it? Once those vile Creed Followers are gone, especially Maurice Gustoff, I will be one very happy man."

He slept deeply that night and awoke with a renewed sense of purpose in his life: make his way up the ladder, decimate Gustoff and his kind, live happily ever after. It was the dream he had always wanted. Hesten was well on his way to total power.

As he entered the gates of the palace, a messenger ran out to meet him. "Commander, I was just on my way to find you." He huffed a little as he waited for Hesten's reply.

Rolling his eyes, Hesten urged the boy on. "Well? What is it? What is the message?"

The boy stood up straight and puffed his chest. With a booming but still pubescent voice, he announced, "Commander Egold, His Majesty the King requests your presence at once to help with an urgent matter."

Urgent? What could be so urgent that a messenger was sent? Hesten started every morning in the king's company, and this would be no different. If something warranted a messenger, it must be imperative.

"Out of my way, boy. I'm headed there now." Nearly knocking the boy over, Hesten took off with haste to the royal quarters.

Did this have anything to do with the queen's private banquet? Had she told Levan what she wanted already? Hesten was loath to have missed it if that was the case. He knew Esme didn't trust him, but perhaps the tables were turning. Being in her good graces would only elevate him more. It took his less than five minutes to arrive at Levan's office door. MacJames let him in quickly, and he found Levan sitting at his desk deep in thought.

"Hesten, I am glad you are here. I need your advice," Levan said, looking up at him. He didn't appear panicked or agitated.

Hesten bowed briefly then stood across from the king. His own mind was too worked up to sit. "My lord, What can I do for you?"

The king lowered the papers in his hands, and Levan looked at him with a furrowed brow. "There is someone I wish to honor. What might you do if you wished to honor someone?" His expression was all seriousness.

Hesten felt almost giddy. Levan wanted to honor someone? Surely, it would be him. Who else would it be? He wished he had time to think more. But he blurted out what came to his mind first. "If I wanted to honor someone who has pleased me greatly, and I was King, I would bring out one of the royal robes and allow this man to wear it. I would give him one of the royal rings and allow him to wear it also. Then perhaps I'd throw a parade in his honor, all the while announcing he has found favor with the king."

A parade in his honor. What a treat. Hesten hoped he would have time to send a messenger to Nicie and the boys that he was having a parade thrown just for him. First private banquets and now this? It was the best day of Hesten's life.

"Brilliant." Levan stood, his face lit at the idea. He clapped his hands and smiled wide. "It shall be done at once. MacJames."

Hesten was so overjoyed he wanted to dance. He would need to find that messenger boy again quickly.

Levan's valet appeared in the doorway. With a flourish of his hand, Levan gave his command. "MacJames, go down to the scribe's room at once and bring up Maurice Gustoff. Also fetch me a royal robe and a ring." He paused in thought. "Make it the ruby ring. We shall be honoring Mr. Gustoff today. Call it, 'Maurice's Day.'"

A ringing in his ears almost caused Hesten to miss the last part of the king's command. "Hesten, you shall lead the processional of his parade. What a brilliant idea." Hesten heard that loud and clear.

He was unable to move. To think. Maurice Gustoff? He nearly choked. Levan wished to honor Maurice? He burned with rage.

Levan rubbed his hands together in happiness. "Oh, and Hesten? As you lead the parade, be sure to call out, 'This man is being honored by the king for his good deeds.' I think that shall bring attention to Maurice," Levan said as he sat back down in his chair and nodded at his own words.

"Y-yes, sir. At once," Hesten stammered.

CHAPTER 30

MAURICE COULD NOT BELIEVE his ears. He looked at MacJames again. "Are you positive this is what King Levan has ordered?"

MacJames, a short man who was beginning to bald, laughed. "Absolutely. He realized late last night he had not done anything to reward you for catching the two thieves who plotted to kill him after his marriage to Queen Esme. He asked Hesten first thing this morning what should be done, and this was Hesten's idea."

Maurice choked on his coffee. "Hesten's idea? You cannot be serious. That man loathes me."

With his belly shaking, MacJames laughed. "That's the best part. I think Hesten thought the honor would be for him. That was what he wanted done for himself, and now he's the one who's going to parade you through town."

"I wish there was a way to document this processional. Where's a portraitist when you need one?" Maurice laughed. "I'll be in King Levan's office in ten minutes. I want to send a message to my wife."

Once MacJames took his leave, Maurice wrote a quick note for Geylis before he found a messenger.

It seems I am to be honored by King Levan with a parade through the streets of Atelina this afternoon. Tell everybody to come outside. It's being called Maurice's Day, no less.

He did not include that Hesten would be at the head of the parade. That would be the big surprise, as if all this recognition wasn't surprise enough. With the messenger sent on his errand, Maurice made his way up the winding stairs to the king's office.

Upon entering the room, he not only bowed, but went down on one knee to show proper respect. While staying down, he asked, "Your Majesty, you sent for me?"

"Indeed I did, Mr. Gustoff. I know we have crossed paths many times over the years, and you are truly a loyal and dedicated subject of the crown." The king rose from his seat and came around his desk to where Maurice knelt. "I realized last night that you were never rewarded for your service to me and your warning of the would-be assassins."

Despite his knee beginning to ache, Maurice stayed where he was. "It was my duty and honor to be of your service, my lord. Any subject would have done the same."

The king extended his hand to Maurice and helped him to stand before clapping him on the back. "Regardless, we will celebrate your accomplishments and your service." He turned to his valet. "MacJames, is the queen here?"

"I'm here, sire," Esme answered as she swept into the room. Her eyes widened upon seeing Maurice, but she said nothing. She dipped into a curtsy before her husband.

Esme was instructed to place the royal robe over Maurice's shoulders. He stooped low for her to drape it over him and fasten it over his chest. As he stood, she met his gaze. "You have not only pleased the king, Mr. Gustoff, but me as well. We thank you for your allegiance."

"My pleasure, Your Highness," he replied to his cousin. No longer was she a meek little girl. Now she stood with her back straight and her head high. Pride swelled in Maurice.

Next, the king himself pushed a gaudy ruby ring over Maurice's finger. He held it in place as he spoke. "You have proven yourself as a trustworthy subject, and we honor you today. Please take this ring as a sign of my gratitude to your devotion."

With a stoic face, Maurice nodded at the king's words. "It is my pleasure to delight the king."

With the finery in place, Levan dismissed everyone. His part of the honoring was finished. Esme offered to escort Maurice out to the courtyard where an open carriage waited for him.

As they descended the stairs, Esme kept her back to him but whispered, "I wasn't sure what I was walking in on, cousin. You are just now being thanked for the tip about those two men?"

"It would seem so. It's a bit odd given that in under a month Hesten plans to have us all killed." He shook his head in disbelief. "And now, he will be leading me though the city in this ridiculous parade."

Esme stopped and turned to him. "He is?" Her eyes were wide, and a playful smile came across her lips. There was his little Cricket.

"Indeed." He wanted to explode in laughter, but the sound would carry and raise suspicion.

As they got to the bottom of the staircase, they were met by the two princes who joined their little processional. The boys flanked his sides while Esme walked in front of them.

"Wow, Mr. Gustoff, isn't it grand you get your own parade?" Lennox asked. He looked just like his father except his hair color more closely matched his mother's—and Esme's.

While he had seen the children, he rarely interacted with them. Maurice realized they were something of step-grandsons to him. "I am delighted, young man," he replied. Then to Esme he added, "And a little embarrassed."

Esme giggled. "I would be, too. This is such a big to-do for something that happened so long ago. I wonder where Levan got this idea."

Maurice gave her a sideways glance. "I understand it was all Hesten's idea, thinking the king planned to honor him."

She stopped and looked at him, surprise and amusement all over her face. "Isn't that hilarious? And he's heading up the whole parade? He must be fuming mad right now."

They approached a large, open carriage rigged with a team of four horses. Maurice thought the whole ordeal completely overdone. A simple thanks and maybe a nice stuffed ham would have been sufficient, but he was not one to argue with the head of the nation. Esme kissed his cheek, and he boarded the carriage. Levan had managed to pull together a small band because before him were a bugler, a flute player, and a drummer. He had his own trio for his parade.

Esme and the two boys waved him off as the carriage jerked into motion. Maurice knew his face was red from all the attention. People everywhere stopped to stare at what was going on.

Hesten, who stood in front of the musicians, began his slow march down the street away from the palace. "This man is being honored by the king for his good deeds," he called out. His voice was clear, but less than enthusiastic, Maurice thought.

Every few seconds, Hesten would call out again, "This man is being honored by the king for his good deeds." Each time he sounded more depressed than the time before. And with each passing moment, Maurice's confidence about having a parade in his honor grew stronger, though he tried to remain humble about it.

As soon he saw Geylis standing on the side of the road, bewildered by the announcement, the musicians, and Maurice, wrapped in Levan's own royal robe. He waved to her, grin plastered to his face. They passed several hundred people by the time they got to her, and as he looked ahead, more people gathered on the roadsides to watch. Geylis waved back, still flabbergasted at what was happening. Before he passed her, though, she blew him a kiss and threw a small bouquet of flowers toward the carriage.

When they rounded the bend back to the carriage house, Maurice knew his five minutes of fame was over, and he would have to return to his hole in the ground—the scribe room where he recorded the news, not made it. He would, however, be recording his very own parade. For posterity, of course.

Descending from the carriage steps, he made his way to Hesten and gave him a nod. "I thank you, sir, for your service. I know that wasn't easy. Please return King Levan's robe and ring back to him."

Hesten spat on the ground at Maurice's feet before taking the items. "You're right. That was not easy. Just you wait, Maurice. In a matter of weeks, your very existence will not plague me any longer."

Behind Hesten stood Esme, who had walked up as they spoke. She cleared her throat, and Hesten turned to see her. "Your Highness. What a lovely surprise," Hesten cooed. "I was going to take these things back to the king then prepare for our banquet tonight."

She held out her hands. "I will see Levan gets these items returned." Hesten had no choice but to give the robe and ring to her. "You can begin readying yourself, Hesten. I shall see Maurice out."

Hesten made a swift exit, leaving the cousins alone. Maurice gave Esme a questioning look. "A banquet with Hesten?"

Esme walked toward the door, robe folded over her arm. "In our three days of fasting, this was the best idea I could come up with. Please keep praying it works. Tonight, I will tell Levan everything."

Maurice nodded. "You are always in my prayers, Esme. May He guide your feet and your words this night." He squeezed her shoulder, aware anybody might be watching them. They parted ways at the door, and Maurice began his prayers, all thoughts of his parade vanished.

THAT WAS THE MOST humiliating moment of Hesten's life. Walking through the streets shouting that Maurice Gustoff had so pleased the king. Gustoff. A Follower. Mindless sheep that he was, of course he did whatever he could to get in Levan's good graces. But it wasn't enough. He might be celebrated today, but soon he would be buried in the ground to rot.

Hesten stormed home, all thoughts of working forgotten. His boots fell heavy on the packed dirt road, and his nostrils flared. He needed to kill something now. Anything.

Inside his own doorway, a housemaid crossed his path. "You." He couldn't recall her name. "Grab my gun." The girl paled and hurried off.

Nicie rounded a corner and stopped short when she saw him. "Hesten? What are you doing back? What's going on?"

"I have never been so mortified and infuriated in my life. Something will die today, so get out of my way," he roared. His chest heaved, and he wanted to punch something, but he knew it should not be his pregnant wife.

So he turned away from her and punched the large clock his parents had given them as a gift. The mechanisms popped from the inner workings, and the face fell to the ground with a clatter. The usually soothing tick-tock of the pendulum turned grating as it now sounded like it was scraping something.

"Get me a bandage," he mumbled to his wife who still stood, dumbfounded. "Bring it to my study. I need a brandy."

Thankfully, his knuckles weren't too scraped up. After a bit, the bleeding stopped, and he could prepare for the second banquet without it. It wouldn't do to show up to such an enthralling event with his hand bandaged.

CHAPTER 31

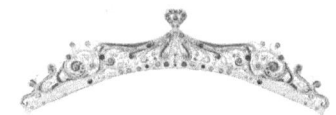

THAT NIGHT, SERVANTS ESCORTED Levan and Hesten to the same room. Levan expected the scene to be a repeat of the previous night, but when the door opened for him and Hesten, he was astounded by what lay before him.

Rich, bright tapestries decked the walls, telling the story of how Geoline came to be its own country. Normally, they hung in one of the outer hallways, but Esme had them brought into this small dining room. The table was ornate with crystal goblets and plates. The centerpiece was candles surrounded by jewels so their colors were reflected onto the walls of the room. Levan felt almost dizzy from the effect.

And there, in the same place as the previous night, was Esme. This time, she stood and came to the front of the table. If she had been stunning the night before, Levan had no words to describe how she looked now. A dress of sapphire blue clung to every curve of her body. Levan could see the outline of her hips before the skirt fell into a dramatic flair of tulle. Again she wore a necklace that covered her exposed collarbone, this time of sapphires and rubies. She wore one of her most elaborate tiaras, made of sparkling diamonds.

She turned to Hesten first and greeted him with a kiss on the cheek and a gravity-defying curtsy, making Levan feel a twinge of jealousy. When Hesten stepped aside, she rose and turned to Levan, giving him the same kiss and curtsy in one of the most graceful displays he had ever seen.

As she rose, she smiled at him. "Thank you, my most wise and gracious king, for coming again."

He took her hand and kissed it, wishing he could pull her into a tight embrace not suitable for company. "The pleasure is all mine, Esme. You have outdone yourself on this night's banquet."

She gave a slight smile and held her arms out to showcase the table. "I can only arrange items that you yourself have provided for me, Your Excellency. So I thank you, most humbly, for the riches you provide that I do not deserve."

The remark caught Levan off guard. Of course she deserved them; she deserved all the riches the world had to offer. He almost thought to comment on it, but then he realized she was doing no more than paying him respect as Guy had most likely instructed her.

The trio sat down, and Esme raised her hand. Once again, three young men attended them, now stepping forward to fill their wine glasses. As they retreated to get the first course, Levan looked around the room again and marveled at the beauty.

The first to compliment her, however, was Hesten. "Gracious Queen, you have outdone yourself. The décor in this room is magnificent. The only thing I have ever seen that could outshine the beauty of this room is the beauty within it. You are as lovely as I have ever seen you."

Esme batted her eyelashes, something Levan was not accustomed to her doing. His wife was not one for flattery. Levan knew something was up. Esme had something to say or something to ask. Levan lit up at the first idea that entered his head. Perhaps she was finally pregnant. But then, why would she have invited Hesten to a banquet if that were her news? Maybe she needed of something, but he could not think what that might be.

Roasted chicken, ham, sweet potatoes, corn, breads, and more put all thoughts of Esme's reasoning for the banquet from Levan's mind. All his favorite foods were before him, with the promise that more was waiting if needed. Esme had even arranged for his favorite strawberry cake with fresh crème on the top for dessert—and strawberries were not even in season. Levan felt like a glutton, but he could not help himself with all his favorite foods displayed before him.

As the last course was cleared away, Levan was fuller than he cared to admit. But he knew Esme had thrown this elaborate feast for a reason. Finally, he brought it up. He took her hand in his and raised his glass to her. "My darling Queen, you have called us here for something. Anything you want—name it. It will be yours. I will give you your own kingdom if you demand it."

Levan's thin and meek page came forward and refilled his wine glass for a third time. Hesten was on his fifth glass of wine. Esme, he noticed, was still on her first. She had been quite restrained with her drink as well as her portions. He raised his glass again to her, and Hesten followed suit, even if he was a little sloppier.

"A toast to my beautiful wife. Please, Esme, tell me your heart's desire."

"Here, here," Hesten said with a nod. He downed his cup in one gulp. It clattered to the table.

Esme looked at Levan, her beautiful aqua eyes staring into his own. Then she looked to Hesten, and her expression changed to one of wariness. Levan wondered what caused her mistrust.

"My most gracious lord, I have but one request," she said, looking back to him, her eyes swimming with unspilled tears. "If you hold affection for me, if you esteem me in any way and love me, I ask that you please spare my life. And spare that of my people. For we face certain death at the hands of one who detests us for no reason other than our existence."

The tears slid down her perfect cheeks, and Levan wanted to collect each one. Yet, she continued. "If I thought perhaps we might simply be relocated as ancient peoples were relocated, I would not bother you, sire, with such a request. But I am certain death would be the only acceptable resolution for he who despises me and my family." Esme's eyes pleaded with him.

Levan shot to his feet, furious. Would someone dare threaten the Queen of Geoline? Heat radiated through his body. Looking from Esme to Hesten, he was ready to demolish any who would dare such an undertaking.

"Who? Who would dare do such a thing? Tell me!" Levan shouted. In his rage, he swept his arm across the table, clearing it of half its contents and spilling them to the floor.

Esme calmly and quietly looked at him then turned her eyes to Hesten. "It is Hesten Egold, my king. He is the one who has made my people into his enemy and wants to destroy them all."

Standing to his feet, Hesten shook his head. "No. Never, Your Grace."

As calm as she could be, Esme snapped her fingers, and an unseen arm delivered the edict Hesten had written and Levan had signed. Esme addressed Hesten. "Do you deny it was your plan to do away with all the Creed Followers in Geoline? Do you also deny that instead of simply moving them out of the country, you planned a mass murder of one hundred thousand people?"

Hesten opened his mouth, but before he could speak, Esme continued. "These are my people."

His commander wanted to annihilate Esme and her entire family? Blinded in his anger, Levan stormed from the room ready to kill Hesten as soon as he could find a tool with which to do it. How could a man he trusted commit such a heinous act? He went to the hallway and paced back and forth for a few moments. Hesten planned to kill Esme? Esme was a Follower? How did he not know that?

As he thought, he realized he did not care what religion Esme followed—Creed Follower, something else, or nothing at all. He loved her and would never let anybody harm her. He wasn't sure Hesten had known either, though. Levan had not read through the entirety of the edict, wishing only to appease his commander. He demanded the copy to be given to him and an unknown servant produced it for him. Scanning the document, he found it. Tucked away where he had not seen was a clause that Hesten could do as he pleased with the people once they were arrested. And knowing his hatred for the people, Levan guessed he would have them all killed.

Hesten's plan would not survive. Neither would Hesten. Then it dawned on him that he had left his wife alone with the monster who wanted her dead.

ALONE IN THE ROOM with Hesten, Esme stood so that she was over him. She was not afraid of him, but now he seemed afraid of her. She folded her hands in front of her body and stared him down, waiting for him to move or speak.

"I-I did not know you were a Creed Follower, Your Highness," he stammered, stepping closer to her.

"I am a Follower, Commander Egold. And for the record, Maurice Gustoff is my cousin and the man who raised me," she said, smoothing out the deep blue dress she wore. She knew she looked powerful in it. She was also aware Hesten would not hold power in Geoline ever again.

Hesten's eyes widened in astonishment, his mouth agape. "No. Surely not."

Laughing, Esme reassured him. "Oh, yes, Hesten. Maurice raised me from the time I was a little girl. I know all about your ridiculous feud with him and your plans to murder all of the Creed's Followers in Geoline. I hope you enjoyed this meal, Hesten, because I have a feeling it was your last."

Stumbling, he reached his hands out to her. "No, Your Grace, I beg of you. Have the king spare me." In that moment, he tripped and fell into her.

Esme fell back into her upholstered chair, Hesten landing on top of her. She cried out under his dead weight, struggling to get out from under him. Right then, Levan reentered the room and saw what appeared to be Hesten assaulting her.

"Get off me! Please!" She cried out as Hesten fumbled in his attempts to stand. His breath smelled foul as he wheezed in her direction.

Levan pulled Hesten, now hysterical and drunk, off Esme and held him up by the lapels. "You would even attempt to attack my wife after making a decree to spill her blood? Who are you, Egold?" Levan let go of Hesten and punched him in the gut as he sagged to the ground. Esme recoiled at the sight.

As Levan shouted, three guards came into the room, and he barked orders at them. Two took hold of Hesten, who could barely stand. Esme stood again and made herself as tall as possible. She looked down at Hesten, only moments ago a prideful man, now falling apart at the seams.

As the guards moved to take Hesten away, he cried out, "Levan, please! You need me to run this country. You can't do it without me. You replaced the queen once already. You can find another one after this one is gone—my sister is still available. But you can never replace me."

Esme turned her face away from the hatred spewed by the vile man. Levan came to her side immediately and held her. She buried her face in his shoulder as Levan gave his final orders for Hesten.

"Have him executed. Immediately. Then dispose of the body. His widow and children are to be on the first ship bound for the Americas. In fact, any relation of his should go. I want nothing of Hesten Egold left in my lands." His voice was firm and cold. Ever the king, he commanded attention.

But then Levan lifted her chin so she looked into his eyes. His face was tender and loving. Now he was a husband, not a ruling monarch. "I will never let anybody hurt you. Or your family. Tell me everything," he said. His voice was gentle and calm. He invited her to sit next to him, amid the chaos and debris in the once elaborately decorated room.

CHAPTER 32

THE WEIGHT OF HER truth pressed on her chest, as if an entire herd of cattle stood on her. It was time the truth came out. "My parents died when I was eight years old," she started. "I lived in a little town and had no other family."

Interrupting her, Levan asked, "What town?"

Esme looked to him, unsure what to say. She opened and closed her mouth before sighing. "It was a little town called Burnside. In Cartrelle." She shrank back a little, unsure what he might say.

With a tender gesture, Levan extended his hand and intertwined his fingers with hers. He held it, cupping his other hand over hers protectively. "Go on," was all he said. There was no comment about her being Cartrellan.

She cleared her throat and continued. "A terrible illness came through Burnside and many other rural towns. My sister and parents all passed quickly. Only me and my younger brother stayed alive. Someone somehow knew we had a cousin here in Atelina and sent for him to get us. But before he came, Aaren died as well, leaving only me."

Levan frowned. "Cartrelle is an advanced country. Where were the doctors, the medicines?"

She shook her head. "We tried medications. The doctor had given us several to help us and other families. Nothing worked. Later, I was told that out of over four hundred people infected, less than ten survived. I was one of them." Esme swiped a tear that escaped down her cheek. "So we buried my family, and Maurice brought me back here to Atelina. He adopted me and gave me his last name: Gustoff."

Levan sat straight. "Wait. Maurice Gustoff? The scribe? He is your cousin?"

With a laugh, Esme confirmed, "Yes, that Maurice. Hesten was shocked as well."

He scratched his head, ruffling the locks that fell into his eyes. "I had no idea. All this time... I just honored him with a parade. I had no idea he was related to you. You did not tell me."

Guilt washed over Esme, but she carried on with her story. "Maurice raised me. We are Creed Followers. When I came to the palace as one of the Final Fourteen, he had asked me not to tell anybody who I was or who my family was. He thought I would not be safe. He did not want me to even come to the palace after I was chosen for the contest. He had not known I applied to be queen at all," she told him.

"So, why does Hesten hate Maurice so much?"

"Only Hesten knows that for sure. But it seems Maurice did not play into Hesten's games of power, and Hesten did not like that. Soon he had transferred his loathing to all Creed Followers, and he made the edict you signed."

Levan's face changed as it dawned on it. "The edict *I* signed. I signed it, didn't I? I wanted him to stop bothering me about this group he claimed was wasting resources and taking up space all over the country. He said Cartrelle planned on invading. I wonder if that was even true. I had no idea who was among them, and I admit to not doing my own research," he said, cupping her cheek. He kissed her forehead. "But now that I know, I can do something about it."

Esme sighed a breath of relief. "There is still time before the edict is set into motion. No innocent blood needs to be shed, Levan." She laid her hand on his arm, feeling safe and comforted. Everything would be fine now.

"Let's quickly get a new decree written and signed. Copies will be sent to every city, every village. Actually, we'll make two. One stating the mistake made and the second an announcement of Hesten's execution and an apology to all Followers in Geoline and elsewhere."

The fasting, the planning, the feast—it had all worked! Followers of the Creed need no longer fear death. The weight on Esme's chest lifted, and she took in her first full breath of the past week. There was hope. Finally.

They rushed to the scribe's office and found Maurice pacing the floor. His dark green coat fluttered after him as he walked. Esme ran to him, still dressed in her finery, and embraced him.

"Maurice. It's over. Hesten is gone. The edict shall be overturned immediately." Tears streamed down her face, and her knees felt like they might give way.

Maurice looked from her to Levan. "Are you certain?"

Stepping closer, Levan held out his hand to Maurice. When her cousin took the offered hand and lowered himself, Levan bowed to him. After several seconds of silence, Levan stood. "Maurice, I had no idea you were the man who raised Esme. Had I known, I would have elevated you to the highest place of honor in my kingdom. But now, as Sovereign Ruler of Geoline, I give you my word that you and your family are protected. And you shall be honored yet again in the city of Atelina."

Bowing, Maurice turned a bright shade of pink. "Your Majesty, that is not necessary. As long as my people are free to continue living in this wonderful land and as long as my little Cricket is safe, I can ask for no more." He looped his arm around Esme's back.

"As we speak, MacJames is drawing up a new edict, renouncing the previous one to put all Creed Followers into exile. We will need the scribes to work all night to make copies. I apologize to you personally, Maurice, for my ignorance in all this," Levan said, his tone serious.

"The Creed teaches forgiveness, and I happily forgive any wrong you have done, sire," Maurice said with a smile.

Levan scowled for a brief moment before he put his hand out for Maurice to take. "Please, call me Levan. After all, we are family now."

After a few minutes, MacJames arrived with several pieces of parchment in his hands. The first was the new edict, rescinding the call to arrest Creed Followers. The second revealed the fate of Hesten and his family. Maurice quickly called in the scribes on duty and told them to get to work. The room was a flurry of activity, and Esme tried to take it all in.

Levan stopped and took a deep breath, looking at Esme. She wondered what he was thinking behind the icy blue eyes he had. But she was in no way prepared for his next words. "Family means everything to me. To us. I want to make a new proclamation."

He snapped his fingers, and a scribe with a writing desk appeared, ready to take down his every word. "Make it known that from this day forth, I will have a new Commander. He shall always be at my right hand and will be consulted on all major happenings in Geoline. He is cousin to the queen, a Creed Follower, and has proven himself to be a man of highest esteem. Maurice Gustoff."

Esme's eyes grew wide. Levan was making Maurice his second in command? Surely, the Eminence was smiling down on them in that moment. How else could their fortune change from a people almost annihilated to the king's right-hand man?

Then a thought made her heart leap with joy. Perhaps, just perhaps, she could show Levan and the children her faith and help them come to trust the Eminence as well. She already made sure to incorporate the basic values into the boys' lessons, but now she could show them the Testaments and have that taught to them as well. Maybe this was a change for the entire nation.

Maurice stood rooted in place, his face blanched, his hands up on his chest.

"What do you say, Maurice? Do you accept?" Levan took three large strides to Maurice's side and put his arm around Maurice's shoulder.

"I—I accept. I am honored and a little overwhelmed, Your Grace."

Tears swam in Esme's eyes as Maurice blinked several times and ran his fingers through his hair. He stepped forward, dressed in his everyday garb, and bowed before them. He kissed Esme's hand and shook Levan's.

Right then and there, Levan gave Maurice the oath of his new position. Esme knew her cousin would take the oath and responsibility seriously, treating all he encountered with respect and dignity. With a snap of Levan's fingers, the signet ring that had once adorned Hesten's hand was now upon Maurice's.

When some of the shock had worn off, Esme and Maurice embraced and both shed tears. Tears for the years they had been apart and tears for the years they would now have together. They cried for the favor they found with the Eminence and that all their people would be free to live and worship without tyranny as they had before.

WITHIN HOURS, MAURICE'S LIFE changed. Moments, really. One moment he had been pacing his office floor—as close to Esme as he could get—praying. He prayed the Eminence would hear them, would liberate them from the hell to which Hesten sentenced them. He prayed Esme would come out unharmed both in spirit and body.

And then... Then Esme and Levan floated into the room, and he had been surrounded with smiles and love. Everything was going to be all right. Hesten was no longer a threat, his fanatical edict was no longer valid, and suddenly normal life resumed. And just as suddenly, *that* had ended, and King Levan made him his second in command. Him! Maurice Gustoff!

He was sure Geylis would faint at the news. How he wished she had been there with him when he had taken his oath, but he knew she would understand. She was the most understanding person he had ever met.

With the other scribes carefully copying the new edict and proclamations, Esme and Levan bid him farewell. Before they left the room, Esme wrapped him in the tightest hug ever, and Maurice recalled all the times he had tried to hug her as a teenager when she brushed him off. He savored the feel of his little Cricket in his arms again.

It felt like he flew home—his feet carried him so fast. Maurice had never needed a horse; his life existed in a relatively small circle within Atelina, and he enjoyed walking. Today, he could not have gotten home faster if lightning bolts had been attached to his feet. People wished him well as he went past, but he did not stop. He hoped they didn't think him rude, but he wanted to get home to Geylis.

She stood outside waiting for him. Even though it was cold and dark, Geylis did not wear a cloak. She jumped as she saw him approach their house, knowing this was the night Esme would make her request to the king. Maurice all but crashed into her as he reached the door. He lifted her up and carried her over the threshold of their modest home.

"Maurice, what has happened? Did Levan reverse the edict?" Her eyes searched his as she held onto his shoulders.

Maurice sat on the couch, then stood and paced before sitting again. Unable to keep still, he stood once more. "Everything happened. The edict is rescinded. Hesten is gone. We are safe. But there's more." He stopped to catch his breath.

"More?"

He ran his hand over his face, still processing everything that had happened. "Esme told the king everything. That we're family. That we're Followers. He— I—"

"Slow down," she said with a laugh. "One thing at a time."

A large, loud breath came from Maurice, and he finally sat still with her. "Geylis, I was made Commander in Hesten's place. Me."

Her eyes grew large. "What?"

Maurice shook his head. "I know it sounds wild, but it's true. The king told me to call him Levan. To his face. And he knows Esme and I are family, and he welcomed me—us. And then, before I could think, I was taking the oath and he was putting this ring on my finger."

He leaned back from her and showed her the ring he now wore on his right hand. He had not even had the chance to inspect it yet. The ring was made of brilliant yellow gold, a circle of diamonds at the top, and the initials L and G—for Levan and Geoline—were intertwined on the face. The ring was a wonderful fit, which surprised Maurice. He would have never thought he and Hesten had the same size hands.

"It's lovely," Geylis said. "I remember seeing an identical one on Levan's hand when I was at the palace. But it looks much better on you." She smiled and kissed him, laying her head on his shoulder.

"This means we will have many changes happen in the coming weeks and months. I don't know the extent of my duties, but I will have to be at Levan's beck and call now. It's a demanding position," Maurice warned her. He wondered then if taking the position had been a good idea. Not that he had been given much choice in the matter.

"I know," came her reply. "And I know you will do wonderfully as both a husband and as commander. I am so proud of you and Esme tonight. I don't know that I could have been as strong as her if I held the fate of so many in my hands."

"Ah, but Geylis, realize it was never in Esme's hands at all. The fate of those people rested in the hands of the Eminence and Him alone. Esme was only a vessel in which to carry out His ultimate plan."

CHAPTER 33

THE FIRST OF APRIL arrived as every other day before it. The sun began it's slow, lazy rise over the horizon. It was a Friday, and already the palace bustled with activities preparing for the weekend. Levan turned to Esme and put his arm protectively around her. Less than a month ago, this day would have meant death. Even if Esme had not perished, those she loved would have, and that would have killed her spirit and brought great heartache. She would not have escaped unscathed.

Levan still bore a certain amount of guilt over not reading through Hesten's words carefully. How could he have been blind enough, trusting enough, to sign something without first reading every line? He had known Hesten despised the Followers. Levan never thought to question the accuracy of the information Hesten had provided him. Upon further investigation, it seemed most everything Hesten told him had been a lie. Hesten craved power over everything. That was a mistake Levan decided he would no longer make.

Power was nothing without love and compassion to balance it. In the past few weeks, Levan spent less time in his office and more time with his family. It helped that his second in command no longer needed him every second of the day as Hesten had. Maurice Gustoff was already flourishing in his new role. Levan could simply give him a task, and Maurice did it without having to run every detail by him. Within a few weeks, Levan noticed a decrease in his stress level and an increase in his contentment.

On this day, instead of the arrest and murder of one hundred thousand people, there would be a celebration for all those who believed in the Creed. Levan admitted Esme's religion often left him confused and asking questions, but he felt wonderful knowing there was something in control over him. Esme had spent weeks explaining the idea of grace and mercy. Levan marveled at the idea of a free gift of salvation where all one had to do to get it was accept it. It seemed too simple. But Esme assured him that was all there was to it, and Levan had accepted it wholeheartedly.

In the three weeks since finding out Esme was Follower, Levan discovered MacJames had been one for years. Guy Hart was one, too. Several of the mayors he had appointed over the districts of Geoline were also Creed Followers. In Atelina alone, Maurice estimated close to forty-thousand Followers. Levan had been unaware all this time.

But now the citizens of Geoline flocked to the faith. They abandoned the idea of leaning on themselves and embraced the notion of an Eminence who would save you from your sins if only you would let Him. In Atelina, hundreds met in the house recently occupied by Hesten's family. It had become a place of worship and praise. Every day, more people came to know about the Testaments and the Eminence who had ordained it.

It seemed that Esme, like Levan, was unready to begin the day as she nestled in closer to him, seeking comfort in his presence. *Well*, Levan thought, *it is a day of celebration. Who says the celebration has to be in public the entire day?*

When MacJames slowly and carefully opened their room door, Levan told him to be gone. The king and queen would spend the morning in a private meeting. MacJames only nodded and discreetly closed the door as he exited.

"Did you send MacJames away, Levan?" Esme asked into his shoulder.

"Yes," he replied.

"Why? Is it not time to start the day?" She lifted her head, her raven locks spilling down his arm onto the bed behind her.

"Today is a day of celebration, my love," Levan said with a smile. "And we shall begin the day with a private meeting. I think it would be best to meet with our eyes closed."

"Oh," Esme said, her grin growing wider. "I see. Or rather, I don't see if my eyes are closed. Shall I go back to sleep?"

"Only for a little while, my love," Levan said, running his hand up and down her arm. "But we do need to celebrate."

That afternoon, a grand package arrived with a message from Raina, the Queen of Cartrelle. Levan asked Maurice and Esme to be with him as he opened it, since they were originally from the country themselves. The gift was a hefty but simple golden yoke along with a message. Levan read it aloud.

"'Greetings, King Levan and Queen Esme. I have heard of the goings on in Geoline of late. I am glad to hear Hesten Egold has paid the price for his wrongdoing, and everybody in Cartrelle prays he repented before his death. We now celebrate with you as we hear many of your citizens are coming to the faith and following the one and only Eminence.

"'This gift is a yoke. I understand the capital of Atelina has a new, large house of worship, and it is customary to adorn houses of worship with a yoke to symbolize the burden borne by our Eminence. Now that your Creed Followers are not hiding, I'm sure they will be overjoyed to display it. May the peace and mercy of the Creed be with you today and always.'"

Levan set the letter aside, picking up the yoke to examine it. It was large—nearly large enough to hold him, and the idea of dying on such a device scared him. "Why is this used as a symbol of your faith if it's the thing that killed the Savior of the Creed Followers?" He turned to Maurice, looking for an answer.

She went to him and laid her hands on his arm. "You see, my love, we don't use the yoke as a sign of His death, but of His life. He lives on forever." Esme smiled at him, so pure and passionate. Levan truly wanted to believe what she said.

Nodding, he returned her smile. "I understand now. He lives on. What an amazing Eminence you serve."

"We all do," Maurice chimed in. "It's a beautiful yoke. I think it will be perfect for the newly designated worship house."

Esme excused herself to get ready for the festivities celebrating her people's freedom. She was as excited as Lester and Lennox, who didn't know exactly why festival rides and fireworks were planned, but neither did they care. Young boys just wanted a reason to have fun, and Esme felt much the same. Everything had been and remained peaceable. Levan hadn't received a single report of Followers coming to harm. Esme was thankful the Eminence had overseen the entire situation.

Guy waited for her with a drink of water and a light snack of apples and grapes.

"Thank you, Guy. You spoil me too much," she said as she sat at the small round table in her personal office just off the bedroom.

"I do no such thing, Chérie." Guy sat in the seat opposite her and popped a grape in his mouth. "I know today is as busy as ever, but I had a quick question for you."

Esme raised her eyebrow. It wasn't like Guy to say he had a question before asking it. Something was going on. "What's wrong?"

Guy laid his hands over hers. "I know everything about you, Esme. This time it might be something very right. You know today's date?"

She eyed him suspiciously. Of course she knew it. "April first. The day of Creed Liberation." When Guy continued to stare at her, she removed her hands from his. "What, Guy? What is it?"

He winked at her. His chocolate brown eyes twinkled. "Unless I'm mistaken, you're overdue for something by at least three full moons."

Which might mean she was pregnant. Could it be? Esme flushed red. "You're right. In all the excitement, I was not thinking. But my monthly cycle has not come for some time now." She jumped up. "How can we be sure?"

Guy jumped up and ran to another room to beckon the palace doctor. Esme paced the floor, her bright pink skirt flowing behind her. She reasoned with herself. She had experienced late cycles before, but as she counted, she realized they were never this late. Still, in just over two years of marriage, not once had she turned up pregnant. Today would be a fabulous day to find out Levan's child grew within her.

Her eyes closed, Esme prayed silently. Every month, she hoped and prayed for her cycle to be absent, and every month, it arrived without fail. This time, she prayed for the Eminence's will in her life and in the lives of her family. If she was meant to have a child, she would.

Guy rushed back in with several ladies maids on his heels. Then the doctor arrived, a serious fellow with strange instruments. A few times over the years, he had been called to check on the royal womb, but Esme didn't know him well.

Instructed to lie back on her bed, Esme watched and waited as the doctor placed a tube to her stomach and listened through the smaller end. He gave no indication if she was indeed pregnant yet. After listening, he had Guy bring Esme's chamber pot to him.

With pure disgust, Esme watched the doctor sniff her urine then drop a needle into it. He waited a minute then retrieved it, leaving Esme perplexed.

Everybody in the room was silent as they watched him perform his tests and experiments. Guy crossed to where Esme still laid and took her hand in his, squeezing it gently.

Finally, the doctor announced, "The queen is with child. Once the quickening happens, we will know when to expect the next royal babe."

The room erupted with cheers, and Esme laid a gentle hand over her stomach. *Finally*. She closed her eyes and thanked the Eminence for all He had done.

While her maids erupted in song, she quietly looked up to Guy. "I can't wait to tell Levan tonight."

"Then we better get you ready," he replied.

Bright orange material slid over her skin for this event, accented with a serene cream color, it looked marvelous on her pale skin. As a maid buttoned her back, Guy came in dressed in a tangy lemon-yellow coat with rust colored pants.

"You'll outshine us all, Guy," Esme teased.

"Hardly, Chérie. Who could complete with a glowing queen?" He bowed to her. "Are you ready?"

"I am. As soon as I am on Levan's arm, I shall tell him. Won't he be thrilled?" When Guy nodded, Esme nodded in return, and they made their way through the palace to the front lawn.

Esme was awed by the sight. The usually sparsely decorated front lawn was now finely decorated and buzzing with activity. Carnival games had been set up, and children ran around without a care in the world while parents chased them from place to place. Young couples held hands and nuzzled heads while hidden away in the dark recesses. As she and Guy walked, people stopped and bowed to her. She quickly nodded or spoke to them.

It had taken some time, but Esme worked hard to gain the trust and affection of the people in Atelina. Her garden had brought people in and made them curious. Handing out produce had given her a few naysayers, but almost all of them had come around in time. Esme was truly one of the people, and they appreciated her for that. She was approachable, kind, and graceful, and the people of Geoline embraced her.

Esme thought over the past few years of her life. He whole life, really. Not everything had been easy: from the death of her family to the almost-death of all Creed Followers. The assassination attempts on Levan's life were also terrifying. But through it all, she persevered, endured, and came out on top with the help of the Creed.

The little orphan girl from Cartrelle was now the queen of an entire nation. She had trusted her faith would guide her every step of the way, and it had indeed. Even when she wasn't sure what the best course of action was, the Eminence had and helped her down the path.

As Esme saw Levan come into view, she smiled at him, knowing she was radiating light and beauty. He approached her and took her hand. "You are looking particularly lovely today, my queen," he said as he kissed her hand. "There's something different, even from this morning."

Her smile was sly, hinting at secrets to be revealed as she looked at Levan. He would be as overjoyed as she was. "Something is different. I have a gift for you, my love. Do you want to know what it is?" She crooked her finger and bade him to come closer to her.

"Tell me," he whispered in her ear. Levan wrapped his arms tightly around Esme, creating a protective shield around her. He kissed her neck and made her giggle. Esme could feel the love radiating between them. And soon, the evidence of their love would be blossoming in her body.

When Levan looked her in the eye and raised his eyebrows, she bit her lip. "You will have to wait a few months to hold it," she teased in a whisper.

"A gift I have to wait months to h—" he stopped. His jaw dropped. "To hold?"

Esme loved every moment of this. She saw his mind working. The arms that had been holding her suddenly released her and hovered over her middle, as inconspicuously as he could manage. "Truly?" he asked with an eager whisper. "You're expecting? We are to have a child?"

She nodded. "Guy realized I have missed several cycles, and the doctor just confirmed it."

Tears swam in his eyes, and they sprung to hers as well. What a perfect way to end the chaos that had been happening lately. And what a perfect beginning to the next chapter of their lives.

Levan picked her up gently and held her tight. He thanked her profusely then he thanked the Eminence for the miracle of life inside her.

And Esme knew she had been blessed. And chosen.

Esther again pleaded with the king, falling at his feet and weeping. She begged him to put an end to the evil plan of Haman the Agagite, which he had devised against the Jews. Then the king extended the gold scepter to Esther and she arose and stood before him.

"If it pleases the king," she said, "and if he regards me with favor and thinks it the right thing to do, and if he is pleased with me, let an order be written overruling the dispatches that Haman son of Hammedatha, the Agagite, devised and wrote to destroy the Jews in all the king's provinces. For how can I bear to see disaster fall on my people? How can I bear to see the destruction of my family?"

Esther 8:3-6

Afterword

This is the last we hear of Esther. We do not know her life after this. Xerxes met a violent end as his oldest son dethroned him twenty-one years into his rule. We can only assume those close to him—Esther and Mordecai included—were also assassinated. We never learn if she had children.

I have been obsessed with the story of Esther for years. I have pored over Bible studies, commentaries, fiction books, and anything else I could get my hands on about her. Did she want to be the queen or was she forced? Was she terrified? Thrilled?

Many texts suggest she was forced from her home. Why else would a young Jewish woman end up in the harem of Ahasuerus/Xerxes (both names seem to be accurate) and potentially become his consort?

Esther 2: 8 (NIV) says, "When the king's order and edict had been proclaimed, many young women were brought to the citadel of Susa and put under the care of Hegai. Esther also was taken to the king's palace and entrusted to Hegai, who had charge of the harem." No version says if she was taken by force or if she went willingly. There was no mention of anything except she was an orphan cared for by her cousin.

I chose to present this a little differently. With nervous excitement. A girl who says "Why *not* me?" Maybe she's a little like Henry VIII's fifth wife Catherine Howard — a young woman who's a little foolish and a lot excited. But in this story, Esme grows up quickly and realizes exactly what's at stake.

So, I wrote them as contemporaries of Henry VIII and his wives, set in a fictitious European country called Geoline. I also have a long love of all things Tudor history. A few times Levan notes how Henry does things, which I added to give this fictional version some historical context.

Over the years in my studies, I've heard rumor that Ahasuerus/Xerxes demanded his wife, Vashti, come before him dressed in splendor and draping in jewels. Other accounts suggest he wanted her only in her jewels and nothing else. According to Esther Rabbah (expanded text) 3:14, it says, "You want me to come naked — even my father, when he judged litigants in a trial, would not judge them when they were naked." Did she mean actually nude or just vulnerable? Scholars have many theories. So in *Chosen* I decided it wasn't Levan's actual words, but Hesten's interpretation. In truth, we will never know.

CHOSEN

We also don't know what actually happened to Vashti. The Bible simply says Esther was made queen instead of Vashti. It would make sense for her to have been killed, but banishment is also an option. In my writing, I opted to have Levan be a little more humane than we tend to think of Ahasuerus/Xerxes with Veva only being banished. Esther Rabbah 5:2 suggests he felt remorseful once he sobered and regretted his action but could not undo it.

All that aside – this is a book about two women who stood up to powerful men. Two women with God-given power.

Vashti refused the demands on a drunken husband that could have endangered her welfare. In the end it endangered her position in the world, but she stood on her morals and showed all the women around her that they had autonomy. It gave women the power to say No.

Esther went to the king unbidden, which could have invited a death sentence. While her kneed shook, she held her head high and spoke up when nobody else could. "And if I perish, I perish." What powerful words. I shudder every time I read them. Make no mistake – she was scared, tired, and weak. But God gave her power. God gave her mercy.

You, too, have that power. Never forget God has given all His children the power and mercy of Christ.

Acknowledgements

Thank you to my biggest cheerleaders: My husband, my kids, my family, my friends.

Thank you a million times over to Brigid for not only her editing expertise, but also her insight.

To Heather C, thank you for your encouragement and love.

Thank to Katie for always being on my team.

To Moms Who Write – you are beyond amazing.

All of your friendships have been the biggest blessing to me.

Thanks to early readers who caught all those typos that make it through a thousand edits and many sets of eyes. You are worth your weight in gold.

I also must thank you, the reader! God bless you. Thank you, thank you, thank you for picking up this book. You have no idea how much it means. Remember you can move mountains.

About the Author

Allison Wells is the author of gritty women's fiction, often with a faith element, and sweet romance books. She is also a certified writing coach and fiction editor. Words truly are what make her happy. Allison is Team Oxford Comma and is proud to be a leader in the Moms Who Write community. She lives near the mountains of South Carolina with her husband, children, dog, cats, and several chickens.

Allison's motto is, "Life is Short. Eat the Oreos."

*Scan to find
my website and
social links!*

Or click here

Also by Allison Wells

A modern retelling of the Woman at the Well in the New Testament, Living Water shows us that no matter our past, it's God's love that truly quenches the thirst of our souls.

What happens when a preacher falls in love with a prostitute? Perfect for fans of Francine Rivers, *Bell of the Night* is a tender romance and heart wrenching reminder that we are never too far from God's healing hands.

Find out more about these titles and all of Allison's Books at whatallisonwrote.com

Scan the QR code to find out more!

www.ingramcontent.com/pod-product-compliance
Lightning Source LLC
LaVergne TN
LVHW021234080526
838199LV00088B/4346